D1274205

BETWEEN
TWO
BROTHERS

ALSO BY CRYSTAL ALLEN

*How Lamar's Bad Prank Won
a Bubba-Sized Trophy*

The Laura Line

The Magnificent Mya Tibbs: Spirit Week Showdown

*The Magnificent Mya Tibbs:
The Wall of Fame Game*

The Magnificent Mya Tibbs: Mya in the Middle

BETWEEN TWO BROTHERS

CRYSTAL ALLEN

BALZER + BRAY

An Imprint of HarperCollins*Publishers*

Balzer + Bray is an imprint of HarperCollins Publishers.

Between Two Brothers
Copyright © 2024 by Crystal Allen
All rights reserved. Printed in the United States of America.
www.harpercollinschildrens.com

Library of Congress Control Number: 2023936917
ISBN 978-0-06-304729-7

Typography by Carla Weise
23 24 25 26 27 LBC 5 4 3 2 1
First Edition

For anyone who needs hope.
Nothing is impossible.

CHAPTER ONE

In parts of Texas, it's illegal to sell Limburger cheese on Sunday or shoot a buffalo from the second story of a hotel. So how is it that no one saw fit to make it a crime for a kid to do chores on his birthday? I'd be lying if I didn't admit I'm a bit salty about this. The way I was planning to roll today had nothing to do with rolling a wobbly wheelbarrow across our farm.

But here I am with a choke hold on the handlebars of this wagon full of hay, corn mix, and table scraps for the animals. I've got a bad case of the birthday blues until my four feathered divas strut out of their coop. I turn on my playlist, and they cluck to the music. I can't help but smile as I feed them.

"Mornin', Aretha, Mariah, Rihanna, and Whitney," I say, bending over to pet each hen before jacking all the eggs they downloaded last night.

From there, I stop at the pigpen, fill their trough with food, and give them clean water. I even make a few mud puddles so they can lie down and dance the waddle.

"Let me show you how to waddle. See, you have to work hard at it, like this."

I break off some hogtastic moves, but the pigs just keep eating, so I grab my wobbly wheelbarrow and move on. My last stop is the horse pasture, but first I grab a couple of apples from our tree to surprise them. "Mornin', Dolly. Hey, Buster. Look what I've got for you!"

They bray a good morning to me and then reach into my open palms for a bite of crunchy sweetness. I can't help but admire my two favorite animals. Their coats and my skin are the same shade of brown, and I keep their thick, black manes natural, just like mine. As they finish their apples, I inhale and then let it out slowly, knowing what I'm about to do is not going to make them happy.

Dolly has a nasty cut on her neck, and today I need to change the bandages. She's been blind in her left eye since some careless person wandered near our farm, playing with a BB gun. Sometimes she runs into things like low lying branches, so I'm always checking her for injuries. Buster is Dolly's only colt, and he likes to stay on her blind side. To me, he's protecting her.

When I think they're ready, I gently rub Dolly's nose with my left hand so she can smell and feel it, then grab my burlap sack for medicine from the wheelbarrow with my right.

"Easy, girl," I say. "I'm coming in. It's bandage-changing day. Scoot over, Buster."

I read a do-it-yourself blog written by a real veterinarian who gives instructions, with pictures, on how to take care of minor animal wounds. All I have to do is put on a pair of rubber gloves, peel off the old bandage, clean the cut, and spread a coat of ointment before putting on the new dressing. "All done. Good job."

I climb out of the pasture and barely finish feeding them when a voice startles me.

"Yo, Ice?"

It's Seth, still in his pajamas and wearing sunglasses. "Is today August twenty-eighth?"

Snapsickles!

I burn off toward the apple tree—maybe I can climb it to get away. The animals watch the action like it's FarmFLiX until . . . *WHAM!*

Seth's all over me as I squirm in the grass.

"Stop, hahaha!!! Stop tickling me; I can't hold it! You're going to make me, hahaha, you're going to make me—"

Pooooot.

Seth's nose wrinkles as he gets up. "Did you fart?"

I'm still cracking up. "I told you I couldn't hold it!"

He flops on to me again. "I'll help you. That's what older brothers are for!"

I'm laughing too hard to defend myself as he swats my butt.

"One, two, three . . . !"

By the time he gets to thirteen, both sets of my cheeks hurt, and we roll on our backs, out of breath. For a minute we lie there, staring at the colorful sky.

Seth chews on a blade of grass as he says, "This time next year, I'll be a college freshman, running cross-country for Texas A&M! And you'll be a freshman at Scarboro High! Isn't that wild?"

Before I can answer, he scrambles to his feet. "Come on! We've got places to go!"

I hustle up. "For real? What are we going to do?"

"Two things you've never done before," he says, walking toward the house.

I'm on his heels. "Okay, but where?"

Seth stops and faces me. "Ever heard the word *surprise*? No more questions."

I like surprises, but what if they're buzzkillers? I guess it doesn't matter if I'm hanging with Seth.

I shower and get dressed, then wait by our bedroom window until Seth finishes. We have more fun together than anybody, but now time's flying by, and I wish it would slow down. On the day Seth signed his scholarship papers, I had two whole years left before he had to leave for A&M. Now I've only got one.

A mist chills the back of my neck, and when I spin around, Seth's holding his cologne.

"Ladies like guys who smell good," he says, spraying himself, too.

"We're not meeting girls, are we?" My palms sweat just thinking about it.

Seth puts a hand on my shoulder. "Dude, you have to work harder on losing that shy guy inside your gut. I mean, other than being a dork, you're not bad. Girls might like you." He chuckles and playfully pushes me. "Let's go eat."

The aroma of bacon and blueberry pancakes lures me to the table, where Dad's scrolling through his phone. When he sees me, his whole face grins. "There he is! Happy Isaiah Day!"

I grin, too. "Thanks, Dad."

Mom's cooking and listening to KPRA, a 24-7 gospel radio station. I cut my eyes to watch her, feeling like I'm five years old again because I still love her like that.

She sees me. "Hey, handsome! Reach up there and grab my fancy fruit bowl, please."

I open the cabinet. There's no fancy fruit bowl up there, but I do spot a colorful gift bag with my name on it. Mom giggles as I set it on the counter and look inside at my new phone. "What?! I read about this one! It's got a longer battery life and more storage space. I love it!"

I reach back inside the bag to grab a paper—what I thought was the warranty, but it's not. Everyone stops moving as I gently set my phone on the counter and stare at the signed permission slip to join the school yearbook staff. For two years I've begged for this. The problem was I needed someone to pick me up from after-school meetings, but Dad works evenings, and Mom doesn't drive in rush-hour traffic.

"I just got moved to the day shift, so I called your school and changed your elective to yearbook class," says Dad.

I'm all in my feelings, until Seth changes the subject. "I transferred everything over from your old phone, loaded some apps and music."

I wipe my eyes and smile. "This is so fly! Thanks, everybody. Let's take a picture."

We all move to the dining room and huddle together. I set the timer for ten seconds, then place the phone on the table so that my awesome breakfast is part of the pic.

"On three, say 'Abernathy!' One, two, thr—"

Click.

Uh-oh. I check the image. My tongue's between my teeth with my lips spread apart like Dolly's before she brays. Seth's checking his phone, and Dad's trying to steal bacon, but Mom's grabbing his wrist. I hold up the photo and grin so hard my face hurts. "It's perfect!"

CHAPTER TWO

After breakfast, Seth slides on his sunglasses—he always wears them because bright light, especially sunlight, hurts his eyes. He taps my shoulder. "It's time for us to get gone."

Dad pushes back from the table. "I've got to get going, too. Can't be late for work. See y'all later."

I chug my milk, hug Mom and Dad, and grab my new phone. Outside, I lean on the side of Seth's truck. "How about letting me drive to the mailbox?"

He tosses the keys. "You're lucky we live in the country, away from real traffic."

I catch the keys and squeeze them. Yeah, baby! That's what I'm talking about!

When I open the driver's door on Seth's old green Chevy truck, heat slaps my face. The air conditioner's busted, so I crank down the window, adjust the mirrors, strap in, and put my foot on the brake before starting it up. I've got a death grip on the steering wheel but a live grin on my face as I drive down our dirt road and turn onto the gravel path that leads to our mailbox and off the farm.

Seth pretends to be a news reporter. "Good people of Scarboro, we have Ice Abernathy behind the wheel, tearing up the gravel road at a blistering three miles an hour."

"It's called safe driving," I yell, laughing.

"I could walk faster than you drive," says Seth.

"Then use your Chevro-legs!"

We both laugh because that was Gramps's joke. I miss him, and I know Seth does, too. At the mailbox, I pull over because I know my driving is over.

Seth puts his phone on the dashboard. "I made you a playlist. This first song is a serious throwback."

He hits the volume as the beat drops and bass vibrates my body. I turn off the truck, and we get out and dance like we're at a party to our favorite oldie, "Walk It Out."

When the song's over, we get back in the truck and Seth sits behind the wheel. My stomach gurgles. Hopefully, it's just gas—if it's Shy Guy trying to ruin my day, I won't let him.

The mall parking lot is packed, and downtown traffic is bumper to bumper. Seth takes a detour, then parks in front of Redd's Barbershop.

I stare through the window at the crowd inside.

"We're not going in there, are we?"

He cuts the engine. "I wasn't kidding about doing new things."

I've never been in a barbershop because Mom always cuts my hair at home, just me and her in front of the mirror. Now my inner shy guy is screaming—there's way too many people in Redd's, and I bet I don't know any of them! What if they start talking to me?

Seth grabs my chin and turns my face to him. "You're going to love Redd's. Remember—you're with me."

My heart's pounding as I look through the window again. "Yeah, okay."

Seth opens his truck door. "Besides, it's mandatory for a guy's fade to be super fly on his birthday. Don't ever forget that. And one more thing. Look who's behind us."

A black Jeep pulls up. Juan Carlos steps out of his ride, pimpin' a red baseball cap with an *E* in the center, a red-and-white jersey with *Escogido* written across the chest, white baggy jeans, and red Nikes.

I rush over and fist-bump him. "What's up! I thought you were still in the Dominican."

He hands me a bag. "Got back late last night. Happy birthday, Ice Pic!"

I open the bag and take out a candy bar wrapped in gold paper as Juan Carlos grins.

"Dominican chocolate is the best chocolate," he says.

Seth rolls his eyes, but I laugh because Juan Carlos is

cooler than a fan on high. He swears his dark skin, dimples, and black curly hair are the reasons girls love him "like candy."

He points at the gift bag. "Look inside again."

I reach in and pull out a white T-shirt with a picture of a camera on it. Underneath the camera are the words *Oh snap!* I can't help but laugh again.

"I'm putting this on right now!"

As I peel off my shirt, Juan Carlos nudges Seth. "All those muscles and only thirteen?"

Seth chuckles. "It's that farmwork he does, tossing hay and rolling the wheelbarrow."

Juan Carlos is Seth's best friend, but I claim him as my brother from a different mother. Even though Seth won't be around next year when I go to high school, Juan Carlos will be because he's only a junior. Sometimes, on the farm, he lets me drive his Jeep to our mailbox while he sits next to me. He even gave me the nickname *Ice Pic*, short for Isaiah's Pictures.

This new T-shirt is perfect. "I love it. Let's take a selfie!"

Juan Carlos poses and points at my shirt. "Oh snap!"

He's hilarious, and I can't stop laughing as Seth joins us. *Click.*

"I'll send it to you," I say, turning toward Redd's.

Juan Carlos pulls a letter from his back pocket. "Seth, I need to holla at you about something. I got an official invite to visit Blinn College!"

Seth high-fives him. "Blinn is just a few miles from

A&M! If you get that scholarship, we could leave Scarboro together!"

I snap a picture of them celebrating before Seth looks my way. "Go on in. I'm comin'."

My balance shifts from one leg to the other as I chew on my bottom lip. Juan Carlos steps toward me, but Seth stops him. "Let him go. He's working on a thing."

Juan Carlos taps his chest. "Whatever it is, handle your business, Ice Pic."

I lock eyes with my brother. "You're coming in soon, right?"

He winks. "Give me two minutes."

I turn the knob and walk in. A cowbell clanks above the door.

Clink-a-link-a-link.

As I step inside, Black, Hispanic, and Latino guys stop chatting and laughing to look my way. I freeze, but then they turn away and go back to their conversations. Gospel music plays in the background as four Black barbers, dressed in matching red shirts, mow heads better than John Deere tractors, and hair falls like fresh-cut grass. I'm all into the scene until someone takes my hand and shakes it. I quickly relax when I see who it is.

"I'm Uncle Jerry. What's your name?"

I've answered this same question for him many times. "Isaiah, but call me Ice."

A voice interrupts. "Don't you mean Ice Cream?"

My knees lock. I'd know Brandon Hart's voice anywhere.

He's sitting next to his best friend, Rhino, Uncle Jerry's nephew. Shy Guy starts going off inside me, and I turn to leave.

Clink-a-link-a-link.

Seth walks in and takes off his sunglasses. "All right, everybody."

Instant respect comes from every corner as Seth hands out fist bumps and man-hugs. All the chairs are taken, so he points to a spot by an empty wall, and I walk past Brandon as if he's not there. As we wait, Seth's phone buzzes three times, all different girls. He grins at me, and I grin back.

Twenty minutes later, a man with dreadlocks strolls over. "You ready?"

Seth playfully palms the back of my head. "Take him first. It's his birthday."

I take a seat in the barber's chair. He snaps a black cape around me. I'm already impressed.

"Happy birthday. I'm Jeremiah."

"Isaiah. Call me Ice."

"What are you getting done today?"

Mom never asked me, but I know what I want. "Could you fade the sides like Seth's but leave the top alone? Oh, and a fly edge-up, please."

He turns on his clippers. "I got you. So are you on your way to college, too?"

Since I don't have to look at Jeremiah, it's easier to talk to him. "No, sir. I go to Brazos Bayou Middle School. Seth's my brother."

"Seth's in here all the time. Where have you been?"

"Getting haircuts from Mom. She covers me with a towel instead of a cool black cape."

He laughs. "Okay, I'll leave that alone. What sports do you play?"

"None. I'm going to be either a veterinarian or a photographer. Or maybe both!"

"Wow, you're not in the game? You're such a tall drink of water. All that wasted height."

I get tight when folks talk to me as if sports are the only thing tall people can do. But Jeremiah's got my fade looking so legit that I'm going to let it slide. Once Seth's finished, I signal Jeremiah to come take a selfie with us. Uncle Jerry joins, too.

Click.

While Seth pays, I admire my fresh look in the mirror until I trip over someone's foot. Brandon stands, glares at his shoe like I damaged it, then frowns.

"Ice Cream, drippin' all over me. Nothin' but soft serve."

Everybody's staring, even Seth. I've got two choices, but only one feels right. I walk around Brandon and leave.

CHAPTER THREE

I can tell from the way Seth jams the key in the ignition that he's salty. "What just happened in there? We need to talk, and I need a smoothie."

He thinks I didn't man up, but I did. And I'm not going to spend my birthday talking about Brandon, either. It's dead-people quiet in the truck as I scroll through my phone and send him and Juan Carlos the pics from Redd's. I know Seth's mad right now, but when he runs off to A&M he'll be happy that I captured these cool memories.

Soon he parks in front of Sir Smoothie and gets out of the truck. A few feet away a man stops jogging and smiles. "You're Seth Abernathy, right?"

Seth smiles back. "Yes, sir."

"I ran cross-country at Scarboro High twenty years ago. Now I'm a member of the alumni club. We're all following your career. Good luck at A&M."

Seth bumps fists with him. "Thank you. I hope to make everybody proud."

"You already have. Take care."

As the man jogs away, I roll my eyes. Random people always treat Seth like a celebrity. He turns to me. "Chocolate power blast, right?"

I nod. "Yep." Maybe talking to that guy was just what Seth needed to let the Brandon talk go. I grab a table, and moments later he hands me my smoothie.

"So what happened in Redd's? You should've knocked that dude into next week."

I grip my smoothie. "And what's kicking his butt going to prove? That I'm *not* ice cream?"

I can't see his eyes behind those sunglasses, but I can tell a thought took him deep. "Hold on—was that the same twerp whose dad called you Ice Cream back when you were nine?"

I try to blink the memory away, but the image of Dad having to carry around my birth certificate for peewee league sports to prove my age is too strong.

His name is Isaiah, but we call him Ice, Dad would say. I loved my cool nickname. I thought the other kids liked it, too.

But I can still hear the voices of the parents on the opposing teams.

He's too big to be nine. He'll play too rough.

It only took a couple of things—like me running off the soccer field to comfort a stray dog in the middle of a game and scoring zilcho points during our entire basketball season—to change their minds. The complaints switched to chuckles, especially from Brandon Hart's dad. And during our last basketball game Mr. Hart shouted, "You said his name is Ice? More like Ice Cream! That boy is soft serve!"

Dad stomped up the bleachers, ready to rumble, but security came and calmed everybody down. Even though Mr. Hart apologized, Brandon made sure the nickname stuck.

Seth takes my silence as a clue that he's right.

"If you want Brandon to stop calling you Ice Cream, then do what Dad was about to do to Mr. Hart. Order him a smack sandwich combo meal with fist fries."

"I don't think Dad was really going to fight. And look, I bet I could shut Brandon up, but I've waited two whole years to be on the yearbook staff. I can't risk losing that over a one-time, worthless fight with Brandon. Does that make me soft?"

Seth sighs. "I'm sorry, little brotha. I didn't know Brandon was still twerpin'."

"Well, he is. And tell me why people assume that just because I'm tall, I have to play sports? If you're smart, do you automatically have to run for class president? Or how about this one: if you're not book smart, does that automatically make you a loser?"

Seth points at me. "I told you how I'd handle it. Go ahead and try it your way, but you're gonna get sick of it.

And when you do, you'll order that combo meal."

I lean back and avoid eye contact. This is too personal, and I'm feeling some kind of way just talking about it. "I don't want to be called soft, because I'm not."

Seth leans over the table toward me. "What do you think it means to be soft?"

"It means you're a pushover, somebody who won't fight back. Bully bait."

Seth nods. "Okay, that's pretty good. To me it means that person can't back up his trash talk and is too scared to fight. Now let's find out what *soft* really means." He looks it up on his phone. "It says here that *soft* means 'emotional, gentle, cares about others'—or it could also mean 'not healthy.' All those definitions could fit a lot of people."

My eyes find his. "Except you. You're a beast at your cross-country meets, total strangers worship you, and I can't even count how many girls are blowin' up your phone."

"First, there's no such thing as having too many girls blowin' up your phone. Second, none of the things you mentioned have anything to do with the real definition. Are we done?"

I've got one more question parachuting from the roof of my mouth, and how Seth answers it will mark this birthday one way or another. "What about you? Do you think I'm soft?"

He sips his smoothie, and I wait for Seth to tell me that I'm going to be just like him. When he leans forward, I'm ready for his boost of confidence.

"Yeah, I think you're soft."

I stand, ready to flip the table as blood rushes from my heart to my face. But then Seth puts up a hand. "Hold on, hear me out. You've got that shy thing going on, and you like to be by yourself. Some dudes might think that makes you soft."

I snap at him. "They're wrong!"

"Can you just sit back down? Look, I agree. Soft is what's inside you, who you are. Like the way you capture the natural beauty in people and nature with your pics, how you handle animals—you've got skills. The livestock on our farm already think they're your personal pets."

I take a seat. "That's not true."

"Right. All farmers name their hens Aretha, Mariah, Rihanna, and—what's her name."

"Whitney."

"See what I mean? I bet Dolly and Buster think you're their daddy. That's because caring is your superpower. So, yeah, you're soft, but the soft in you is hard-core."

I don't know what to think. "But being called soft isn't a good thing."

Seth searches on his phone again. "Okay, fine! How about *smooth*? It says right here that a smooth person is 'someone who's not rough or hard, but soft and easy.'"

I can't help but grin. "Same thing, different word. But *smooth* sounds a whole lot better."

He nods at me. "Then ask me if I think you're smooth."

I feel myself blushing, but I fight through it. "You think I'm smooth?"

"As a baby's butt."

We laugh, bump fists, and after we climb back in the truck, Seth puts his hand on my shoulder.

"Listen up, it doesn't matter to me if you're smooth or rough with jagged edges. I see you, and I always will. Between brothers, right? Say it or I'll tickle you."

He reaches for me, but I lean away. "Okay! Between brothers! There. Happy now?"

He shifts the truck into drive. "You good?"

I don't know what I'm going to do when he leaves for A&M. Seth's always kept it real with me, even when the conversations are hard. That's why I love him so much. I fasten my seat belt and smile his way. "Yeah, I'm good."

CHAPTER FOUR

We're cruising down Main Street when I notice Seth
checking his rearview mirror.

"That BMP truck's got to be doing sixty."

Before I can turn to look, it blows by, making Seth's
Chevy rock side to side. It swerves in and out of traffic
before taking the industrial road exit.

"'There and back in a dash makes more cash!' Dad hates
it when the truckers say that." He loves working for Bayou
Meat Packing, but not that part. "Anyway, where are we
going?"

Seth cuts a right onto Worthing Street and pulls over.
"New thing number two." He points to the big marquee in
front of the Worthing Recreation Center. "You're finally old
enough to be in the sibling rivalry competition! You in?"

Dang. Buzzkiller. "It's just a jock fest, isn't it?"

He cuts the engine. "I thought you wanted us to do fun

stuff together before I leave for A&M?"

I sit up. "Oh! So it's just for fun? Yeah, I'm in."

He pulls up the website. "It's definitely for fun, but we'll be in it to win it! If you win your one event, you get a medal. But if you win yours *and* I win mine, we get a trophy!"

He checks out something on their website and sighs. "Never mind. They always have a bunch of different categories, but now there's only two events still open. Distance running and free throws. I know basketball isn't your thing."

Seth's the best distance runner in the state. The last time I shot a free throw, I missed the rim and hit the referee.

"Unless . . ." He turns to me, fired up. "What if I teach you how to shoot free throws? You'd snatch up the gold."

My palms sweat. "But I stink at basketball."

"All you need is practice, and you'll wreck. I know it."

The thought gets me hyped. "For real? You think so?"

"The competition isn't until September ninth. You've got almost two weeks to practice!"

"Two weeks? Okay, let's do it!"

Seth types in our information and hits the send button, then shows me the response: *Thank you for registering! Look for your confirmation email from us shortly.*

He starts the truck. "While we're out, we can pick up a rim and net."

Inside the sporting goods store, it doesn't take long for reality to set in as I stand in front of a wall covered with basketballs. What did I just do? And I bet the rec center is going to be packed! Maybe I can still back out.

Once we're home, I'm still thinking of how I can weasel out of this until a whiff of Mom's spaghetti and meatballs gets my attention. I rush to the dining room, where Dad's scrolling through his phone. I throw a napkin at him, then hit the record button on my phone.

"Yo, Dad, Mom made spaghetti and meatballs. You down?"

His head stays still, but his eyes rise to meet mine. "All the way down."

"Cool," I say. "Check this out."

I bob my head and move my body to a silent beat that turns Mom's meal into a rap song.

> *I got my mind on spaghetti, all those meatballs on*
>   *my mind.*
> *Momma's Saturday spaghetti makes her family*
>   *unwind.*
> *Because she made it for my birthday, it's the best*
>   *you'll ever find.*
> *I got my mind on spaghetti, all those meatballs on*
>   *my mind.*

Second verse, same as the first, except Seth adds beats with his knife and fork. I keep filming everything: Mom shuffling to the table in her sauce-splattered apron, carrying a steaming dish of heaven. Dad watching her with a grin and a sparkle in his eyes. Seth answering his phone and whispering to a girl. I smile, knowing this footage is money. Later, I'll send it to everybody.

We bow our heads as Dad blesses everything he can think of, but as soon as he eats a forkful of spaghetti, he stands with a piece of garlic bread in his hand and calls to Mom.

"Come, my queen. Food's so good, makes a king want to dance." He grins at me and Seth as Mom gets closer. "If your gramps was still alive, he'd say to me, 'Ah, sookie, sookie, now, Ray.'"

Seth chuckles and nudges me. "If you really want to video something, this is it."

I press record as Dad butchers some old-school song, but Mom doesn't seem to care. He's still in his work uniform of blue jeans and a dark green shirt with *Abernathy, Meat Production Supervisor* stitched over the right pocket. He's worked at Bayou Meat Packing for years, making his way up from a driver to the front office supervisor.

When the dance is over, Dad gets back to eating. "Ice, you diggin' that new phone?"

I try not to laugh at his slang. "Yes, sir. I'm going to make something special before Seth leaves for A&M—like a story with pictures—a countdown to college. I'll create a share file with everything in it."

"That sounds legit," says Seth.

Dad nods. "I like that! When will it be ready?"

I shrug. "How about the day he burns off for college?"

Seth grins. "Way to look out for the family, little brotha."

"I like that, too! What else did you boys do today?" asks Mom.

Seth puts his arm around my neck. "We entered Worthing Rec's sibling rivalry!"

Dad's face lights up. "What? I've got employees who have kids in that every year!"

Great. First Seth, now Dad. Looks like my chances of backing out just disappeared.

"Mark your calendar. September ninth," says Seth.

Dad winks at me. "We'll be there."

After dinner, Seth uses a big piece of wood for a backboard and paints a red square in the center before nailing it to the rim he bought. He climbs a ladder and attaches all of it to the oak tree out front. Once he climbs down, he draws a free throw line in the dirt with a stick.

"Watch carefully." Seth dribbles twice, bends his knees, and throws the ball underhanded toward the basket. It hits the center of the painted red square, *boomph* and then . . . *swish*.

I back away. "Game over. There's no way I'm shooting underhanded. That's granny shots! Guys are already calling me soft. I'm not trying to shoot like I'm old and wrinkly, too!"

He puts a hand on my shoulder. "You've gotta trust me! I know what I'm doing."

I shake him off. "I'm not getting laughed at again."

"If you do what I tell you, and don't quit, laughter won't

be what you'll hear. It'll be cheers and claps. Just try it. You'll see."

I step up to the free throw line, and after fifteen tries I finally make a basket. Seth gets the ball and tosses it back to me. "Make the ball kiss that red square. It's called a bank shot."

I try again and clank it off the front of the rim.

"It's okay. Shoot it a little harder," he says.

The next one sails behind the tree and into Mom's vegetable garden. Seth jogs in between the rows of veggies to get the ball and throws it back to me. I take a deep breath and shoot again, hitting the backboard but still missing the shot.

I'm sweating a river, and so is Seth as we bake in the sun while I shoot enough bricks to build a city.

"Stay focused, Ice."

"I am!"

"You can do this. Make the ball kiss the red square."

"I'm trying!" I hold the ball, bend my knees, and let it fly. *Boomph. Swish.*

Seth celebrates. "Yes! Shoot fifty like that every day and you'll wreck at the rivalry."

He snatches off his T-shirt and wipes his face and neck before sliding his shades back on. His chain with the golden running shoes dangles from his bare chest and throws off a reflection from the sun. "I'm going to shower and then hang with Juan Carlos, okay?"

I shrug. "Yeah. Thanks, Seth—you know, for today."

He half grins. "Tomorrow's Sunday, and you know what that means?"

I nod. "Jesus Jail. Better have fun while you can."

He chuckles and nods at me. "You, too! Later."

After he leaves, I sit under the apple tree. The colorful sky looks magical, which makes me remember something I should've done this morning. It's still my birthday, so maybe it's not too late.

Gramps used to say, "Isaiah, if you talk to the almighty wish granter, you've got a good shot at getting what you ask for." I still make a wish every year because Gramps's advice was on point. The first time I tried it, I was eight and got a BMX just like Seth's. Wished again on my ninth birthday and—*bam!*—an Xbox with two controllers. But now I'm thirteen, Gramps has passed away, and what I want, money can't buy. This request may be outside the wish granter's mojo, but there's only one way to find out. As the sun goes down, I close my eyes and open my heart.

Wish granter, please make me better at basketball and help me get rid of my shy guy so this last year with Seth is the best one ever.

I open my eyes, then grab the basketball and practice for a while longer. If we win, it'll be because I gave it my best. But if we lose, it won't be because I didn't try.

CHAPTER FIVE

Every Sunday morning, we all pile into Dad's truck and go to Center Street Baptist Church. The service is long, and on top of that, we go early so Mom can talk to her best friend, Ms. Hannah, and Dad can hang out with Mr. Johnny Earl, his friend and coworker.

When the organist plays a few chords, it's everybody's cue to find their seats. My family takes their spot on the fourth pew from the front, like we always do, behind Ms. Hannah and her family, and directly in front of Mr. Johnny Earl and his family. When the choir marches in, led by Pastor Holloway, everybody stands and sings "Hosanna in the Highest."

But Seth and I changed the words and sing it as "Yo Santa is the fly-est."

We're not allowed to bring our phones, so when the preaching starts, Seth and I play the pinching game. The rules are simple: We take turns pinching each other.

The person *getting* pinched counts to five using their fingers, and then the person *giving* the pinch has to let go. Then we switch. The first one who taps their knee because they can't handle the pain loses.

As soon as Pastor Holloway starts preaching, the sanctuary goes quiet and Seth grabs the skin under my elbow, near my armpit, and squeezes. My eyes water as I clench my teeth to stop from screaming. I quickly count it out using my fingers. *One, two, three, four, five*. Seth lets go.

Now it's my turn.

I snake my fingers under his oversized shirt and pinch a tiny piece of bare skin. His body flinches, and Mom looks our way, so I have to let go to keep us from getting in trouble. Dang it.

I'm braced up and on guard, waiting for Seth to make his move, but he seems totally zoned into Pastor Holloway's sermon on being thankful. So I listen, too.

Just as I fully relax, Seth snatches that same patch of skin right under my armpit. I wasn't ready, and the pain streaks up my arm and out my mouth.

"Oooooowwwwwww!"

The pastor stops preaching. I feel the whole church watching me in silence, and my inner shy guy goes rock-concert loud at the unwanted attention. Desperate for an excuse that will keep me and Seth out of trouble, I go with the first one that pops in my head. With eyes closed, I wipe away fake tears, snort back invisible snot, slowly raise my hand, and speak up.

"Thank you, Jesus."

Pastor lifts his hand, too. "It's okay, Isaiah! Let it out, son! We all need to thank Him!"

The organ player mimics my words, over and over on the organ with musical notes, *La la, La-la!*

Pastor holds out his fist toward us and copies me and the organ player. "Thank you, Je-sus!"

But when the choir stands and the organ player cranks out a song, the place turns into a thank fest of dancing, singing, clapping, and shouting.

Seth's bent over, biting his lip to keep from howling, but I feel Mom and Dad shooting hot eye arrows at the side of my face. I guess they didn't buy my performance since our pew is the only one not rockin'.

After church, Ms. Hannah convinces Mom that I wasn't faking the holy spirit in the middle of Pastor's sermon. I get a bunch of hugs, and one old lady gives me a stick of gum and a quarter. Soon we grab our phones from under the truck seat. Mine pings with a text from Seth.

Got gum? That was hilarious watching you cover up for losing the game.

I text back. **Lose? I didn't pat my knee. And . . . I got paid.**

I show Seth my quarter, and we laugh as Dad orders chicken from Binky's drive-through so Mom doesn't have to cook, because Sunday is family day at the Abernathy house.

Dad laid that law down a long time ago. *There's nothing more important than spending time with family, and we're going to dedicate our Sundays to doing just that.* Mom doesn't cook, and Seth and I can't leave the farm.

We call it Jesus Jail.

At home, Seth and I do anything we can to pass the time—practice free throws, play video games, listen to music, even play thumb war. I take pictures of Dad with his arm around Mom as they nap together on the sofa. I practice more free throws for a while before Seth and I call it quits and go sit in our favorite spot—under the apple tree. I'm drinking a sports drink when Seth twists the top off his chocolate milk and nudges me.

"I was proud of you yesterday when you went into Redd's without me. For what it's worth, your shy guy took a big hit when you did that."

I get serious. "I want Shy Guy to be gone before you leave for college. Think I can do it?"

"You can do anything as long as you don't quit and speak up for yourself. I've got cross-country practice early in the morning, so I won't be here to remind you of all that. Don't forget."

"I won't," I say.

Later that evening, as Seth lies across his bed texting, I lie on mine getting mentally ready for my first day in yearbook class tomorrow. I must fall asleep, though, because next thing I know, my alarm blares. Seth's already gone, so I feed the animals, then grab the basketball and do what he showed me.

Boomph. Swish. Yes!

Clank. Dang it.

Four shots go in, but twenty-one of them are bricks. I'll try another twenty-five after school.

I walk to the mailbox every morning to catch my bus. It's about a mile from my house, but I use the walk to take pictures of cool things like snakes, turtles, whatever I see. When the bus comes, I give Mr. Williams—my bus driver since first grade—a big grin.

"Hi, Mr. Williams."

"Good morning, Isaiah. How's Seth?"

I take a seat. "He's good."

Two high school boys talk in the back, and four elementary school kids sit up front behind Mr. Williams. We all ride the same bus because the Scarboro school district can't afford to send three buses out here to pick up only seven or eight kids. When Mr. Williams pulls into the Spring Elementary School parking lot, the little ones rush over to the school building to find their teachers. For the rest of us, two more school buses wait. One goes to Scarboro High, the other to Brazos Bayou Middle School. As I get on the middle school bus, a loud voice makes me cringe.

"Rhino, you just stepped on my new Jordans! What's wrong with you?"

"My bad. They still look good," Rhino says.

Brandon keeps loud-talking him. "Lucky for you, or

else I'd make you clean 'em!"

If anyone needs to order a smack sandwich for Brandon, it's Rhino. He used to be such a happy, cool dude, but something changed, and whatever it was flipped him in a bad way.

Brandon yells from the back of the bus. "Caution, Ice Cream in the aisle!"

I take a seat up front and ignore him. I know he's looking for a fight, but I've got bigger dreams, and he's not in them.

CHAPTER SIX

It's just my bad luck that Brandon and Rhino are in my morning advisory before first period. I always sit as far away from them as possible while attendance is taken and Principal Cochran broadcasts the announcements. And as soon as the bell rings, I burn off down the hall.

Mr. Whitaker's standing in the doorway of yearbook class, greeting everyone. My inner shy guy tries to shut me down, but I stay strong. When it's my turn, I hand Mr. Whitaker my permission slip.

He attaches it to his clipboard and puts a check by my name. "Good morning, Isaiah! Welcome to the yearbook staff."

I nod but then remember what Seth said about speaking up. "Oh, uh, thank you."

"Do you like writing? Photography?"

"Photography."

"Perfect! We need another photographer. Let me introduce you to our editor."

I poke my head inside just enough to notice that even though the bell hasn't rung, it's already as busy as a news room. Mr. Whitaker calls out, "Zurie?"

Zurie Mitchell? We've ridden the same bus to Brazos since sixth grade, but I've never really talked to her. Rumor has it she's as mean as a honey badger, which is why she got the nickname Zurie Fury.

There's no shuffle in her steps or clickity-clack in those ankle boots as she pushes her glasses up the bridge of her nose with the back of her hand. Zurie's hair twists are all the same size, and almost as fly as my fade. She's a lot shorter than me—but everybody is.

"Isaiah Abernathy? What a nice surprise! You're always so quiet."

I prove her point, but not on purpose, as Shy Guy revs up my insides, making them goink and gurgle so loudly that Zurie notices.

"Wow. Your stomach speaks more than you do! Are you a writer or photographer?"

Speak up for yourself, Ice.

My face warms. "I, um, take pictures."

She looks over the top of her glasses at me. "Just because you like to take pictures doesn't make you a photographer. If you stand in a garage, does that make you a car?"

"It does if I use my Chevro-legs."

No I didn't just let Gramps's joke slide out of my mouth!

Mr. Whitaker laughs as Zurie just stares. I'm about to find out the truth behind that Zurie Fury nickname.

But instead she giggles. "Follow me, Isaiah Abernathy."

I grip the straps of my backpack as she introduces me to the department leaders, Jacob, Collin, Savannah, and Rashad. Then we walk to a cluttered space near the back of the room with a long table covered in stacks of yearbooks, photos, and other materials.

"This is the photography department. You and I are the only photographers on staff."

I peel my backpack off and set it on a chair. "And, uh—you can call me Ice."

Zurie's eyebrows gather. "Really? I didn't think you liked that nickname Brandon—"

"Just Ice."

"Got it. You can check out some of the other departments while we wait for Mr. Whitaker to let us know it's time for lecture."

"Okay."

I walk around, feeling good about speaking up for myself. This class is everything I hoped it would be as I listen in on conversations about where articles should be placed, whether certain pictures should be big or small, rectangular or round, even whether the sixth-grade or the eighth-grade pictures should be first in the yearbook.

I'm locked into the discussion when Mr. Whitaker asks for our attention. "Please turn your chairs toward my desk and answer this question: Why are yearbooks important?"

Hands go up everywhere. Mr. Whitaker calls on Collin.

"To remember friends, clubs, teachers, and when you get old, to show your kids."

Bam. He nailed it.

"That's true, Collin, but it's not the answer I'm looking for. Anyone else?"

When no one responds, Mr. Whitaker sits on the front edge of his desk. "You're not giving yourself enough credit for the valuable work you do! Every yearbook is a recording of people and events. When this one is finished, you will have created a history book."

He walks around the room again, stops behind me, and puts a hand on my shoulder. "What we design in here is more than just arts and crafts. A yearbook represents the happenings of this school, this city, even this world, one year at a time."

The bell rings, but nobody moves. It's as if Mr. Whitaker put us under a thinking spell and we can't break it. This is the first time I've ever not wanted to leave a classroom.

"All right, get moving to your next class," he says.

I step into the hall like a boss and walk like I'm important because I totally understand that I'm now a part of something huge. When I played sports, I tried—but it didn't matter to me what happened at the end of the game, and I felt bad about that. Now it's clear that it wasn't because I'm not a team player. I was just on the wrong team.

Zurie's in my second-period class, too, but for some

reason, Shy Guy jacks my confidence and I don't feel as comfortable around her as I did in yearbook. I kind of want to sit next to her, but I get nervous and shuffle to a desk three rows away.

Zurie's eyeballing me. I should get up and go sit with her—but she might already be salty, and I don't want her going all Zurie Fury on me in front everybody. I stay where I am, and after class, I rush out without looking her way. Ugh, that was such a Shy Guy move. If I could reach inside my chest and snatch him out, I'd drop-kick him to the moon.

After third and fourth period, I head to lunch and find an isolated table outside in the courtyard. I pop a fry in my mouth as I rip open the ketchup packets and squirt them all over my basket of cheese fries. So far my favorite class is yearbook, but I'm still trippin' on how I treated Zurie in second period. I've got to apologize.

That opportunity comes right after lunch as I'm heading to fifth-period science. Our eyes meet, and Shy Guy tries to shut me down again, but I take a deep breath and speak up.

"Hey, Zurie, can I— You got a minute?"

She frowns and goes off. "Oh, so you can see me now?"

I'm looking around, taking more deep breaths, and letting them out slowly. "Look, I just wanted to say—uh, see, I didn't mean to—"

I'm doomed when the last two guys I'd ever want to

hear me struggle walk up and interrupt my flow.

"Spit it out, Ice Cream, before Zurie drops her fury on you! Ha! Check 'em out, Rhino! Are they the perfect couple or what? One talks too much, and the other doesn't talk at all!"

As they stroll into science class, Zurie watches them, her head tilted. I clear my throat and pick up where I left off.

"Anyway, in English, I was going to sit next to you . . ."

Zurie slowly turns my way with a smile I can't read, and I brace for a fury buster as she takes her glasses off and dead-eyes me.

"You know what, Ice? I owe *you* an apology. And I should thank Brandon for reminding me that you're just not a talker. Who cares! He's right about something else, too—I can do enough talking for both of us. So we're cool, right?"

I force my nervous lips to part. "Yeah. We're cool."

The silence is awkward, so I try to keep the conversation going and not let Shy Guy take over. "What's your last class? I have history."

Zurie pushes her glasses up the bridge of her nose. "Algebra. Ugh, I hate math, but I love science. Is that weird? Anyway, we better get inside. I'm glad we talked about this."

Actually, she did all the talking, but that doesn't matter. When we walk into science class I sit next to her. She smiles, and I smile back as my knees jump and sweat rolls down the center of my back. But it's all good because, today, Shy Guy got punk'd by a girl who talks more than he does.

I can't wait to tell Seth.

CHAPTER SEVEN

After school, I swish six out of twenty-five free throws. That's two better than this morning, but I still stink. I shuffle inside and fall across my bed to enjoy the cool air. When Seth's truck rolls up, I open the window because I can't wait to tell him my news.

"Check me out! I'm the new photographer for the Brazos Bayou yearbook!"

He answers me. "And I'm the new office coordinator for Haylon, Price, and Green!"

I forgot what I was talking about. "Wait. What?"

He heads for the back door. "Hold on, I'm comin' in!"

Seth steps into our room, stripping off his backpack and taking off his sunglasses. Maybe I didn't hear him correctly, so I give him all my attention as he explains.

"I applied for a work internship through my career class at school. I got a voice mail from my teacher telling me about a job possibility, but the employer needed someone right away. Lucky for me, I had my clip-on tie in the truck, so I interviewed with this attorney named Trish Haylon, and bam, she hired me! How cool is it that we both had an awesome first day?"

I sit on my bed and stare at him. I used my birthday wish to ask that we have the best year ever. How's that going to happen if he has to work? "You didn't tell me you were looking for a job."

Seth's smile fades. "Are you salty?"

I quickly clear the air. "No, no! Just wondering, that's all."

"A&M gave me a one-year scholarship. What if they don't give me another one? Dad's not Mr. Moneybags. This job won't pay much, but I need my own cash flow for school if I want a college degree."

"Are we still going to do the sibling rivalry competition and other fun stuff?"

He bumps fists with me. "Of course!"

I tap the camera on my phone. "In that case, let's take a pic to remember Monday, August 30, when both of us did our thing on the same day! What are the odds?"

Click.

He takes a seat on his bed. "Okay, now tell me about this photography gig."

"The editor is this girl named Zurie Mitchell. I've known her since sixth grade."

He rubs his hands together. "I like how this is starting out! Did you talk to her?"

"I did in first period, but after that, my shy guy took over, and I avoided her."

He sighs. "And how'd that work out for you?"

I shrug. "Instead of apologizing to her, *she* apologized for not remembering that I don't talk much, and then said, 'I can do enough talking for both of us.' What'd she mean by that?"

"I'm not sure, so we better get you ready for tomorrow. Pretend I'm her and you want to be friends. What would you say?"

I think about it, relax my face, and hold out my empty hand. "Hi. Would you like this apple?"

Seth closes his eyes. "Oh my God. Shut up."

"It works for Dolly! She's a girl—okay, I know she's a horse, but talking to girls at school . . . I freeze and . . ."

"Okay, slow down. You sound a little . . . swaggravated."

I chuckle without meaning to. "No, I don't."

"Did *anything* go right with her?"

"Well, I said Gramps's Chevro-legs joke by accident, and she laughed."

"Girls love dudes who make them laugh! My little brotha's a smooth operator!" He stands. "You'll be fine. Okay, I smell pork chops. Let's go eat."

Seth and I playfully push each other on our way to the table, where Dad's complaining about BMP. I tell him about the truck Seth and I saw on my birthday, and his whole face tightens. "Two more drivers got speeding tickets over the weekend! Their belief that 'there and back in a dash makes more cash' has got to stop."

"But it won't as long as it's true," says Mom as she puts dinner on the table.

Dad surveys the meal Mom made and drops the conversation about BMP. He says the blessing, and the conversation changes when Seth taps his glass.

"I've got good news. I'm the new office coordinator at Haylon, Price, and Green."

Dad's face lights up like he's got bulbs in it. "You got a job at that law firm on Beacon?"

Seth's grinning. "I sure did! It's an internship through my career class."

Mom lifts her hands. "Hallelujah! God is good!"

Dad raises his glass of tea, and we all clank it for a toast. "Here's to my boy working for a big shot law firm. What are your hours?"

"It's part-time, so I'll work two-thirty to five. Check this out. If I work twelve hours a week, I'll earn college credit! Bonus! And it won't interfere with school or cross-country. He turns to me. "Ice has good news too, right?"

"Yeah! I'm officially a photographer for the yearbook! On Tuesdays and Thursdays, I'll have photography assignments after school until five."

Seth turns to Dad. "I get off work around the same time Ice gets out of his yearbook gig. I can swing by and pick him up after work on those days. Guaranteed brother time twice a week!"

Guaranteed brother time? Sounds like the wish granter is on the job!

Dad nods. "Sure. That okay with you, Ice?"

I playfully roll my eyes. "I guess so."

Seth gobbles down the last of his food. "That settles that! Now, if you'll excuse me, I've got an employee handbook to study and a few calls to make before bed."

Once I check on the animals and watch two episodes of *Law & Order* with Mom and Dad, I get ready for bed. I don't remember falling asleep, but I wake up to a sound I'm not used to hearing. I check my phone—it's two in the morning.

Seth's already sitting up. He walks to our window and lifts it. "What is that?"

I listen closer. "It's coming from the chicken coop."

Squaaaaaaawk!

I peel off my covers. "Something's wrong."

Seth grabs a flashlight as we rush outside barefoot and in our pajamas. He scans the ground with the high-beam flashlight—there, dragging Aretha by one of her wings, is a raccoon.

Squaaaaaawk! Squaaaaaawk! Buc-bucaaaaaaah!

Seth grabs the hose, squeezes the nozzle and drenches the chicken thief. It drops Aretha and scurries out of sight. Aretha drags her wing in obvious pain.

I tell Seth, "Stay with her! I'll be right back!"

I run toward the house to grab my tablet, then dash to the barn for my medicine bag. When I get back to the chicken coop, I pull up the vet website that helped me with Dolly's first aid. I find "wing care" and then hand my tablet to Seth. "Hold this—and I need more light."

"No problem," he says.

I read all the instructions, then check her wing. "No pieces of bone sticking out, and other than her dragging it, nothing's out of place. It's bloody, and she's got a patch where her feathers are missing, but there's no bite marks. The raccoon must've pulled the feathers out when he grabbed her. Maybe her wing is just sprained or dislocated."

I pull bandages, antiseptic wipes, and wound ointment from my bag, pet her again, then signal for Seth. "Dude, prop the light, then grab some gloves and hold Aretha. Be gentle—she's in pain."

As Seth keeps her still, I gently clean the area where she lost her feathers, then wrap her wing close to her body. "I have to make sure I don't accidentally wrap her vent."

"You mean her butt?" asks Seth.

"Chickens lay their eggs and poop out the same hole. It's called a vent."

"That's nasty, and you're nasty for knowing it. Hurry up and get done."

Moments later, I'm finished, and Seth gently places her on a stack of hay in the coop. She seems calmer now, and so do the others. Dad walks in. "What's going on out here?"

Seth and I tell him, and he looks in the direction where

the raccoon escaped. "I'll get some rodent control and spread it near the coop. Raccoons don't like the smell."

"Make sure that stuff won't harm the chickens," I say.

"It won't. You boys get back to bed. It's after three, and we have to get up soon."

Seth's about to leave the chicken coop, but I stop him. "Let's take a pic with Aretha."

Click.

He puts an arm around my shoulders. "Good work, Dr. Abernathy."

Back in our room, we both plop into our beds, but all I can think about is how amazing I feel right now, knowing we saved Aretha's life! When I become a vet, I'm going to have a free site, too, so I can help others do what I just did.

CHAPTER EIGHT

When my alarm goes off Tuesday morning, I'm fired up about hanging out with Seth later and reliving what we did for Aretha last night. As I sit in advisory and wait for the announcements to be over, I even daydream about what we might do. But once the bell rings, and I take a seat in yearbook class, all my mental noise shuts down.

Mr. Whitaker's gentle smile greets us again as he sits on the front of his desk. "Good morning, staff." When it's time for lecture, we all give him our attention. "My question for you today is, what makes the perfect collage?"

Answers come from all sides of the room—themes, contrasts, colors, even movement.

"What about camera angle? Can you create the perfect collage using positions or views?" Mr. Whitaker looks my way. "Isaiah, what are your thoughts?"

I shake my head and shrug him off. I'd rather eat rocks than get called on to speak, especially when I'm not sure I'm right. So Mr. Whitaker puts the question back to the class.

"Anybody have thoughts on this?"

I'm mad at myself for letting Shy Guy win, especially when Seth told me to speak up. I'm not a quitter. I'm part of this crew, and I've got something to say, no matter if it's right or not.

"Mr. Whitaker, I . . . uh . . . changed my mind. I'd like to say something about camera angle. See, if you've got the right camera angles, they can definitely help you make the perfect collage, even if all the pics are of the same thing."

Everyone's staring at me, and I'm tempted to change my mind again, but I've got to do this. "Let me show you what I mean. May I use my phone?"

Mr. Whitaker nods. "Yes, you may."

I focus on my pictures. Once I find the file, I hand my phone to Collin. "Okay, check it out. These are pictures of my horses, Dolly and Buster. I like to use different angles when I'm snapping pics of them, you know, angles that show their personalities, their strengths, their beauty."

Zurie's looking over Colin's shoulder. "You have horses? Seriously?"

Oh no. Having horses is a dead giveaway that I live in the boonies on enough land to own cattle. Shy Guy's going off, calling me a country bumpkin and telling me that the laughing's going to start any minute. But it doesn't, so I keep talking.

"Sometimes the horses aren't in the mood for photo shoots, so I have to get creative."

Collin passes my phone to Savannah. Rashad and Jacob lean in to look at the pics with her. Mr. Whitaker's on the move. "And how would that help with a collage?"

"It helps me separate the images into categories. The collage could be about different moods. Sometimes I'll squat or lie on the ground and snap pics. That makes Dolly and Buster look huge and powerful. When I want a habitat pic, I'll stand on something above them."

My classmates are all into the pictures. I start to walk as I talk, just like Mr. Whitaker.

"Or maybe I'll take close-ups of their faces to focus on something specific, like their kind eyes or their flaring nostrils. That's why photos that use different angles can combine to make a perfect collage."

Savannah passes my phone to Mr. Whitaker. He checks out the pics, smiles, then hands my phone back to me. "I call that the perfect answer, Isaiah."

"Thank you." I take my seat, wishing I had recorded this proof that Shy Guy is definitely getting weaker. When the bell rings, I start to strut toward my next class, but Zurie catches up with me.

"Your pictures were incredible," she says.

"Thanks."

"Sit by me in English. I want to look at more pictures of your horses."

"Okay."

I show her pictures of Seth and me riding Dolly and Buster, two of Buster and Dolly galloping around the pasture, and one picture of them eating hay. Zurie can't seem to get enough, so I keep showing her more pics until the bell rings. She even looks at them during class.

When it's time for lunch, I'm ready for a little alone time, so I find a spot in the courtyard. I almost jump out of my skin when someone touches my shoulder. It's Zurie.

She sets down her lunch tray. "I love horses," she says. "I'm going to be a veterinarian."

I sit up straighter. "Really? Me, too!"

She side-eyes me. "Okay, this is getting weird. Do you have any other animals? I mean, I've got two dogs and a gerbil, but that's nothing like having a horse. Where do you live?"

I keep my eyes on her. "On a . . . farm."

She playfully rolls her eyes as she inhales, but then exhales a smile. "Now I'm super jealous."

I chuckle. "But not fury jealous, right?"

Our smiles fade at the same time as Zurie drops her head. What was I thinking?

"I didn't mean that the way it sounded—I'm sorry," I say.

She shrugs and pushes her veggies around her plate. "You know what it's like to get a bad nickname."

"I do" is all I can say.

"I bet you didn't deserve yours just like I didn't deserve

mine," she says, now looking at me. "See, last year, I tried out to be the kicker for the seventh-grade football team, and I made it! But some of the guys complained about a girl being on *their* team and stopped blocking for me. Finally, I totally lost it on the field and quit. As I walked away, one boy yelled, 'Watch out for Zurie Fury!' Coach made him run sprints, but it didn't matter—the tag stuck anyway."

I don't say anything until I can't hold it anymore. "You got your nickname from a jerk. I got mine from one, too. The world is full of 'em. I'm scratching *fury* off my vocab list."

She slings her backpack over her shoulder. "That's pretty extreme, but I believe you. You're a good listener, Ice Abernathy. Hey, do you have an Instagram page?"

"Nope."

I hope my face can lie as well as my lips because there's no way I'll let her know that I've been IcePicAbernathy on Instagram for two years. All my posts are private because I get enough bullying in person from Brandon—I don't need it in hashtags, too. I just use IG to check out other people's pics, follow veterinarians, and watch funny reels.

"Seriously? With all those gorgeous pics of your horses? You should create one—you're awesome with a camera. Let me know if you change your mind, and I'll follow you. Later, Ice."

I spend the rest of lunch wondering how many more people in the world get ridiculous nicknames like Ice

Cream or Zurie Fury because they don't fit what others want them to be.

Later, as I shuffle into fifth period, I'm in a fantastic mood. For the first time ever, being quiet was a good thing, and it pays off when I step into science class and Zurie calls out, "Hey, Ice, over here. I saved you a seat."

Brandon interrupts. "Why did Zurie Fury call him Ice? Ice isn't soft. Right, Rhino?"

Rhino doesn't answer, but the whole class watches as Brandon keeps going. "Ice Cream, you're the only tall Black dude I know who can't hoop. I bet you granny-shoot free throws like an old lady!"

Snapsickles! What if some of my classmates show up at the competition? They'll know Brandon's right! Suddenly, I get a wild idea. If it works, I might lose my horrible nickname. But if it fails, Brandon's going to blow, Rhino's going to charge, and everything could get out of control.

Stay calm. Be smooth. Say it like you mean it.

Without a smile, without a blink, I stand strong and pray I don't throw up. "I'm better than you'll ever be at free throws, and that includes granny shots."

Phones light up around the room.

Brandon takes a step closer. "Excuse me? Is that a challenge?"

Easy, don't rush. Breathe. Be smooth. Now say it!

I take a step toward him. "That's exactly what it is. Ever heard of the sibling rivalry competition? Seth and I are signed up. He's running. I'm shooting free throws."

Brandon smirks. "I'm signed up for free throws, too. You'll never beat me."

Stay calm. You got this. Now bring it home.

"I think my grandma could've spanked you at free throws. So, in her honor, I'm going to granny-shoot all mine at the competition."

His grin gives me chills. "When you lose, you'll wear a T-shirt with a chocolate soft-serve ice cream cone on it for a whole week!"

I counter him. "When I *win*, you have to stop calling me Ice Cream. Forever!"

He holds out his fist for me to bump. "Deal."

I leave him hangin' and take a seat. "Deal."

CHAPTER NINE

After science class, I stand in the hall, trying to find the rhythm in my breathing. Other kids, even sixth and seventh graders I don't know, hold up their hands for high fives and fist bumps.

"Take him down, Isaiah!"

"Dude, I'm rooting for you."

What's happening? Why are they talking to me? Shy Guy goes berserk as I try to avoid other kids and get to my next class. Zurie pulls up next to me.

"And just that fast, hashtag 'thebrazosbayoubet' is trending on Instagram. You should really think about signing up. All you need is a cool username."

"I'll think about it," I say.

She smiles. "I would love to see a reel of Dolly and Buster. I'd watch it all day! See you after school."

I rush into sixth period and plop in the last desk in the

last row against the wall, thinking about the bonehead bet I just made. What if I don't win? Will everybody think Brandon was right to call me Ice Cream? I can't tell Seth. The competition is for siblings, but this bet is all mine.

After school, I stroll into Mr. Whitaker's classroom for my first after-school meeting. I'm still thinking about the bet when Zurie hands me a 35mm camera.

"Ever use one of these? The shutter speed is lightning fast, just point and shoot."

Thrill chills rush from my head to my feet and back again. "I can handle it."

"Good. We've got a photo shoot with Mr. Cochran in five minutes. Let's go."

I carry all the photography equipment while she talks. "We're doing a spread on his ten-year anniversary as principal. Rashad's already started the interview. I'll do the video. You handle the still frames."

"Got it."

As Rashad and Mr. Cochran greet us, I'm thinking about angles and positions for this camera shoot. Mr. Whitaker said we're creating a history book, so once we begin, I take pictures of anything and everything in Cochran's office that would make this year memorable.

When we're back in Mr. Whitaker's room, the obnoxious honk of Seth's Chevy causes everyone to stop working. I look out the window into the parking lot, then quickly give the camera to Zurie and shrug.

"It's my brother. That horn is brutal."

I turn to leave but then, before I can chicken out, I spin back around to face her and let her know: "There may be a guy named IcePicAbernathy on Instagram. You should check out his pics."

"Okay. I'll let you know if I find him." She smiles.

Outside I'm grinning when Seth calls out. "Come on! I'm still on the clock!"

I buckle up, and he burns off. "Hey, Seth. You good? Why are you early?"

"It was either now or way later because I've still got a bunch of things to do!"

I grin. "What are we going to do after you finish? That new superhero movie—"

His phone buzzes.

"Shhh! It's my boss."

I roll my eyes so hard that it turns my head toward the window.

"Hi, Trish. I'm around the corner from the client's office. Yes, ma'am. Goodbye."

He winks. "Ms. Haylon lets me call her by her first name because I'm fly like that."

He pulls up in front of a building but doesn't turn off the ignition. "I'll be right back."

Minutes later, he hands me a manila envelope. "Hold that for me."

I try again. "Okay. So, I read online that the new super-hero—"

Bzzz. Bzzz.

Seth presses the speaker button, and a man talks to him as he merges in traffic. "Yes, sir, I'll be there in two minutes."

Soon he pulls over on Beacon Avenue in front of Haylon, Price, and Green and points across the street. "You can pick up that coffee shop's Wi-Fi from here. The law firm's Wi-Fi is protected."

Seth takes the envelope and jogs to the office. I tap on my Instagram account, looking to see if Zurie followed me yet, but then a voice makes me drop my phone in my lap.

"Hi! I'm Uncle Jerry! What's your name?"

I smile so he won't think I'm upset. "Ice."

Uncle Jerry's whole face fills my window. Rhino's on the sidewalk behind him, texting.

"We're going to the store. Wanna come? You can get a free cookie," he says.

I shake my head. "Maybe next time."

Uncle Jerry's face saddens as he turns to Rhino. "He doesn't want a free cookie."

Rhino calls softly. "It's okay, Unc. Let's go, because it's getting late."

Uncle Jerry's expression changes to all smiles. "We have to go. Goodbye!"

"Goodbye, Uncle Jerry."

I don't understand how Rhino can be so caring with his uncle *and* be best friends with a jerk like Brandon. I'm still thinking about it when Seth comes back.

"What a day—I got my mind on a smoothie."

I buckle up. "Me, too!"

He pulls up to Sir Smoothie and orders us the usual while I snag a table. I'm already chilled, happy to just hang out with my brother. Seth hands me my smoothie and takes a seat.

"Dude, the partners like me. They moved into this office two weeks ago. You wouldn't believe all the boxes I had to unpack. Yo, I worked hard today. My whole body hurts, but it's a good hurt, know what I mean?"

I nod. "Not the same hurt you would've had if you worked at a slop joint like BMP."

Seth leans in. "About that. See, there's this one huge thing. I'll tell you, but you can't tell Dad."

His voice has fear in it, so I inhale big and exhale slowly, hoping it'll calm him. "Sure."

"A few days before I got this job, I got a call from this dude named Deacon at BMP to set up a job interview."

"You did? That was probably Dad trying to hook you up."

He closes his eyes. "I didn't want the job because I'd have to wash the inside of those trucks after they delivered raw meats. The smell alone could kill my swag. When Deacon called, I didn't have any other job offers, so I set a date to go in. But then the law firm gig came through. It was the job I really wanted. So I ditched the BMP interview. Don't tell Dad."

I whisper out of fear. "Dad will crap a cow if he finds out you blew off the interview."

Seth leans back. "You've got to keep that on the down-low."

"Don't worry, I got you."

After dinner, Seth studies his work manual again, does his homework, and shuffles to bed because he has cross-country practice in the morning. I step over to the chicken coop and lift Aretha up on the hay with the other hens, and then shoot my free throws. Fifteen out of twenty-five. That's three better than this morning! I wish Seth could've seen.

Later that evening, I'm about to get in bed when my phone dings.

LadyZurieM would like to follow you.

CHAPTER TEN

I thought this week would be live and legit, but it's been deader than disco. Seth picks me up again on Thursday, but we go straight home because he has a cross-country meet early in the morning. So when my alarm goes off at five on Friday, I feed the animals and then crawl into the back of Dad's truck, still half-asleep, and we head to Seth's meet. Mom's behind us in her van because Dad has to go straight to work when it's over, so she'll take me to school.

We get there just in time, and when the starting pistol pops, a human stampede takes off, with Seth and Juan Carlos running stride for stride as I get it all on video. But twenty-six minutes later, there's nobody even near Seth as he breaks the winner's tape. Mom's waving, and Dad's pumping his fist. I turn around and catch Juan Carlos finishing with his hands raised in the air.

"You guys wrecked," I say, giving Seth and Juan Carlos high fives.

"Thanks. See you when I get home from work, okay?" Seth says, still out of breath.

I nod and head to Mom's van. After she drops me off, I'm standing on the sidewalk in front of the school, checking out Instagram reels, when someone smacks my phone out of my hand.

Crack.

No! Dang it! I grab it off the ground and stare at the fresh scratches on my shiny screen protector as Brandon tries to crowd me.

"That's what I'm going to do to you at the competition, Ice Cream. Crack your face."

I snatch a handful of his shirt. He tries to overpower me, but instead I slam him against the brick. His mouth opens, and I'm close to ordering that combo meal when I realize . . . fighting isn't what I do. Free throws isn't, either, but Brandon just gave me more determination to beat him in a way that will hurt him more—and not get me in trouble.

"Abernathy, no! Don't do it! Let him go!"

Principal Cochran runs toward us. "Back up, Isaiah. What's going on here?"

Brandon goes for the Academy Award as he straightens his shirt. "What happened was, he—uh—attacked me— for—accidentally cracking his phone."

Mr. Cochran puts up a hand. "I don't believe that, and the way you're stuttering, you can't even make *yourself* believe it. If I catch you two tangled up again, I'll send both of you home, got it?"

"Yes, sir," I say.

"I didn't do anything," says Brandon.

Officer Simms, our school's security guard, rushes outside. "Everything okay out here?"

Mr. Cochran nods toward the front doors. "Both of you, git."

Brandon follows me to my locker. "I promise you'll regret what you started back there, Ice Cream."

I slam my locker door as Brandon walks away, laughing. The day continues in the wrong direction when I knock over a chair in advisory and then trip over it. Brandon snickers. On my way into first period, I bump into Mr. Whitaker, and he spills coffee on his tie. Dang it.

"My bad, Mr. Whitaker."

"No worries, Isaiah. I've got a backup tie in my desk drawer."

In gym, I get a zero for the day because I forgot my gym clothes at home, and then I fail a surprise quiz in science. I just want to get on the bus, go home, and hang out with Seth. So after Mr. Williams finally drops me off at the mailbox, I exhale all the bad school air and take in a big breath of country calm.

But Seth's not there. When he's still not home before dinner, I plop into my seat, and as soon as Dad finishes blessing the table, I ask.

"Where's Seth?"

Dad answers. "He's spending the weekend with Juan Carlos, and going to church with his family. He didn't tell you?"

"No, he didn't."

As soon as I'm finished eating, I call Seth. "Why didn't you tell me you were spending the weekend with Juan Carlos?"

There's loud music in the background. "I didn't? My bad, Ice. I'll be home on Sunday. We'll suffer in Jesus Jail together."

Jesus Jail? The way my brother's been bailing on me, I feel like I'm in Seth Jail.

I spend the weekend hanging out with the animals and practicing free throws. In church, Mom and Dad make me sit between them because of my "Thank you, Jesus" moment last Sunday. Jesus Jail feels slower than snails in molasses until Seth drags in just before bedtime.

"What happened? I waited for you all day!"

He smiles. "Dude, you're going to have to give me a pass. I partied all night on Friday, again on Saturday, and today, after church, I played outfield in a pickup baseball game. I need to sleep."

If I say something, he'll think I'm salty—and maybe I am because we don't have that many days left before the sibling rivalry. He's supposed to be helping me with free throws. I worked so hard on them this weekend that I banked seventeen out of twenty-five today! And tomorrow is Labor Day, so maybe we'll do something fun.

I wake up to someone nudging me. "Ice, I'll be back this afternoon."

I rub my eyes. "What? Where are you going?"

"To a special brunch for seniors. Don't forget to practice your free throws. Later."

I don't say anything. What good would it do? Instead, I get up and feed the animals, then boomph-swish eighteen perfect shots! I'm on a roll, and Seth's not even here. I should've never agreed to this sibling rivalry thing. Seth said it was something for us to do together, and now I feel like he played me.

When he gets home, all he wants to talk about is what he did today, and then a girl calls him. I become invisible, so I grab my tablet, leave the room and go sit under the apple tree.

Early Tuesday, I'm sitting on the bus, still angry, when my phone buzzes.

Trish is closing the office early. Don't catch the bus. We'll do Sir Smoothie.

I answer with a smiley emoji because I'm not trying to get pumped up for no reason. But when the last bell rings, and I spot Seth's truck in the student pickup line, all my anger dies.

"What's up?" I ask, belting myself in.

"Yo, little brotha, I hope you didn't feel like I was ghosting you this weekend. It wasn't like that. I made some promises, know what I mean? We good?"

I nod, happy to have my brother back. "Yeah, we're good. Between brothers."

He grins. "All day. Let's get gone."

Soon, he parks in front of Sir Smoothie then walks inside to order. I'm about to get out of the truck when I see an open envelope on the dashboard. It's from Texas A&M. Is Seth about to drop some awesome news on me? I bet that's why he brought me to Sir Smoothie! We're celebrating! I've got to know what it says! He's not watching, so I pull the letter out of the envelope but feel sick after reading the first line.

> *Dear Seth Abernathy,*
> *It is with great pleasure that we can inform you that your request for early enrollment at Texas A&M has been approved! Please make arrangements to be in College Station on Tuesday, January 14, for orientation, and to meet with your counselor. We will send more information in the coming weeks to help you transition to campus life. We look forward to seeing you in January!*

My brain numbs. I can't think, I can't do the math, but that's got to be at least six or seven months we just lost. I read the letter again to make sure I didn't miss a word or a sentence that would make better sense of this. My eyes drift from the letter to the windshield, where I spot

Seth standing in front of the truck, holding two jumbo smoothies, staring at me.

He opens his door and stands there. "Why are you reading my mail?"

"Why didn't you tell me about this?"

He sets the drinks in the cup holders. "Let's go somewhere else and talk."

I blast him. "No! Let's talk it out right here!"

Seth gets in and slams the door. "Fine! Here's the deal. I'm eligible to graduate high school in December, so I got offered a chance to begin college in the spring. A&M has a huge campus and I'm already stressin' about leaving home. If I start in the spring, I can begin training with my team and even knock out a few classes so I won't have as many when cross country takes off in the fall. Starting early will help me adjust, you know, get my mind right because when A&M cross-country season begins, I want to be ready to do my thing. I thought you'd be happy for me."

"I am! Seth, listen to me! I couldn't be happier for you."

"Then what's this about?"

I shake my head. "It's not about you! Or me! It's about *us*. Once you leave for A&M, days like today won't happen anymore."

He frowns. "What? Dude, I'll be home for winter and summer breaks."

"But it's the *right now* that I'm talking about! You promised to help me with my free throws but you haven't. You said we'd do fun stuff, but we haven't. It's as if what you

66

said wasn't true, like you've been playin' me."

He gets serious. "I'm not playin' you, Ice."

And right there, he takes off his necklace with the golden track shoes and puts it in my hand. "This isn't just a pair of shoes on a chain. It's who I am. But I'm giving it to you. Between brothers. I won't be gone forever—I promise I'll be back."

He puts the truck in reverse. "I didn't realize you needed more help with your free throws. We'll get it done. Now, let's go check out that superhero movie."

I'm all in my feelings. Seth always seems to know how to make everything all right.

Tuesday and Wednesday evenings, Seth's with me as I work extra hard on my mechanics and my focus, but Shy Guy's got me trippin'. I wipe sweat off my face.

"What if I get tight? What if the crowd distracts me?"

"Have you forgotten? You're Ice Abernathy, the cold-blooded transfer from Shy Town, the nastiest free throw shooter in Scarboro. How are you going to represent? Like this."

As soon as our song comes on, we walk it out. I spin around and spot Dad walking it out, too, old-school style. Look at us Abernathy men, getting rid of our stress without caring who's watching! I video the moment for proof because who would ever believe I'd practice a game I hate just to beat someone I hate while spending time with people I love.

CHAPTER ELEVEN

Thursday morning, I'm jolted awake by Seth's yelling. "Wake up! It's game day, baby!"

It takes a minute to clear my mental cobwebs, then I yell back, "That's right! Let's go!"

Seth helps me feed the animals, and as he drives me to school we're hyped, listening to music. But when he pulls up to the curb, suddenly I don't feel good. "Either I've got butterflies in my belly or Shy Guy's acting up," I say.

He frowns. "Butterflies? Shy Guy? Dude! Release your inner dragon—free that giant cyclops and let it deliver a combo meal to Shy Guy! See you at five!"

We both laugh, but as soon as Seth's gone, I rush to a trash can and puke my guts out. Seth doesn't know about the bet, but it seems everybody at school has something to say.

"We're with you, Ice."

"Do your thing, Ice."

My stomach stays queasy all day. I avoid Brandon, in and outside of class. At ten minutes to five, I wait on Seth inside the school doors but there's a different familiar truck at the curb.

"Hey, Dad. You didn't have to pick me up. Seth's coming."

I buckle up, and he drives off. "Call your brother."

His sharp tone puts me on red alert as I call Seth, who picks up and whispers, "Dude, I got a call this morning from my A&M coach. He's in meetings not far from Scarboro and invited all the incoming A&M athletes in the area, along with our parents, to a gathering. He apologized for it being last minute, but I told him I'd be there. Mom's with me. We're only thirty minutes from Scarboro, so don't worry. I'll be at the competition in time. Gotta go. My phone battery's—"

"But, Seth—hello?"

I turn to Dad. "He said he'll be there."

When we arrive at the rec center, Dad smiles. "Don't stress, he's coming."

The lady behind the desk types as I give her my information.

"Where's your sibling?"

"He's on his way," I say.

She nods, then pins a number on my back. "I'm Ms. Scott. We're going to get started in just a moment." She turns on a microphone. "Please clear the floor for round one of the free throw competition. Isaiah Abernathy,

Brandon Hart, Gail Lyons, and Maria Sanchez, please report to center court."

My breaths come shorter and faster as I walk across the gym floor. Shy Guy's screaming for me to leave when Brandon bumps me. "You better granny-shoot all your free throws, Ice Cream, or you lose the bet."

I'm trying to swallow my nerves when a referee asks me to follow him to a free throw line with a rack of basketballs near it. "You have five minutes to shoot fifty shots. I'll be recording your hits and misses on this sheet, and someone will rerack the balls for you as you go. Once the buzzer sounds, you can begin. When I blow my whistle, stop shooting."

I take a deep breath and let it out slowly. "Yes, sir."

My heart's banging against my rib cage like free throws hitting the backboard. *Boomph-swish. Boomph-swish.* Where's Seth?

BUZZZZZZZZ.

Snapsickles! I dribble twice and release the ball just as Rhino shouts, "Hey! Look at Granny shoot her free throws!"

Clank.

Everyone's laughing until the referee blows his whistle. "Rhino, do that again and you're out."

Rhino heads to a side door but gives a thumbs-up to Brandon, who gives him one back.

The ref looks my way. "Are you okay?"

No, I'm not okay. I'm blowing it! "Can I start over?"

He shakes his head. "Unfortunately, that shot counts as one miss. But I'll give you thirty seconds to regroup before I signal the timekeeper to hit the buzzer again."

Seth, where are you? I can't do this by myself. I'm not ready.

Suddenly, my brain pushes all my stinkin' thinkin' aside, and reminds me what Seth said.

You're Ice Abernathy. The cold-blooded transfer from Shy Town, who's now the nastiest free throw shooter in Scarboro. How are you going to represent?

I put my earbuds in, close my eyes, and take deep breaths. The music energizes me to release my inner dragon, free the cyclops, and kick Shy Guy off the court.

BUZZZZZZZZZ.

My eyelids open, and I turn my feet, bend my knees, dribble twice, and pretend I'm practicing at home.

Boomph-Swish. Boomph-Swish. Boomph-Swish.

Soon, the referee moves my rack from me.

I take my earbuds out. "What's wrong now?"

"You've taken your fifty shots. And I must say I've never seen anyone granny-shoot like that! You rocked the house! You've set a new sibling rivalry record for free throws—forty-nine out of fifty. The only way you'll lose is if someone gets a perfect score."

I look at the scoring sheet. "What? Can I take a picture of that?"

The referee shakes my hand. "You sure can."

Click.

I'm mentally taking back that shame Brandon and his

dad put on me when I was nine. Now it's *my* dad's turn to be proud. "Dad! Where are you?"

He pushes through the crowd. "Over here!" He hugs me close. "I'm so proud of you."

Ms. Scott announces, "Free throw competitors, please clear the floor, and participants in the two-mile run, report to the track. Last call for Seth Abernathy. Report to the registration desk immediately."

Dad checks his phone, then shakes his head. "I'm calling your mother."

I can tell he's listening to a voice message as Ms. Scott approaches us. "We haven't heard from Seth, so I'm afraid you'll have to forfeit as a team. But after all the free throw shooting is finished, if you win an individual medal, we'll contact you."

Dad nods. "Thank you. Come on, Isaiah."

I follow him through the crowd, begging my tears to wait until I'm alone. Kids fist-bump me, and I thank them, but none of it makes me feel better.

Someone grabs my hand. It's Zurie. "Ice, you did it! Brandon only made forty-two!"

Right now, all I can do is nod and keep walking, hoping she'll understand.

Juan Carlos man-hugs me. "Where's Seth? I can't believe he missed it! Tonight, you became a legend!"

I thank Juan Carlos, but he's wrong. I didn't become a legend. I became invisible. Seth ghosted me.

* * *

I'm still fuming when we get home. Dad and I are on the sofa watching TV when a key jiggles in the lock. As soon as the door opens, Dad gets up and speaks for both of us.

"We've been trying to get hold of you!"

Mom puts down her purse. "I'm so sorry. We didn't mean to miss it."

Dad's still upset. "Why didn't you call?"

"Seth's phone died, and I left mine on the nightstand. Then the coach wanted to speak to Seth. I'm so tired, Ray. I'm going to bed. Isaiah, I'm sorry, baby. We'll talk tomorrow, okay?"

"Yes, ma'am."

As soon as she closes her bedroom door, Seth picks up where she left off. "I'm sorry. I tried to get there but . . . man, this is the worst."

I can't be quiet any longer. "How could you miss this, Seth? You promised!"

He explains, looking from me to Dad. "After the gathering, my track coach asked to speak to me. I couldn't leave."

"The whole place laughed at me for shooting granny shots!"

He sighs. "I hate that I wasn't there for you, but what I was doing was important, too."

I grab the gold shoes from the necklace and hold it up like a badge toward him. "A promise is a promise, but you chose A&M over us. What's between brothers? I guess nothing."

Dad steps in. "Okay, that's enough. Go get ready for bed."

I storm into the bedroom, slamming the door behind me, then I take off his necklace and fling it against the wall. Even through the closed door, I can hear something going down in the living room.

"Let's talk about you deceiving me," says Dad.

Seth's voice rises. "What? I didn't deceive you!"

"Really? Then why didn't you tell me you blew off the interview with Deacon at BMP?"

Uh-oh. I get closer to the door so I can hear everything. It's quiet, but not for long.

"I'm sorry, Dad. I just couldn't tell you."

"You didn't show up, and you didn't let Deacon know you weren't coming. You have no idea what I went through to get you that interview! I'm so disappointed in you, Seth."

"I didn't mean— It's— I don't want to work at BMP!"

Dad hollers. "Why not!"

Then the house referee steps in. Her sharp but calm voice puts a padlock on that argument. I rush to the window and pretend I'm staring out as Seth storms in, changes clothes, and gets in bed. I wait to see if he's going to say something, but he doesn't. Fine. I won't, either.

CHAPTER TWELVE

I'm in a deep sleep when someone grabs my arm. "Wake up!"

My eyes flip open as I try to clear my mind and sit up. "What's wrong?"

Seth's frowning, his grip getting tighter. "Why'd you go off on me last night?"

Everything's coming back, but I'm extra salty about the way he woke me up, and I yank myself away. "You ghosted me, remember?"

"What? How can you think I skipped the sibling rivalry on purpose?"

I'm still trying to clear the cobwebs. "It doesn't matter, just leave me alone."

"It does matter! You act like I ditched you for a date!"

My body tightens. "Making us forfeit last night was just like ditching me for a date!"

Seth puts his hands on top of his head. "Listen to your-self! Me, me, me!"

I'm getting tighter. "You skipped me, just like you skipped your interview at BMP!"

His eyes have fire in them. "I can't believe you went there. Did you tell Dad?"

"No!"

"I bet you did. I should've never trusted you with that."

We're toe to toe. "I didn't tell!"

"Why should I believe you? You don't believe me!"

I'm shaking. "Shut up, Seth, I mean it."

"I thought you really cared about my future, about us being brothers."

He better back up off me, all in my face.

Seth shakes his head like he's disgusted. "I guess between brothers is no longer a thing for us since all you care about is yourself!"

"Shut up!" My fingers curl and, without thinking, I unleash a punch on Seth's mouth that I'd been saving for Brandon. My hand throbs, bringing me back to my senses. Blood oozes from a cut on his bottom lip, and my heart drops. What have I done?

"Seth? I didn't . . ." I stare at the blood trickling from his lip, wondering how things got so out of control. "See, I was asleep, and you woke me up, hollering and saying stuff that—"

He grabs a T-shirt from the hamper and holds it to his mouth as he walks by. "Save it."

Tears blur my vision as I follow him to his truck, barefoot and still in my pajamas. "Seth, wait! Please."

But he doesn't.

I head back inside to the bathroom sink and scrub at the guilt on my knuckles, but it won't come off. I should've apologized right away. I sit on the bed and try to call him, but then notice it's already after six. My bus comes at seven, and I haven't fed the animals. Dang it!

I rush outside, fill the wheelbarrow, and roll it to the chicken coop. I don't have time to pet them or collect the eggs. I toss them food and leave before they gather around my feet. A quick dump of food to the pigs and some hay to Dolly and Buster gets me back to the house so I can get dressed. But first I need to call Seth.

Ring. Ring. Ring. "You've reached Seth. Leave me a message."

He's never been so mad at me that he didn't answer before. I really messed up this time. His cross-country meet is out of town, which means I won't see him until after school. I grab a blueberry muffin off the table, fake a smile to my parents, and try to leave before they ask questions.

Dad hollers, "Everything okay? You need a ride, Isaiah?"

"No, sir, I can make it."

Outside, black smoke rises in the distance. Must be a neighbor burning trash. But I've got my own fire to put out. I call Seth again, and it goes to voice mail, same as before. This time, I leave a message.

"Seth, it's me. I'm so sorry. Please call me back."

I barely make it to the mailbox before my bus pulls up. I take my seat, then send a text.

I'm trying to call you and apologize. Will you at least text me back? I'm really sorry.

"Looks like a bad fire somewhere," says Mr. Williams.

I don't respond because I'm too busy staring at my phone, waiting for Seth to text back. Dad's truck zooms by, and now I'm thinking the fire must be at BMP. I hope it's not too serious.

When Mr. Williams finally pulls into the elementary school parking lot, my second bus is waiting. As I walk down the aisle, someone claps, and others join in—I'm sure it's a smart-aleck response to me making everyone late. Zurie moves her books so I can sit next to her.

The kid sitting across from me leans my way. "Congratulations. You wrecked last night."

"Got the whole thing on video," Zurie says.

I nod because I've still got Seth on my brain. "Thanks." Snapsickles! I didn't even tell Seth how well I did at the free throw line last night.

Maybe it would be more fun to celebrate if he would just text me back. As I step into advisory, everyone claps except Brandon and Rhino. I take a seat near the window and hide my phone on my lap. *Come on, Seth, text me back.*

Just before the bell rings, an office helper comes in and holds up a pass. "Isaiah, Mr. Cochran needs to see you."

Brandon laughs. "What'd you do, Ice Cream? Commit armed robbery?"

One of the football jocks interrupts. "Yeah, he stole the free throw title from you!"

Everybody's laughing, except the office worker. "Mr. Cochran said it's important."

I grab my backpack and pick up the pace. When I step inside his office, Mr. Cochran's at his desk. "Come in, Isaiah, shut the door and take a seat. Do you have your phone with you?"

I slip my phone inside the pocket of my hoodie hoping I didn't get busted, and then take a seat. "Yes, sir, why?"

"Your mom wants you to call her. There's been an accident. I've paged Officer Simms to take you . . ."

I scoot to the edge of my chair. "Mom was in an accident?"

Mr. Cochran's eyes drop as words seep slowly from his mouth. "Not your mom. It's Seth. He's at Mercy Methodist."

I stand and stumble out of my chair. "He's okay, isn't he?"

Mr. Cochran's expression tells me he's not. My breathing loses its rhythm as my heart explodes into tiny heartbeats, thumping my face, my arms, my entire body. I take a step without meaning to. That must be my signal to get gone, leave now!

Mr. Cochran's voice is behind me. "Isaiah, wait!"

I run like an escaped convict, body pulsing, legs trembling, and confused because I'm suddenly lost in a school

I've attended for three years. Is this the eighth-grade hall?

"Isaiah!" It's Officer Simms.

I burn off again, spot the front doors, and run to them as my backpack bangs against my spine. I break out of school and then sprint down Main Street. The hospital's on Lexington Avenue. If I keep this pace, I'll be there in no time.

CHAPTER THIRTEEN

There's a crowd-control barricade stretched across Main, guarded by police. I reroute and cut a left on Worthing, then a sharp right on Pine, but the smell of smoke and the crowds of people cause a panic inside me that makes me call out—

"SETH!"

By the time I turn onto Lexington I'm in full-blown fear mode. A smoky breeze pushes my tears toward my temples. I've made it to the other side of the police barricade, and Mercy Methodist is just across the street. The sign says "Don't Walk," but I can't wait, and cars honk and brake as I make a run for it.

When the emergency room doors open, I run toward three adults in scrubs until a nurse seated at a desk puts up a hand. "Whoa! Slow down! Can I help you?"

Words stick in my throat. "Seth . . . Abernathy? I'm . . . his brother."

She taps the keyboard, then her eyes meet mine as she stands. "Follow me."

I'm on her heels as we walk down a long hall that smells like rubbing alcohol and bleach, She knocks on a door then opens it. Mom's inside, wiping her eyes with a tissue.

"I thought you were the doctor" is all Mom says.

When the nurse leaves, I hug Mom and check out the room. There aren't any windows, and the brightness from the bulbs is night-light-low, giving the place a creepy vibe. A table with four chairs, a counter with a microwave, a basket of snacks and a small fridge fill one wall. On the other side is a dark blue sofa with a coffee table. There's even a bathroom. But then I count five boxes of tissues in here. This must be a holding spot where they have families wait when the news is going to be bad.

I can barely speak, afraid of her answer. "Mom, where's Seth?"

She sniffles and sits on the sofa. "In the trauma room."

"What's a trauma room? Where's Dad? What did the doctor say? Have you seen Seth?"

She pats the sofa. "Come sit. I don't know much because we were brought in here to wait on updates about Seth. So far I haven't been told anything."

I'm trying to calm down, but I can't. "Is Dad with him?"

"He went to the emergency room to check on Johnny Earl. He was the other driver."

All the internal chaos that jacked my body comes to a dead stop.

"Dad's friend who sits behind us at church?"

Johnny Earl owns an old Toyota Camry, but he also drives an eighteen-wheeler for BMP. Mom won't look at me as she rubs her thumb over the cross on her necklace, and now I'm wishing I had a cross to rub, too, as I speak as calmly as I can.

"Mom, please tell me Johnny Earl was driving his Camry when he hit Seth."

She raises her swollen eyes to meet mine. "He wasn't."

Blood races up and down my body and jump-starts the turmoil inside me. I'm shivering, but I'm not cold; I've got more questions, but I can't talk; I need to call somebody, but I don't know who. Seth didn't text back because he couldn't.

Mom's phone rings, and she breaks down in tears as she says hello to her friend, Ms. Hannah. Her crying rattles me even more. I step over to the table and google *trauma room.*

A trauma center is prepared to deal with severe and life-threatening conditions, with medical staff who are highly trained in traumatic injuries.

Dad comes in while I'm reading, and I can tell he's fired up but not in a good way. He's rubbing his forehead, as if he's got a bad headache. Mom ends her call and walks over to him.

"Ray, is Johnny Earl going to be okay? What did he say happened?"

He keeps rubbing his forehead. "I didn't talk to him—he doesn't want any visitors. While I was down there, though, I saw Seth's truck."

Mom takes his hand as he tries to talk without choking up.

"My dad bought that Chevy truck back in 1979 because the frame was rock-solid. But I just saw it on the back of a flatbed wrecker. A paramedic told me they—they had to use the Jaws of Life to pry Seth out."

He's crying, and so is Mom, but my eyes won't blink, my body won't move, and my mind has completely shut down. Dad wipes his face with the sleeve of his shirt. I don't blame him. I'm not touching those boxes of tissues, either. When he starts talking again, there's anger in his voice.

"If I find out Johnny Earl was speeding and hurt my boy, friend or not—it'll take the national guard to keep me off him!"

His words jolt me back into panic mode. "Dad, I'm really worried."

He wipes his eyes. "I was worried until I saw his truck. Now I'm scared."

Another knock, and the door opens. It's Pastor and Mrs. Holloway, Ms. Hannah, Coach Samuels, and Juan Carlos. Coach is still in his khaki shorts and Scarboro cross-country polo shirt. Juan Carlos's track uniform is still stuck to him from sweat. Dad covers his mouth with one hand and shakes his head as Pastor Holloway hugs him.

"Come walk with me, Ray. Let's find the chapel."

Coach Samuels goes with them, too, but Juan Carlos stays. He nods at the church ladies, then hugs Mom. "I'm here, Momma Abernathy. Whatever you need me to do."

Mom's friends sit with her, holding her hands and listening as she talks. Juan Carlos man-hugs me, then he snatches a bottled water, plops into a chair at the table, and questions me like a detective.

"What happened? Where is he? Don't leave out anything."

"He's in the trauma room. There was a bad accident," I say.

He leans in and whispers. "I saw his truck on the back of a flatbed. Who hit him?"

I don't want to be a snitch, but Juan Carlos deserves to know. "This dude who goes to our church named Johnny Earl Sutton. He works at BMP and drives an eighteen-wheeler."

Juan Carlos squeezes the plastic bottle until it crackles. "He was speeding."

"I'm not sure." I shrug, wishing he'd hit the pause button on all these questions, but instead he slams the bottle on the table and leans toward me.

"If you saw Seth's truck, you'd know that dude was speeding. I bet your dad wants to beat some brakes into that guy until he understands the speed limit—I know I do!" Juan Carlos turns to Mom. "Sorry, Momma Abernathy."

Mom and her church friends watch quietly, and I wish Seth would walk in right now so we could all go home. Juan Carlos leans back and closes his eyes, breathing heavy air in and out like an angry bull. Moments later, he opens his eyes, and his face is no longer as intense.

"My bad, Ice Pic. I'm just all in my feelings right now. I need to move around."

"Okay," I say.

We bump fists, then he hugs Mom and leaves. I sit at the table alone again, not really sure what to do or say. Soon Dad and Pastor Holloway come back without Coach Samuels. I'm tired of phones ringing and knocks on the door. I pull the hood of my jacket over my head and rest at the table until another knock startles me. The door opens and a lady wearing a white lab coat and blue scrubs walks in. "Abernathy family?"

Dad answers, "Yes."

"Hi, I'm Dr. Parker. I'm here to speak with you about Seth."

CHAPTER FOURTEEN

Even though they wanted to stay, Mom and Dad convince Ms. Hannah, Pastor, and Ms. Holloway to leave by telling them they'll call with updates. Dr. Parker waits for Pastor Holloway to pray and the room to clear of guests before she speaks.

Most of Dr. Parker's brown hair is pinned on top of her head, except for a few strands that dangle on the sides of her face like broken tree branches after a storm. Before she can say any more, Mom fires off a question.

"Seth's going to be all right, isn't he?"

"We'll know soon," she says. "For now, I believe our trauma team saved his life."

Mom puts her hand over her heart. "Dr. Parker, I'm so grateful."

She steps closer to my parents. "Of course, Mrs. Abernathy. Unfortunately, Seth is not completely out of the woods. We were able to stabilize him, but he's heavily medicated."

Dad sniffles as he speaks. "What kind of injuries does he have?"

"Abrasions, bruises, a collapsed lung—those injuries were addressed in the trauma center. Surprisingly he has no broken bones, but there is a head injury causing cerebral edema."

Dad jerks as if someone slapped him. "Wait. Cerebral edema—his brain is swelling?"

Dr. Parker nods. "It is."

They exchange a long look, but I'm not sure why swelling is such a bad thing. I mean, his brain is swollen, not broken. I'm feeling good enough to take the hood off my head.

Dr. Parker continues. "At the moment, we have Seth in a medically induced coma to give his body a rest. These next couple of nights will be critical. In a few days, we'll know more."

Mom steps forward. "You'll know more about what?"

"Seth's brain. His head injury is significant and has us concerned."

Mom won't let it go. "He's not going to—to die, is he?"

The air in our room gets thick, and I lose my breathing rhythm again.

Dr. Parker stuffs her hands in her lab coat. "Speaking as Seth's attending physician, there's a seventy percent chance he may not make it through the night."

I hold my breath because Dr. Parker's words are still floating around the room, and I refuse to inhale them. My body tingles, so I exhale, but I'm breathing faster than normal. While Dr. Parker consoles my parents, it takes everything I've got just to say one word.

"Help."

Dr. Parker comes to me. "You're hyperventilating. Try to relax."

Relax? I want to cry, but I don't have enough air for that. This morning, I wanted Seth to know how sorry I am for hitting him. Now I just want him to live.

Dr. Parker holds a finger over one of her nostrils. "Isaiah, do this. Let's breathe together."

I put my finger over one nostril, then exhale and inhale in rhythm with her. Soon the tingling and numbness goes away. I'm breathing better, and Dr. Parker smiles.

"Good job." She stands by the door and speaks to us. "I've asked Seth's nurse to take you to see him. Just so you're aware, he's in the intensive care unit on a ventilator. He's receiving several different medications, and we're monitoring his vital signs. Here comes Seth's nurse now. I'll see you later this evening."

"Knock, knock," says a woman in white scrubs at the door. "Abernathy family?"

"Yes," says Dad.

"Hi, I'm Sofie. I work in the ICU, and I'll be Seth's nurse this evening. He's in his room now, so I'll take you to see him. Bring your things because you won't be back."

I grab my backpack and follow Mom and Dad down a cold and creepy white hallway with no windows, posters, or signs on the walls. When Nurse Sofie pushes the elevator button, I cover one nostril, just in case.

The elevator stops on the third floor, and my heart pounds so hard that I'm sure everyone can hear it. Sofie leads us to two big doors with a sign above that reads: "Intensive Care Unit."

"Please turn off all electronic devices. They can interfere with the medical equipment."

We all power down as Sofie points to a keypad. "The code to enter is zero-one-one-zero. If you forget, ask the receptionist in the waiting room. Please don't share the code with others."

When the doors open, a gust of cold air chills my face as we all stand inside what looks like a top-secret laboratory with long, bright, rectangular ceiling lights. This mega room is shaped like a semicircle with ten individual patient rooms lining the walls. A massive desk sits in the middle, where doctors and nurses type and watch the patients on tiny TV screens.

Sofie stops in front of room four. "This is Seth's room. Upon entering, wash your hands and put on a mask. If you have to leave, when you return, rewash your hands and get a clean mask before reentering."

Mom and Dad stop in front of room four's big glass window and look inside. Mom's crying again. I give Sofie all my attention because I'm not ready to look at Seth yet.

"You are not allowed to visit other patients. If there is an emergency, you must leave quickly and quietly until we say you can come back. Any questions?"

"No questions," says Dad with his arm around Mom.

"Don't hesitate to reach out to me. You can go in whenever you're ready," she says.

Mom and Dad go in first. I stay outside the door because my legs feel shaky. When it's my turn to wash and mask up, I keep my head down and shuffle to the sink. Mom's sniffling, so I close my eyes and take two deep breaths. *Man up. Seth needs me.*

I dry my hands, put on a mask, and fight the urge to run at the sight of my brother lying motionless on his back. White bandages cover everything above his eyebrows, with two long cuts—one on his cheek, and the other on his chin—closed together with stitches. Two strips of tape hold a tube in his mouth that's connected to a machine that clicks and breathes for him.

Click . . . phwww . . . click . . . phwww . . . click . . . phwww.

Seven skinny chrome poles on wheels surround Seth like an iron fence. Each one holds two big medicine bags that drip into tiny tubes connected to his arms and other places underneath his sheet that I can't see. On a flat screen, numbers flash by faster than I can read them—heart rate, blood pressure, oxygen level. I look away. It's too much. And it's freezing in here—Seth hates being cold. Shouldn't he have more than a sheet on him?

Mom wipes her eyes. "He's got cuts everywhere. Look, he even has one on his lip."

All the tape they used to hold that plastic tube in his mouth didn't cover up what I did. Knowing I'm responsible for Seth's busted lip causes a cry I can't control. Mom hugs me.

"It's okay, Isaiah."

No, it's not, and I can't even tell you what I did! How would you treat me if you knew some of his pain was my fault?

CHAPTER FIFTEEN

We've been in Seth's room for an hour before I get up enough courage to ask, "Can I talk to Seth? Alone?" I know Mom and Dad want to be near him, too, so if they say no, I'm okay with it. But I'm mentally pleading with them not to ask me why I need alone time with him. I'm hurting in a place I can't identify deep inside me and could easily break down and confess what I did. I'm so ashamed, and I can't take a lecture from them right now.

Mom's smile is weak. "Sure. That will give your father a chance to explain some of this medical stuff to me. He understands it since he's had all that first aid training at BMP."

"Except they didn't say what to do when it's happening to your own child," says Dad.

Mom nods, and I feel that, too. As soon as they leave, I drag a chair as close as I can to the bed. "Seth, can you hear me? I need to tell you something. I didn't snitch to Dad about you not going to your BMP interview. I swear. And . . . one more thing."

I stare at the floor for a second, shaking my head. Why should he listen to me now when I didn't listen to him this morning? I wasn't trying to hear him, and now I'm not sure he's even trying to hear me. What if he was salty about all the grief I gave him and didn't see Johnny Earl?

There's a knot in my throat that I can't swallow. I pretend to be okay when my parents come in, wash their hands, and get new masks. Dad hands me a sports drink, but I can't hold back the tears. He cries, too, as he pulls me from my seat to wrap me in his arms. "It's okay to cry, Isaiah. This is hard. If you want, you can take a break and go to the ICU waiting room. You can use your phone in there."

I stash the sports drink in my backpack, remove the mask, and wipe my face. "Okay. I'll be back soon."

The waiting room isn't far from the ICU, but I have to sign in with the receptionist before I can even pick a spot to sit. This place isn't much bigger than our living room. Two people lean on each other and nap while another lady eats and watches a soap opera on the television braced on the wall. There's an unoccupied corner far from the receptionist desk with an electrical outlet. I toss my backpack in one chair, set my drink on the floor, and claim that space.

It's already six o'clock. School's been out for hours. I scroll through my phone as it charges, but it's depressing

94

to see all the missed texts and calls, especially knowing they're all from people asking about Seth. Zurie sent multiple messages.

Ice, what's going on?

It's me again. What happened to Seth? OMG, pls call me.

Are you okay? It's all over the news. Do you need help? I'm panicking. Pls call.

I text her back.

Can't talk right now. Will text when I can.

It feels as if I've been in the waiting room for hours, but the clock says it's only been twenty minutes. I don't like sitting in here, especially when my brother needs me. I unplug my phone, turn it off, and go back to the ICU. I wash my hands, get a new mask, and stare between the bed rails at Seth's bandaged head before my eyes roam down to his busted lip. I cross my arms, tucking my guilty hands under my armpits, and take a seat.

Soon the intercom crackles again. "Attention, visiting hours are over in one hour and will restart at nine tomorrow morning."

Mom presses the call button. When Nurse Sofie answers, Mom's almost crying again. "I can't leave him. I won't. Not tonight."

I can hear the patience in Nurse Sofie's voice. "I understand. I'll request special permission for extended visiting hours for your family."

"Thank you, Sofie."

Later Dr. Parker comes in, washes her hands, gets a clean mask, and examines Seth. She gently opens his eyes and flashes a light in them before typing on a computer near his bed.

She smiles at us. "I've approved special visiting hours, but it's important that you stay awake, just in case we need to get to Seth quickly."

"Thank you," says Dad.

After visiting hours are over, we hold hands as Dad prays, but I keep my eyes open. How could God let this happen? We're in church every Sunday, Mom and Dad volunteer for everything, and we even spend Sundays together as a family. Pastor Holloway says, "God is always watching. He never sleeps." But this morning, God either fell asleep or wasn't paying attention.

Maybe he doesn't even exist.

After dinner we head back to the waiting room, where we're given blankets and pillows.

"I'm not sleepy, so I'll take the first shift with Seth," says Dad.

Mom nods. "I'll come relieve you at midnight."

I'm nervous about sleeping in the waiting room. I've never slept in a room full of people I don't know. There's a mix of Black, Asian, and Hispanic folk in here—all looking broken and tired. Everybody has tear-stained faces, messy hair, and wrinkled clothes.

One lady turns two chairs to face each other and lies down on them as if it were a bed. A Hispanic woman approaches Mom and me. "Is this your first night? Turn the chairs to face each other to make a bed. Get some sleep, Momma, so you'll have energy for another day," she says.

I make chair-beds for Mom and me, then the lights dim, and the waiting room is quiet. I finally fall asleep, but a few hours later my eyelids flip open. It's three in the morning. Dad's curled up in a chair next to me, head tucked like a bird as he sleeps. Mom's chair-bed is empty.

I sign out at the desk and head to the ICU. As I pass the nurses' station, I get stopped.

"Can I help you?" asks a nurse behind the counter.

I point to room four and whisper. "Going to sit with Seth. I'm Isaiah, his brother."

She smiles. "I'm Sasha, Seth's night nurse. Please stay quiet, okay?"

"Yes, ma'am."

I get Mom to go back to the waiting room, then take a seat close to Seth, put my earbuds in, and listen to music. I don't realize I've drifted off until an alarm makes me jump. I take out my earbuds, confused by the flashing lights, and someone gives me a hard nudge. It's Sasha.

"You have to leave now," she says.

I stumble out of my chair and check on Seth. Even though it's freezing in here, sweat beads on his face. Red lights blink on the flat-screen monitor as blood pressure, oxygen, and heart rate numbers flash in rhythm with the blinking red lights. I reach for his hand.

"Seth! What's wrong? What's happening! Sasha, why is he sweating?"

A voice speaks over the intercom. "Code blue, code blue. ICU. Bed four."

"What does that mean? Seth!"

Dr. Parker rushes in. "Isaiah, you have to leave."

I hold on to the bed rail with one hand, and nudge Seth with the other. "Wake up! Seth! Please don't leave me!"

Dr. Parker speaks stronger. "Get him out of here, now!"

Sasha pries my fingers from the bed rail and escorts me out. "Try to understand, Isaiah. We need all the space in Seth's room to help him."

The ICU doors close, and I'm standing outside in the empty, silent hall, breathing faster, trying to keep up with the thumping of my heart. My face numbs, and then my lips. *Oh no, not again.* The tingling spreads until nothing on my body feels normal. I try to cover a nostril but I'm too dizzy, and slowly I slide down the wall until I'm sitting on the floor. *Please somebody help me.*

CHAPTER SIXTEEN

Mom's yawning as she rounds the corner, but when she sees me she starts to run. "What's wrong?"

I'm propped against the wall. "Seth's dying, and it feels like I'm dying, too."

Instead of using the code, Mom forces a crack in the ICU doors and hollers inside. "Help! Please help us!"

Seconds later, the doors fly open. Sasha sees me and gets down on one knee. "Isaiah, slowly breathe in through your nose as if you're sniffing flowers. Then slowly breathe out through your mouth as if you're blowing out candles. Smell the flowers, blow out the candles."

Mom's frantic. "This is the second time today. Why is this happening?"

"I'm not sure. Hyperventilation can be triggered by many things."

"What about my other son? Is he okay?"

Sasha touches Mom's arm, then gets up. "Dr. Parker will speak with you soon."

As Mom and I lean against each other, I try not to unleash a cry that will wake the world. Soon Dad comes around the corner, and when he spots us, instead of asking questions, he joins us on the floor. How can the world be asleep while Seth fights for his life?

Thirty minutes later, the same Hispanic woman who showed us how to make a bed with chairs shuffles toward us, stretching her arms and wiping her eyes. "Excuse me, but the receptionist said the ICU is closed because of a code blue. I was just wondering if you knew—"

When she sees Mom's face, she stops speaking and gets on the floor with us, taking Mom's hands in hers. "I'm sorry, Momma. I wasn't thinking. My daughter, Isabella, is in there, too. I've been here nonstop for a whole week, and sometimes I lose my common sense."

Mom tries to smile. "It's my son. Are you a praying mother?"

The woman smiles back. "Is there any other kind? I'll pray with you. What's his name?"

Mom's already crying. "Seth."

And right there on the floor, with me doing my breathing exercises and Dad's arm around Mom, these two mothers hold hands, and with eyes closed, the woman begins to pray for Seth. She prays that my brother wakes up, and that he gets to go home. She prays for our family, and for peace. She doesn't mention her own daughter once.

When she finishes, Mom hugs her before she leaves and heads back to the waiting room. I wish that lady would stay because I could feel her strength, and my whole family needs that right now.

Soon Dr. Parker steps out of the ICU and stops in front of me, nodding. "Smell the flowers, blow out the candles. Great calming exercise." She sits on the floor and touches my hand. "Are you breathing better now?"

I nod, but everything inside me is on standby, waiting on what she's going to say.

Please don't tell me he's dead.

"You have a strong brother. He's stable again, and we'll continue to monitor him through the night, but I'm concerned about your well-being as much as Seth's." She hands me a granola bar.

It feels good knowing she cares about me, too, but her words make me blush.

She lets go of my hand. "Sasha told me the two incidents of hyperventilation you've had today have never happened before. Is that correct?"

"Yes, ma'am."

"Hyperventilation has many different triggers, but in my opinion, yours was caused by fear. I want you to practice the breathing exercises we've taught you. Both methods work well."

"Okay."

"I'm also concerned about what happened during Seth's code. We had to ask you multiple times to leave the

ICU during critical moments that should've been given to Seth."

I feel horrible—no doubt I was wrong, but that was my gut reaction to Seth needing help. I unwrap the granola bar she gave me and take a bite as she keeps talking.

"Isaiah, I know you love your brother, and this is extremely difficult. But for your sake, and Seth's, I'm going to recommend that your parents take you home, or to stay with someone they trust, until Seth's condition improves."

I frown at her. "What? I can't leave! Seth needs me!"

Mom and Dad talk to each other without saying a word as Mom's eyebrows rise, followed by Dad's.

Then he drops the verdict. "Isaiah, we agree with Dr. Parker."

I stop eating the granola bar. It feels like a bribe now. "You don't understand. I can't leave him alone. I promise I won't do it again. I . . . I was scared."

Dad gets up. "Go wait for me by the elevators. I need to speak with your mother."

I turn to my last hope. "Mom . . ."

Her tears are still falling. "I can't have both my sons on breathing machines."

Dang it! I storm off, wanting to hit a wall with my fist. Dad could've told Dr. Parker that Seth and I are tight, but he didn't. He could've let her know that as soon as Seth hears my voice, he's going to wake up. But he didn't, and I'm so salty that when he comes to the elevators, I ignore him.

We're still not talking when the emergency room doors open and we head to the truck. With each step away from the hospital I feel like I'm deserting my brother.

It's a quiet ride until Dad sighs and says, "We're doing this for your own good."

I'm almost screaming. "Seth needs me, and you know it!"

"You hyperventilated twice! Seth's struggling. You want us to watch you struggle, too?"

I stare out the window, furious because he has a good point.

"And what if Seth had another emergency, but you refused to leave, and they lost those few precious minutes to save him? How would you ever get over that?"

Dad's two-for-two in the "good point" column, and I can't think of a comeback.

"Isaiah, you're still a kid, and being at the hospital is affecting your health, causing you to make bad decisions, and putting things in your memory that no child your age should ever have. The best thing for you is to get back to school. It will take your mind off—"

"No way! What if I never get another chance to see Seth alive, and you made me leave? It'll be your fault! How would *you* ever get over that?"

He stares at the road in silence, and I'm already mad at myself for saying something so cruel. When a tear falls down his face, it breaks me, and I have to make it right because that's what started my horrible drama—I did something to Seth and didn't apologize right away.

"I didn't mean that. I'm so sorry, Dad. Everything's just so messed up."

He sniffles. "It is, but we have to stick together. You must believe Seth is going to live."

"Yes, sir."

"You need time to process all this. It's a lot for a kid to take in."

I roughly wipe at my tears because Dad doesn't understand, and I can't tell him the truth. I don't need to process—I need to tell my brother I was wrong for hitting him, and I'm sorry.

CHAPTER SEVENTEEN

When we get to the house, our bedroom door's open, inviting me in. Instead, I sit on the sofa and turn on the television. The house smells awful, so I walk to the dining room table, where full coffee cups sit next to two plates of half-eaten food. I scrape all the scraps into a bag for the pigs, dump the coffee in the sink, and sit back on the sofa.

Soon Dad comes out of his room in clean clothes, carrying a small suitcase. "Your mother asked me to pack her some things because she's staying at the hospital with Seth until he gets better. I'll swing back through here at lunch, then sleep here at night before heading back to the hospital early in the mornings. That's how I'm going to roll until we can all be together again, okay? I'll see you for lunch. Love you."

When Dad leaves, I grab the bag of scraps and toss it

in the wheelbarrow, get food for the hens, feed for the pigs, and a slice of hay for Dolly and Buster. Now that I'm alone, the farm feels and looks so much bigger. I stop at the chicken coop, but instead of waiting for the hens to come out, I go in.

"It's just me." I sit on the ground and sprinkle corn mix around me.

My divas ruffle over, and I gently pet their heads. Aretha sticks her neck out of her nesting spot.

"I see you," I say.

I help her to the ground and unwrap her bandage. She flaps both wings, then struts over to eat breakfast with the others. After that, I go to check on Dolly's cut. It's completely healed.

"I'm glad you and Aretha are doing better."

I thought hanging out with the animals would calm my mind, but it doesn't. Instead, I can't erase the stress of Seth fighting for his life, or the fact that the hospital kicked me out for accidentally being extra and wouldn't even give me a second chance.

I've got to be more positive. Dad said I have to believe Seth's going to be okay. So I go inside to our dining room table and make a list of things Seth and I can do when he gets out of the hospital. Sitting under the apple tree is definitely number one, but I can't think of anything after that—I'm too tired. I've been up since three, and a nap sounds good. I put my list away, shuffle over to the sofa, and sleep until the jiggle of a key wakes me. Dad walks in with a bag from Torchy's Tacos.

I jump up. "Is Seth okay? Is he awake?"

He sets the food on the coffee table and grabs the remote. "Not yet."

I don't remember the last time I ate, so I grab two tacos out of the bag. Dad takes a couple, too, and we're putting salsa across them when Seth's picture appears on the television.

"Dad, look! Turn it up!"

The reporter's standing in front of Mercy Methodist. "According to a hospital source, the Scarboro High School cross-country star is in a medically induced coma, fighting for his life. Skyler Mills is standing by at the corner of Center Street and Main. Take it away, Skyler."

My stomach flips as I stare at a familiar spot downtown.

"I'm at the scene of a horrific accident involving high school standout Seth Abernathy and an eighteen-wheeler owned by BMP, the employer of Seth's father, Ray. The speed limit on Main is thirty-five, but reports say the BMP driver may have been traveling at a speed closer to seventy."

She moves to a big pile of things in the grass. "There's been an outpouring of support with hundreds of flowers, cards, even a cross-country jersey placed at the site of the collision."

A lady sets a plant near the pile, and Skyler approaches her. "Excuse me, do you know the Abernathy family?"

The lady shakes her head. "I've seen that young man's picture in the paper, and I hurt for his parents. I'm outraged that our community has complained again and again about those BMP truckers roaring through Scarboro like it's their own personal racetrack, but nothing's been done about it. Now look what's happened. What's it going to take to make them stop?"

Skyler turns back to the camera. "There will be a special ten o'clock prayer service for Seth Abernathy tomorrow morning at Center Street Baptist Church for anyone who would like to attend. This is Skyler Mills, reporting live, Channel Two News."

Dad rubs his forehead. "You know, half of me wants to do something bad to Johnny Earl. The other half understands the pressure he's under to provide for his family."

I'm feeling tight and salty at Dad. "But it's his fault Seth's in the hospital!"

He sighs. "BMP's unofficial motto of 'There and back in a dash makes more cash' promises bonus money to drivers willing to break the law. And they know which drivers need money the most. Seth's injuries are serious, and he may not fully recover—when he wakes up, he may be different. But Johnny Earl's changed forever, too, just because he was trying to feed his family."

Dad tells me to stay positive, so why is he talking about Seth being different after he wakes up? Different how? Why is everybody hatin' on Seth? First Dr. Parker said he might not make it through the night. Well, guess what, Doc? He's still here! Now Dad's talking ridiculous, too. I put my earbuds in and listen to music because I'm not trying to hear that. The only different I'm hoping for is that Seth's no longer angry with me.

On Sunday morning, Dad's already gone when Ms. Hannah and her friends come by with food. They even tidy up and do a load of clothes. When they finish, I walk them to the door.

"Thanks for the food and all your help," I say.

Ms. Hannah hugs me. "You're welcome. We're on our way to the prayer service for Seth. We'll come back on Tuesday with more food and to help again."

Once they leave, I text Zurie. I need someone to talk to. Maybe she'll understand.

Seth's still in a coma. No change. I'll be at school tomorrow. Dad's making me go.

Less than ten seconds go by.

I'm so sorry, Ice. I'll save you a seat on the bus.

Later, Dad comes home for lunch. "The house smells good. Looks good, too."

Since he's not talking negative, I leave my earbuds in the case. "Ms. Hannah and her crew came through. How's Seth?"

"He's having an MRI tomorrow. It's a procedure that will take pictures of his brain and let the doctors know if the swelling has stopped."

Stopped? "You mean his brain may still be getting bigger? I thought we were just waiting for the swelling to go down."

"We'll know more tomorrow."

"Dad, I should be there with him. I can help keep him calm before those tests."

"It's not up to me. Let's just pray the tests come back with . . . positive results."

I hope this isn't connected to that "Seth may be different" nonsense Dad was talking about yesterday because now he's scaring me. And tomorrow, while all Seth's testing is going on, I'll be stuck at school, so worried that I'll probably be doing the same thing Seth's doing right now. Nothing.

By the time my alarm would've gone off Monday morning, I've already fed the animals and taken my shower. Now I'm sitting on my bed, dressed for school, but I can't get my mind right. This is the first time I've sat on my bed since the argument, and I'm fighting tears all over again. Mom and Dad think I can go to school as if everything's cool. But it's not.

Yesterday one of the ladies who came with Ms. Hannah made our beds. Now Seth's side of the room looks all wrong. His covers should be half on the bed and half on the floor, with his pajama bottoms flung across the footboard, and the top should be off his cologne. I can't see him, talk to him, or even hear him in here. I can't even smell him.

Snapsickles! His cologne! I spray myself, then squirt some in the air before heading down the road to wait for my bus. I've never loved the smell of this cologne the way I do right now. It's as if a part of Seth's with me. Twenty minutes later, Mr. Williams pulls up in front of our mailbox and opens the bus door. "Mornin'. Is Seth doing any better?"

"No, sir, not yet."

"I went to that special prayer service," he says as he closes the door. "Seems like everybody in Scarboro was there. I hope your parents make BMP pay for what they did."

I don't say anything because "making them pay" sounds gangster, and my parents don't roll like that. I hope today isn't filled with questions about Seth. The last thing I want is everybody all up on me about my brother. I can already feel Shy Guy trying to shut me down.

As soon as I step on the bus to Brazos Bayou, it gets creepy quiet. Even Brandon and Rhino stare at me. I slowly walk down the aisle toward the seat next to Zurie.

She moves her books so I can sit, but all eyes are on me like I'm new. I keep my head down as Zurie whispers. "It's okay, don't worry about them."

But I am worried about them. I can feel their looks, their unasked questions, their pity. I don't want this attention. It's all making me tight, and the only person who can possibly help me is in a coma.

CHAPTER EIGHTEEN

In the hall at school, students separate like oil and water to let me by, and when I get to advisory, I turn my chair to face the window. Brandon mutters something and then snickers. If he says something wrong to me, I'll rip his lips off.

After advisory, I keep my head down walking to yearbook class, but Mr. Whitaker stops me at the door. "Good morning, Isaiah. May I have a word with you?"

"Yes, sir."

I follow him to his desk before he turns to me. "My wife and I went to the prayer service. It was so crowded that hundreds of people had to stand outside. But we all managed to hold hands from the choir stand to the curb and pray for Seth. I just want to let you know if you need me, I'm here."

I've got that knot in my throat again, so I just nod

and hope he understands.

Yearbook class keeps my mind busy, but when the bell rings, I'm back in the hall, thinking about Seth. Zurie catches up with me, and just walking with her calms my mind until Brandon and Rhino pull up.

"About the overrated sibling competition—you got lucky. I had a bad shooting night."

Zurie calls him out. "News flash! You lost the bet."

"Are you his bodyguard now, Zurie Fury? Is that why you blasted that text about leaving Ice Cream alone while he deals with his family drama?"

I turn around, ready to rumble. "Shut up, Brandon."

Rhino backs up as Brandon steps forward. "What'd you say?"

Zurie pulls at me. "Here comes Officer Simms. Don't do this. You'll get suspended."

I stand there a few seconds longer to let Brandon see the fire in my eyes before walking away. He doesn't know that the fear I've felt for the last three days is a radical, heart-thumping, emotional bully, so much tougher than anything he's ever dished out. And if he had a clue how much stronger I am because of it, he'd shut his mouth and keep moving.

Later, during lunch, I head to the courtyard and look for a table away from everyone, but Zurie finds me and softly asks, "Can I join you?"

When I don't say anything, she takes it as an invitation

to sit. "Don't be mad at me for blasting that text. After you told me you didn't want to talk, I texted the yearbook staff, that's all! They must've sent it to their friends. We're just trying to protect you—give you some space."

I snap at her. "But I didn't ask you to do that, and you didn't ask if you could."

There's so much sadness in her face. "I was only trying to help."

I can't deal with her right now, especially when I need to text Dad for an update on Seth's tests. Just as Zurie took my silence as an invitation to sit, she must take my texting as a signal to leave because by the time I look up, she's gone. Dang it. I'll apologize later. When the bell rings ending lunch, I turn my phone to vibrate in case Dad texts back.

There's a group of teachers in the hall, including my science teacher, Mr. Avery.

"We're so sorry about Seth's accident. We all went to the prayer service," he says.

"Thank you," I say.

Mr. Avery nods toward his classroom. "I'll be in shortly."

In science class, almost all the seats are taken, but Zurie's holding one for me. Before I can reach her, though, Brandon cuts me off.

"Right here is where it all started, Ice Cream—it's where we made that stupid bet. And that's all it was to me—something stupid."

Zurie yells at him. "You're a jerk, Brandon!"

Heads nod as cell phones point toward us.

Brandon snaps. "Mind your business, Zurie Fury! This has nothing to do with you."

I take a step toward him. "You're right. It isn't about her. It's about you losing, isn't it?"

Zurie's furious as she talks to the class. "In case you didn't know, last Thursday night at the sibling rivalry competition, Isaiah beat Brandon at shooting free throws underhanded, just like he promised right here in this classroom. Now Brandon wants to—"

Brandon pushes her with both hands. "I told you to mind your business!"

Her tiny body bangs into a desk, then falls to the floor. Without thinking, I grab a handful of Brandon's shirt and ram him into the back wall. He tries to get away, but I slam him to the ground, raise my fist, and drive it twice into his face.

He hollers. "Get off me! Rhino, help!"

Rhino doesn't charge, so I stand Brandon up and give him two more hard punches to the gut. "That's for cracking my screen protector."

Mr. Avery rushes in. "Isaiah, stop!"

A whistle blows, and Officer Simms yells. "Abernathy, let him go!"

I do, and Brandon crumbles to the floor. I know he's hurt, but he's been hurting me for years. That ends today. Mr. Cochran arrives, grabs me on one side, and Officer

Simms has the other, but I pull away and power-yell out my anger.

"Aaaaahhh!"

Mr. Cochran points at me. "I won't hesitate to call for backup if you don't get your behind over here and sit down. Don't make me tell you again!"

There's fear in his eyes, and in everyone else's. As Officer Simms hands Brandon paper towels to hold against his busted nose and mouth, our eyes meet. He looks away first, so I take a seat.

Mr. Cochran pulls a walkie-talkie from his belt. "Nurse Hopkins, please come to Mr. Avery's room, 110. There's been an altercation between two students. One's bleeding."

A staticky voice responds. "On my way."

My knuckles and arm throb in rhythm with the pounding in my head. I hold one nostril closed to slow my breathing while I close my eyes in triumph. It's over. I've finally shut Brandon down. Nurse Hopkins rushes in with a backpack.

"Isaiah, can I trust you to walk with me without any trouble?" asks Mr. Cochran.

"Yes, sir," I say, keeping my finger over my nostril.

Zurie's waiting at the door. "Ice? Are you okay?"

"Zurie, I'm sorry."

She shakes her head. "It's okay. He deserved it."

"I'm not talking about Brandon," I say as I'm forced to keep moving.

A half hour later, Officer Simms, Dad, the school

counselor, and I are all crowded in Mr. Cochran's office. They're all firing questions my way. Everyone except Dad.

The counselor speaks up. "Brandon Hart is still not talking. How did the fight start?"

"He shoved Zurie really hard into a desk, and she fell to the floor."

Mr. Cochran leans over his desk. "Why didn't you call a teacher?"

I cross my arms. "For what? Tried that before. Didn't work. Brandon's the biggest bully in this school. I'm not proud of punching him, but I'm not upset about it, either."

"So you stop a bully by beating him up? Does that make sense to you, Isaiah?"

I glare at him. "Nothing makes sense to me right now."

Mr. Cochran opens his drawer, pulls out a stack of papers, and fills them out. Then he passes them around. Once everyone has signed, including me, he takes the papers back. "Isaiah, you've been a student here for three years, and you've never been in trouble. If I hadn't seen it myself, I would never believe you participated in something so violent."

I look at him. "Me, either. I don't believe in fighting, and there's really nothing you can do to me that's going to be worse than what I'm already doing to myself."

Mr. Cochran tries to act all concerned. "You're going through something much bigger than anyone in this school understands. You need time to reclaim the real Isaiah."

Reclaim? He's got a lot of nerve, and I call him on it.

"What do you mean 'reclaim the real Isaiah'? You don't know me. When have we ever had a real conversation? I bet you don't even know where I live."

He leans over his desk. "I know you're not the same upbeat photographer who snapped pictures of everything in my office during my interview for the yearbook."

My head droops, and I can't look at him as he continues.

"I'm going to give you time to find yourself again. So instead of the usual three-day suspension for fighting, I'm giving you this entire week. Brandon will get the same. You can get your assignments from the school website. Any questions?"

"No, sir." I turn to Dad. "Can we go now?"

Dad leads me past the crowd in Cochran's office, eyeballing me as if I don't belong here.

Seems like all I do lately is get kicked out of places.

CHAPTER NINETEEN

At first, Dad gives me the silent treatment on the drive home, but then he stuns me. "Was that Nathan Hart's son, the boy you played ball with back in the day—the one who bumped into you on purpose at the sibling rivalry?"

I nod. "Yes, sir. You saw that?"

"Uh-huh. You okay?"

"Yes, sir." I don't want to talk about the fight even though my knuckles are still swollen. That makes me think of Seth. "Did the swelling stop?"

"We're waiting on Dr. Parker to talk with us about the test results. I'll let you know."

He stops in front of the house to let me out. "I'll swing by later to check on you."

"Dad. I'm sorry about fighting and getting suspended from school."

"I'm sorry, too, Isaiah, that you didn't feel comfortable

enough to talk with me about what you've been going through with that boy. You and me, we'll have to work on that."

"Yes, sir."

Dad leaves, and I shuffle over to the apple tree where Seth and I always have our talks. Only now, I'm alone, feeling like the world is against me. School, home, everything in my life is messed up, and I can think of only one person who can help me. I sit under the tree and look up.

Wish granter, I know it's been a long minute since I've spoken to you. I'm sorry. I still believe in you, but things are really bad. Will you please help?

A gentle breeze, along with the sounds and smells of our animals relaxes me, and soon I fall into a deep sleep until the sound of tires crunching on gravel causes my eyelids to flip open. A black Mercedes rolls slowly toward the house. I stand, and it stops as if I scared it.

The back door opens, and Zurie gets out. "Is it okay for me to be here?"

I put a finger over one nostril to keep my breathing in check. What's she doing here? Zurie says something to the driver, who backs down the hill and leaves.

"That's my cousin. She'll be back in a half hour," Zurie says as she walks toward me.

I look around the farm. The animals are staring at her, too. I've never had a visitor, and it feels as if I just lost the biggest game of hide-and-go-seek I've ever played.

"How did you find me?"

She gives a half smile. "A good reporter never gives up her sources."

I keep staring until that half smile becomes the whole truth. "Okay, a friend of mine works in the office. She hooked me up. I wanted to thank you in person for what you did for me."

I'm still mad at myself. "I should've handled Brandon a different way."

"Everybody's tried to stop his bullying, but thanks for having my back."

"Okay, well, your cousin could've stayed because that only took—"

She steps closer to me. "Ice, wait—I'm also here because I'm worried about you. Can we talk? Please?"

I shrug and offer her a spot under the apple tree. We sit with our backs against the trunk. It helps that I'm not facing her because I'm still trippin' on the fact that she's here, and Shy Guy's trying to shut me down.

"I didn't get a chance to ask you about Seth. How is he?"

I stare at the grass. "Haven't seen him since Saturday morning."

"Why? Is it because it's too hard to see him like that?"

Even though I've got a lot to say, I'm not comfortable. But if it were Seth sitting under this tree, I'd spill my guts—and I can hear him in my mind, encouraging me to speak up.

Zurie keeps talking. "I'm sure Seth being in the ICU is scary."

"I can't even describe it."

"Why don't you try? Sometimes it helps to talk things out."

She puts her hand on mine, and Shy Guy goes ballistic. *Smell the candles, blow out the flowers. No . . . wait. That's not right.* I have to make sense of this on my own. Zurie cares. For her to look for me, even travel down a gravel road, way out here in the country, is proof.

So, for the first time, I open up. "He . . . uh . . . he doesn't move, Zurie. Not even a little. There's a machine that breathes for him because he can't even do that on his own."

She holds my hand tighter. "Oh no. I'm so sorry."

That knot's back in my throat. "To see him like that, it's like—he's—"

Zurie's crying, so I close my eyes and keep swallowing, hoping I can stay strong enough to finish what I'm trying to say. "When my gramps died, there was a funeral, and I said goodbye to him in his casket. We buried him at the cemetery. It was over, and I knew it, understand?"

She's sniffling. "Yes."

"This is different. My mind tells me Seth's not moving, the same way Gramps didn't in his casket—like he's dead but not yet dead enough for a funeral. So I keep wishing, hoping for something to happen. If he would just . . . move."

"Maybe he just needs more time."

I slowly open my eyes because I'm about to tell her something I haven't told anyone, and now I can't control my tears. "I think something's wrong with Seth. I'm still hoping he'll be okay when his brain stops swelling . . . but I'm scared he won't be. And what about his scholarship to A&M? What if he can't go? Running cross-country for A&M is his dream."

She moves her hand from mine, and cries harder, trying to talk through her tears. "Have you talked to your parents?"

I shake my head. "I can't tell them. They'd be so angry if they knew."

"What are you talking about?"

I want to confess what I did, and Zurie seems like she could be the right person for that. But my words hurt as they try to come out, so I squeeze a handful of grass and hold it to help me get started. "Not all the scars on Seth came from the accident."

"What do you mean? What happened?" She stands with her hands on her hips, fuming. "Did something happen at the hospital? Who hurt him?"

I just squeeze more grass because I need to say this at my own pace. This is either going to be really bad, or it will be just what I needed.

But she keeps talking. "You've got to tell your parents! There's abuse laws—"

My body tightens, and I let go of the grass. "It was me! I did it! We had a bad argument the morning before the accident. I wanted him to shut up, so I hit him! I busted his lip. It was bleeding, and . . ."

I cover my face again, hurting from somewhere deep inside me, and crying from that same place. *Seth, I'm so sorry. I didn't mean it. I swear.*

A soft hand grabs mine, pulling it away from my eyes. She's still crying.

"Don't worry about that, Ice. I'm sure Seth knows you didn't mean it."

"But I don't know for sure that he does. I have to be sure. Seth has to wake up, and when I tell him I'm sorry, I need him to forgive me."

We sit under the tree in silence, giving each other space and time.

"We just have to believe." She lies down on the grass and watches the clouds. "Sometimes, when I feel pressure, I'll stare at the sky until I get back on my game."

I side-eye her, sniffling. "Do you feel lots of pressure being the yearbook editor?"

She flips her hand at me. "My grandpa was a psychiatrist. His father was a surgeon, my uncle's a dentist, my mom is an obstetrician, and Dad has a general practice. *That's* pressure!"

I lie next to her. "Last week, a raccoon tried to drag one of our hens away, but Seth and I stopped it. I was able to fix her wing and take care of her. I felt like a real vet."

There's kindness in her eyes as she smiles. "I can't wait to do stuff like that."

I nod and smile back the best I can. "Thanks for finding me."

She sits up. "That's what friends do. And you know what else? Everybody makes mistakes. Always leave space for grace. Mom told me that."

I get up, pluck an apple from the tree, and rub it on my shirt. "Here, this is for you."

She takes a big bite. "Thanks! I love apples."

I grab two more from the grass. "Come on, I'll introduce you to the animals."

She meets my diva hens and the pigs, and when Dolly and Buster trot over to the fence, Zurie giggles as she feeds them. I take selfies of us, and soon my mood is much better.

She shakes her head. "I can't believe you're not making reels of these adorable animals!"

When Zurie's cousin returns, I wish she didn't have to go.

She hugs me. "You're a good brother, Ice. And you can call or text me any time you need to talk. See you in school next week. Until then, stay out of trouble, you big troublemaker."

I laugh. "Whatever."

As her cousin drives away, Zurie waves, and I wave

back, holding my arm high in the air to make sure she sees it. Until she showed up, I didn't think I could open up to anyone besides my brother. There may be fury in Zurie, but today, she was the friend I needed.

CHAPTER TWENTY

Monday evening, I'm working on my English assignment when Dad calls. "Good news! The brain swelling is going down! Dr. Parker says the next step is to slowly bring Seth out of the coma, and then get him off the ventilator. He may be awake by Friday!"

I stand and jump in place. "I knew Seth would be okay! Can I see him?"

"Haven't heard anything about that, but as for Seth, we still need to pray."

I can't stop grinning. "Right! Wooo-hoooo!"

"Are you okay by yourself for the night? I was going to stay at the hospital with your mom and then swing by the house tomorrow for lunch."

"Yeah, Dad, I'm good. Are you okay?"

"Yes, since Seth seems to be out of danger I feel comfortable enough to go back to work tomorrow—at least for half a day. I've got plenty of sick days and vacation days, so it shouldn't be a problem."

I remember what Dad said about blaming BMP. "Are you sure you're ready? Especially after what you think about them now?"

He sighs. "It's hard being here in the ICU, and it'll be hard going back to BMP. But the only thing more important to me than being with my family is providing for them. I love you."

"Love you, too, Dad."

Sometime after two cooking shows and a western, I fall asleep.

When I wake up on Tuesday, life doesn't feel quite as hard as it has the last two weeks. Seth's getting better!

Ms. Hannah and her crew stop by to clean and drop off food. Once they leave, I take extra time with the animals. I switch things up and feed the pigs first, letting water run out of the hose inside their fence until they've got a huge puddle to play in. "Let me see you waddle!" I laugh as they roll in the mud like dancers. I remember what Zurie said about posting pics of the animals on Instagram. I guess now is as good a time as any to change my profile to public.

I snap pictures of my diva hens, and even make a video of Dolly and Buster running and kicking around the pasture. Maybe they've missed me as much as I've missed them. It's the first time I've had fun with my phone since

Seth's accident, and it feels good.

Once I finish, it's time to sit in the shade under the apple tree and post my favorite pics to Instagram. I watch the reel of my pigs and laugh again, then upload it with the caption, *I'm having this kind of good day*, tagging Zurie. There. I did it.

The sound of tires crunching gravel makes me look up. It's Dad. He stops and rolls down his window as I walk over to the truck.

"Hey! How'd it go on your first day back at BMP?"

He reaches out the window and fist-bumps me. "Better than I expected! Mr. Douglas seemed surprised to see me, and when I asked to work half days until Seth gets out of the ICU, he said he'd let payroll and human resources know."

"That's great, Dad."

He holds up a bag. "Chicken sandwiches with fries. I'll see you inside."

By the time I clean up and get to the living room, Dad's got the television on. The Channel 2 reporter Skyler Mills is surrounded by five people, but one man seems to be doing all the talking for everyone.

"We are local members of WATCH-US, a worldwide watchdog group that stands up for civil and human rights and environmental awareness by holding corporations accountable for their actions."

I take a big bite of my sandwich. "Ever heard of them, Dad?"

"Uh-huh. They're a huge thorn in BMP's side. Always sending letters about health and safety violations or requesting information. They're relentless."

The man continues. "We're planning a peaceful demonstration to protest Bayou Meat Packing's continuous health and safety violations. The march will begin at the corner of Center and Main on Friday morning at seven and will end in front of BMP's executive offices. Please join us."

I look at Dad. "There's a lot of people mad at BMP for what happened to Seth."

"Including me," he says, folding his arms across his chest. "But I have to work, and I want to believe that, somehow, BMP's going to make this right. At work this morning, Mr. Douglas was super supportive and asked how we were doing. I could tell he feels terrible about what happened."

"Did he come to the hospital to visit Seth? Have any of the BMP guys come?"

When I feel terrible about something, I always try to make it right. Dad taught me that, but now he doesn't answer.

After lunch, he gets up and I follow him to the door. "We're getting low on animal feed."

He nods. "I already ordered some from BMP's feed store with my discount. See you tonight."

I grab a sports drink, my phone, and my tablet and head back to the apple tree. It's only two o'clock. Zurie's still in class, but I text anyway to give her the good news.

Seth's getting better. He may be awake by Friday!

Moments later, I get a response: **Yay! That's great news! The pig video was funny!**

I pull up Instagram and realize my pig video has fifteen likes with invitations to follow others. Six likes are from the Brazos yearbook staff, including Zurie. I'm cool with that, and press "Follow" on all my yearbook friends.

After dinner, I shut down early, but on Wednesday, I'm brushing down the horses when Dad's truck rolls by. It's only ten thirty. He probably forgot something, so I walk to the house just in case he needs me.

"Dad?"

He's in his room, crying hard and praying. "Why, Lord? I don't know what to do."

My mouth opens, but words won't come out. My heart thumps harder with every step I take toward Dad's room. *Please don't let this be about Seth.* I rush to his door. "Dad, open up!"

"Not now, Isaiah."

"Dad, please! You're scaring me!"

When he opens the door, I wrap my arms around him and hold on as he hard-cries again. I'm not sure what to do, but I don't let go because he may have to do the same for me if this has to do with Seth. "I'm here, Dad. What's wrong?"

He reaches in his pocket and hands me a pink paper before drifting back to take a seat on his bed. I sit next to him and read the paper. Dad's talking, but it all sounds like scrambled noise until my eyes meet his and he starts crying again.

"I've worked for BMP for over twenty years. I've never had a disciplinary write-up or a complaint about my performance. But this morning, I got a notice that I'd been laid off."

CHAPTER TWENTY-ONE

I don't know what to say to help Dad because I can tell by his tearstained face that everything hurts right now. So I just listen.

"Your mother and I split the responsibilities. She takes care of everything in the house, and my job is to make sure she has money to do it. How will I do that without a job?"

I take a breath and exhale slowly. "You'll figure it out, Dad. You always do."

He rubs his head. "What a difference a day makes. Yesterday Mr. Douglas was surprised to see me. Now that I think about it, he probably thought I was going to quit. That would explain why this morning when he came back from a board meeting, he handed me that layoff letter."

He puts his head on my shoulder, and I realize he needs me as much as I need him. "It's going to be all right, Dad.

You should lie down. That will help you feel better. And I'll put your résumé online for you. That should help."

He stretches across his bed. "Yeah, that's a good idea."

"Turn off your phone. I'll wake you in an hour," I say, then close his door.

With Dad laid off, and Seth in the hospital, I should get a job because we're going to need money. I walk outside, sit under the apple tree, and search site after site for an after-school job, or even holiday work since Thanksgiving and Christmas are coming up in a couple of months. Seth told me he needs money for school, and I know Dad needs money to pay bills. I have to help them. I could cut grass, or even take pictures for people during special occasions. I come across a cool site for posting your résumé. I'll have to tell Dad about it.

I'm deep in the online classifieds when my phone rings. When I see who's calling I jump to my feet. "Mom? Are you okay? Is Seth all right? What happened?"

Her voice cracks. "Your father's not answering his phone. Is he there?"

"Yes, ma'am. Are you sure everything's okay?"

"Isaiah, you and your father need to get here because Ray and I have an important meeting in half an hour, but more important—Seth just opened his eyes."

I sprint to the house. "Daaaaaaad! Wake up!"

I open his bedroom door without knocking, and when he sits up, I hand him my phone and burn off to my room to fill my backpack with things Seth's going to need—deodorant, toothbrush, toothpaste, cologne, clean boxers, pajamas. Dad and I come out of our rooms at the same time and climb into his truck. I can't wait to see Seth.

When we get to the ICU, Nurse Sofie greets me. "Hey! Are you doing okay?"

"Yes, ma'am."

She hugs me. "I'm glad. Go see your brother."

Dad and I step inside room four, wash our hands, and mask up. I give Mom a long hug. She looks tired, but her smile is the same. "Hi, baby, I missed you. I haven't seen your handsome face for days," she whispers.

"I missed you, too," I say.

Dad and Mom stand on one side of the bed rails, and I'm on the other. The monitors still beep, but I don't care how annoying they sound because Seth's eyes are open— until the tube in his mouth reminds me that everything is not okay.

Click . . . phwww.

Seth stares at the lights above his bed, and when he blinks, it's much slower than normal.

"Dad, why is he staring at the lights? Seth's eyes are super sensitive to brightness."

Mom's crying, and Dad puts his arms around her as he begins to cry, too.

Dr. Parker walks in. "Isaiah, welcome back. Good afternoon, Mr. and Mrs. Abernathy."

To me, she's still a hater, but I listen to her report with Mom and Dad.

"I've slowly taken Seth off the coma medications, and we're monitoring his reaction. I also lowered the number of breaths the ventilator was giving him, so Seth's now taking breaths on his own! Our goal is to get him off the ventilator completely."

"That's great news," says Dad.

Dr. Parker nods. "Yes, it is. Let's talk about his nutrition. Seth is still not ready to eat normal foods. Up through today, he's received his daily requirements through one of the medicine bags hanging from the poles, but he's losing weight, which concerns me. He's not ready to eat table food, so I've scheduled him for surgery at four o'clock this afternoon to have a feeding tube inserted, unless you decline."

I don't understand feeding tubes, but I know what surgery means.

"Does he have to have it?" Mom asks.

Dr. Parker nods. "In my opinion, it's vital."

Dad's getting upset. "Well, I'm not going to let my son starve to death. Fine. Do it."

I thought Seth just needed the swelling in his brain to go down. When did starving become a possibility? What else have they kept from me? What's really going on with Seth?

Dr. Parker types on the computer at the end of Seth's bed. "The surgery usually takes less than an hour. We'll make a small incision and place a tube in his stomach."

A chill runs down my back. "They're going to cut his stomach open?"

"The cut is very small, Isaiah," she says. "And if everything goes well, and there are no complications, I'll sign an order for Seth to be moved to the rehab floor."

"He keeps staring at the light. Why are his eyes not moving?" I ask.

She looks at Mom and Dad before answering, "Some of that may be due to . . . his very low brainpower right now. But a neurologist will provide us with a more accurate answer later."

Dr. Parker examines him again, then types on the computer. "Any more questions?"

Mom and Dad must have at least a hundred of them, but they stay quiet.

Dr. Parker smiles. "All right! I'll be back to check on Seth after his procedure."

As soon as she leaves, a lady dressed in a blue suit, who I've never seen before, comes in, washes her hands, and masks up. She's a tall Black woman with brown eyes and black hair past her shoulders. "I wanted to wait until the doctor finished before I came in."

Dad's voice sounds mechanical. "Seth's having surgery to insert a feeding tube."

She nods. "He needs more food. A feeding tube will help him get it." She steps over to my side of Seth's bed. "You must be Isaiah. I'm Patricia Haylon—call me Trish. Seth worked for me."

She leans over the bed rails and pulls Seth's sheet over his chest and shoulders—as if she cares about him.

Our eyes meet, and she smiles. "I was a nurse before going to law school. Seth brought a real love for life to our firm, and he talked about you all the time."

I hate that she's talking in the past tense, as if he won't ever do those things again. "Trish, it might take him a while, but Seth will get better. He might even be back to work in a couple of weeks. You didn't fire him, did you?"

She wipes her eyes. "Seth will always be welcome to work at my firm."

I grin, feeling like I just saved Seth's job, and knowing he would've done the same for me.

CHAPTER TWENTY-TWO

While Mom and Dad meet with Trish, I stay with Seth. I grab a chair and bring it closer to his bed. "Hey, it's me. Are you okay?"

His eyes open again, and I get excited. "Blink once for yes, twice for no."

But he just stares at the light as if I'm not there. I've only seen magicians and hypnotists make people stare like that. I lean in a little more. "I can't tell if you can hear or understand me, but in case you can, I—uh, I'm sorry for hitting you. And that Deacon dude must've told Dad about you skipping out on the BMP interview because I swear it wasn't me."

I look for a twitch of his hand, a wiggle of his toes—anything to let me know he's with me—but there's nothing. "And guess what? I ordered Brandon a combo meal like you told me."

That should get him going, but it doesn't, so I keep talking. "I got a week off for that. But then Zurie came to the house—you know, our yearbook editor! I gave her an apple, and she ate it. So you were wrong, bruh. All girls like apples, whether she's a horse or a human."

Normally Seth would've made a big deal out of this, but not today. He just stares at the ceiling. Maybe if I keep going, he'll snap out of it and tell me I'm talking too much. "I'm trying to be more active on Instagram. I changed my profile to public. Using Instagram lets me communicate with people without worrying about that shy part of me. Shy Guy's not even a factor."

I don't mention the protest that's happening on Friday because it might upset him. And I don't tell him it was Johnny Earl Sutton who hit him. Instead, I'm telling him about Ms. Hannah and her crew when someone turns on the water at the sink.

Juan Carlos takes off his baseball cap and masks up. "Hey, Ice Pic. How's he doing?"

I man-hug him. "His eyes are open but—"

Juan Carlos grins and struts over to Seth's bed. "Yo, Seth! It's about time you woke up!"

Seth just keeps staring at the lights in the ceiling, and soon Juan Carlos's smile fades. He reaches between the rails for Seth's hand. "Can you look at me?"

"He's still trying to get all those coma meds out of his system," I say. "It may take a minute before he starts recognizing us."

Juan Carlos nods. "Oh, okay."

"There's something else. He's having surgery this afternoon. Something about a tube in his stomach so he can get food because he's losing weight."

Juan Carlos sits in the chair next to Seth, squeezing his baseball cap. Tears leak from the edges of his eyes. "Can I have a minute with him? Alone?"

"Sure," I say, and leave.

I stand outside Seth's room, like I'm guarding it. After a few minutes, I look over my shoulder and see Juan Carlos bent over in his chair, shoulders bouncing in rhythm with a cry, and hands folded in prayer. He's always been so cool and smooth—seeing him like this makes me break down, too. It seems like I cry all the time now—when someone else is crying, when I look at my brother, or just thinking about my parents, it doesn't matter. You'd think I'd be sold out of tears, but they keep restocking.

Juan Carlos shuffles out of Seth's room and takes off his mask. "Can we talk?"

"Yeah."

He sniffles and wipes his nose with the sleeve of his shirt. "How are you holdin' up?"

I shrug because I'm not sure. Juan Carlos turns to look through the glass at Seth, and then starts crying again, not caring who sees him.

"I can't lie. I'm messed up, and I don't know how to be okay. He looks bad, Ice Pic."

My own tears come harder. "I know."

Juan Carlos hugs me, and for a minute we cry together. Then he grabs my shoulders.

"We can't give up. Seth is all about long distance, not short sprints. He'll be back."

I wipe my eyes again, happy to hear someone finally talk positive. "You think so?"

He puts his baseball cap on and winks. "All day! I have to go now—I promised I'd help my dad with yardwork. But I'll swing by again when I can." He gives me another hug. "All right, then."

"All right, then," I say back.

When Mom and Dad come back, they pray over Seth again before the nurses unhook his monitor, secure all his medicine bags on one pole, and push his bed out of room four. My lip hurts knowing I cut his, and now the hospital's going to cut on him, too.

Dad walks toward the door. "Let's go to the cafeteria and grab a sandwich. It may be our only chance to eat before they bring him back from surgery."

When we get there, none of us order food. I guess we're all feeling the same way.

Dad sips his coffee. "I saw Juan Carlos. He didn't look like he wanted to talk."

"He doesn't," I say. "How did your meeting go with Trish?"

Dad looks around and then whispers. "We'll talk later. Oh, and thanks for texting me that link to the online résumé site. I think that's going to help me find a job."

Soon we're back in Seth's room waiting on him. When the nurses wheel him in, Mom lifts his covers to see what the doctors did. Dad turns away. "I can't look at that. Let's go."

"Why? Does it look horrible? Is it a big cut? Dad?"

He walks toward the door. "Isaiah, I said let's go."

He's quiet in the elevator, in the hall, even in the truck. When we're halfway down Lexington, he opens up. "Trish's firm is going to represent Seth in a lawsuit against BMP."

I'm trying to wrap my head around this news when Dad drops another bomb.

"And she's adding my layoff to the lawsuit as a wrongful termination of employment. She thinks BMP let me go to scare the other employees into keeping their mouths shut, or they'll get laid off, too—it's called a chilling effect. She's been working with your mom and me on the paperwork. The lawsuit's getting filed tomorrow."

I don't understand this legal stuff very much, but Dad sounds serious.

"When we add up the cost for Seth's medical bills, it could easily be in the millions."

I can't think. I can't talk. It's all too much. And the worst part is that Dad didn't say a word about Seth getting better.

CHAPTER TWENTY-THREE

Thursday morning when Dad and I step inside the ICU, we wash our hands, mask up, and hug Mom before walking over to Seth's bed. He's been in this hospital for seven days, but it feels like a whole month.

I'm about to say good morning when I realize— "The breathing machine's gone!"

Mom's clapping. "Surprise! They just removed it thirty minutes ago. He's breathing on his own! Praise the Lord for some good news!"

I check Seth's lip—I can barely see the scar now. I lean over and whisper, "Congratulations on getting that tube out. Maybe you'll be able to talk soon."

The white bandages are off his head, and his hair has grown into a small Afro. It's been three weeks since we went to Redd's for my birthday. Now both of us need haircuts. I bet Jeremiah could hook us up in no time.

Sofie and another nurse walk in and turn Seth from his back to his right side.

I tap Nurse Sofie on the shoulder. "Excuse me, why are you moving him?"

"To avoid skin breakdown. If he lies in one spot too long, he could develop sores, but we're not going to let that happen," she says.

"Okay, but his left side is better. He gets stopped up on his right—you know, congested."

Sofie nods. "Sure, thanks for letting me know!"

As they move Seth around in his bed, Dad seems bothered. "I'm going to step out for a minute," he says.

I understand Dad a hundred percent. All these people touching Seth, making decisions for him has got to be annoying. Maybe it will bother Seth enough that he'll wake up sooner.

It's not long before Dad comes back. He grabs his keys and hugs Mom. "I just got a call from a lumberyard owner who saw my résumé online and wanted to know if I could come in and talk with him about a manager position. I told him I'd be there in thirty minutes. Wish me luck."

"Good luck, Dad."

But an hour after he leaves, he's back at the hospital. "That didn't go as well as I'd hoped."

Mom hugs him. "It's okay, Ray. Give it some time."

He grabs the television remote. "It was more than that. The guy kept staring at me, then asked me if I was related to Seth, the kid in the hospital. I told him I was his father, and immediately, our interview ended. I think BMP may be putting the word out to other businesses not to hire me."

I look to Mom, and she shakes her head with that *Don't say anything* shake.

I grab my backpack and head to the waiting room. "I'm going to finish my schoolwork."

I find a quiet spot in a corner and plug in my tablet to keep it charged while I work, then turn on my phone. There's a text from Zurie.

> **Hey! How's Seth doing today? Wanted to let you know I picked you to be my partner for a project in science. You down? It's for a major grade. Topic: The similarities between the brain and modern technology. Due before Thanksgiving break. Call me later.**

I smile, feeling good that Zurie picked me as her partner. I'm excited to get back to class—I don't remember the last time I could say that. I always thought school was boring, but nothing could be worse than doing homework in an ICU waiting room. I pull up Instagram, take a panoramic pic of the place, then post it with a caption:

Mercy Methodist ICU. Ever been in here?

Once I finish my homework, I turn off my phone, gather my things, and head back to the ICU. Dad's watching television when I walk in. I dry my hands and mask up. "Where's Mom?"

"In the cafeteria having coffee with Hannah, Pastor Holloway, and his wife."

"Why didn't you go?" I ask.

"I'm not in the mood."

Two people in scrubs knock on the door. "Hello. We're here to take Seth for an MRI."

Dad watches as they unhook Seth from the monitors, transfer all his medications to one pole, and unlock the wheels on his bed. "Can I go with him?" he asks.

"You're welcome to come if you'd like, but you don't have to."

Dad checks his pockets. "I left my phone in the truck."

I walk with Dad as they roll Seth to the ICU doors and then hold out my hand. Dad smiles as he drops his keys in it. "Thanks, Isaiah, and let your mom know I'm with Seth, okay?"

"No problem," I say as they head down the hall. I wonder how much longer Seth's going to be in here. When will he open his mouth and say, "What's up, little brotha?"

In the elevator, I think about how I wish I could hear his voice right now. When the emergency room doors slide open and I step out, a crowd of people rush at me with cameras and microphones.

"Are you Seth's younger brother, Isaiah? Is Seth awake? Are you aware of the lawsuit?"

I don't know what to do, what to say, or even how to act with all these microphones and cameras in my face. I burn off to Dad's truck, scramble inside, and lock it behind me. It's scorching in here, and if I don't get the AC blowing soon, I'm going to pass out. I put one finger over a nostril, but it's not helping.

The reporters surround Dad's truck. I yell at them, "Go away! Leave me alone!"

Suddenly, they back away and there's a knock on the window. It's Mom.

I unlock the door, and she takes my hand to help me get out. "Hurry, Isaiah."

Pastor Holloway, his wife, and Ms. Hannah are with her, and as Mom and I rush to the emergency room doors, our church calvary stares down the reporters, daring them to follow us. As soon as we pass the information desk, Mom nods to the lady sitting behind it.

"Thanks for paging me."

"From one mother to another, Mrs. Abernathy. I got you," she says.

I'm still shaking. "Dad's with Seth. What was that all about in the parking lot?"

We're in the elevator before Mom explains. "BMP got served with our lawsuit, and somebody at the courthouse leaked it to the press. Stay in the ICU. You'll be safe in there."

I'm still wiping sweat off my face. "So we're trapped in the hospital?"

"For now," she says. "You can go to the waiting room and the restroom. That's all."

The more I sit in Seth's small ICU room, the more I feel like a prisoner. I even have to eat lunch and dinner in the waiting room. So when Dad says it's time to go, I'm ready. It's dark outside when we leave, and the reporters are gone. And when Dad's truck tires leave the smooth roads and crunch the gravel toward home, I open my window and fill my nose with country calm air. As soon as we walk in the house, I curl up on the sofa and go to sleep.

In the morning, after I feed the animals, Dad and I head back before the sun comes up. On the way, he turns down an alley and cuts through another back street to avoid the crowds gathering near Main and Center for the protest march, then drives inside the Mercy Methodist parking garage to avoid the reporters who are already gathered near the ER doors.

We rush to the elevators and make our way to the ICU. Who would've thought I'd feel safe inside this lab-looking place?

"Seth had a good night," Mom tells us as we wash our hands and mask up.

I now understand that *Seth had a good night* means nothing happened. He's still staring at the lights, he still hasn't moved, and he's still not talking. How can that be good?

Dr. Parker washes her hands and nods. "Hello, Abernathy family. I have good news. Seth's vital signs have remained stable, and he's breathing completely on his own. No reported issues with his feeding tube, which means he's ready to leave the ICU! Congratulations!"

Mom hugs her, and Dad shakes her hand. "Thank you for everything," he says.

"You're welcome. I've signed the order for him to be discharged from the ICU. There's a private room ready for him on the rehab floor. Things will begin moving much faster there."

Dad's phone rings. "I'm sorry, I forgot to power down," he says, rushing out.

"Happens all the time," she says. "I'll be back before you leave the ICU."

Mom hugs me, and it feels like the beginning of a good day. Dad comes back in, smiling. "I just got another interview, this one at a grocery store. When it's over, I'll come find you on the rehab floor."

"Good luck, Dad. Be careful," I say.

After he leaves, Mom and I sit with Seth since the press still has us cornered in here, but thirty minutes later, Nurse Sofie walks in. "It's time to leave the ICU! Hooray for Seth!"

I lean over the bed rail. "We're bustin' out of here, bruh. And you need a haircut."

"I can start cutting his hair again," says Mom.

I picture Seth's eyes rolling so hard that he's staring at the back of his head. I bite my lip to hide a laugh.

Now we have to get him to talk, and walk, and everything else that will make him his old self again.

CHAPTER TWENTY-FOUR

Just before noon, Sofie unhooks Seth from the monitor and places his medications near his feet, then releases the brakes on his bed and rolls him out of room four. Mom follows behind Seth's bed, carrying his wallet, shoes, and sunglasses in a bag. I walk behind her as the ICU staff smiles and waves goodbye.

"Good luck, Abernathy family," says a clerk at the desk.

Mom smiles. "Thank you for everything."

Other families wave from their loved ones' doors. I spot the lady who prayed for Seth in the middle of the night. Through the window behind her, there's a young girl on a ventilator like the one Seth had. That must be Isabella. Mom waves, and so do I. Everybody needs a little hope.

Dr. Parker presses the button to open the doors for us, then she hugs Mom and grabs my hand again. "You're a good brother and a good son, Isaiah."

"Thank you."

We take a short elevator ride to the fifth floor, make a left, and follow Sophie and Seth down the hall.

"Here we are, room five-fifteen. The sofa lets out into a bed," Sofie tells us.

"Mom, can I stay overnight with Seth? Or how about the whole weekend?" I ask.

She smiles. "Sure. It'll give me a chance to sleep in my own bed."

Sofie winks. "Mrs. Abernathy, I'll just need you to sign a waiver saying it's okay for Isaiah to be here with Seth. The rehab nurse will bring it to you. All right, folks, I'm so sorry we had to meet this way." She hugs Mom and then me.

"Bye, Ms. Sofie. Thanks for taking care of Seth. Can I use my phone in here?"

"You sure can, but not on the speaker setting."

"Okay."

The first thing I do is text Zurie.

Seth's out of the ICU. In Rehab Room #515. I'm staying with him this weekend.

My phone buzzes.

Yay for Seth! May I visit tomorrow? We can talk about the science project.

Whoa. Seth's not ready to have new visitors. He needs more time.

But before I can text her no, a Hispanic man in a blue suit

comes in. "Hello, Abernathy family. I'm Dr. Ramirez, I'm a pain management and rehabilitation doctor. Congratulations on Seth's discharge from the ICU."

"Thank you. I'm his mom."

"And I'm his brother, Isaiah."

"Wonderful. I've been following Seth since his admission to Mercy Methodist, and while he's on the rehab floor I'll oversee his care. If you're not feeling well, we ask that you wear a mask. Other than that, we only ask that you keep your hands washed. His therapy begins in the morning. In the meantime, have a good evening, and I'll see you tomorrow or Sunday."

Later, a young Black man in burgundy scrubs strolls in and introduces himself as Jason, Seth's evening nurse. "Are you Mom and Isaiah?" he asks.

"Yes," Mom answers.

"Perfect, let me update some information for you."

Jason steps over to a blank erasable board on the wall, picks up a marker, and writes:

MY NAME: SETH ABERNATHY
NURSE: JASON, DOCTOR: RAMIREZ
ROOM NUMBER: 515
TODAY IS: FRIDAY, SEPTEMBER 17
THERAPY SCHEDULE FOR: SATURDAY AND SUNDAY
MORNING: 10:00 OT, 10:45 PT
AFTERNOON: 2:00 OT/PT

"The board will keep everyone, especially Seth, oriented while he's here. Mom, I need you to sign this consent form for Isaiah to stay overnight."

"Sure," she says.

"Thank you. I'll be back later to feed Seth. If you need anything in the meantime, just press the call button."

"Okay, thanks, Jason," Mom says, just as her phone rings. "Oh, it's Pastor Holloway!"

There's excitement in her voice as she tells our pastor all about Seth moving to rehab, but then her expression changes as she listens. "Uh-huh, yes, I'd like that. Thank you! Okay, goodbye."

I'm looking at her, waiting for her to spill the beans, but she doesn't. Good news is hard to come by these days, and I can't believe Mom's holding out.

When Dad walks into Seth's new room, his eyes widen. "This is a castle compared to the tiny space he had in ICU."

Mom flashes a huge grin. "Guess what? Pastor offered me a job at the church daycare, and I took it! And he said when Seth gets out of the hospital, if I need to, I can bring him with me. I can start whenever I'm ready!"

Dad's smile is weak as he hugs Mom. "Congratulations. We sure needed that."

She kisses him. "And how did your interview go?"

He looks at her, then me, then at Seth, and shakes his head. I remember what he told me the day he got laid off. Making money to pay the bills is part of his responsibilities, not Mom's.

He takes Mom's hand. "Let's go, we can't be late to our meeting with Trish. There are protesters and reporters everywhere. Isaiah, I'll feed the animals. Oh, and don't watch the news."

I call to him on his way out. "Did you get the feed?"

He waves as he heads out the door. "I'm working on it. Love you."

Seth's still staring at the lights.

"Dude, you're going to hurt your eyes! Stop it! If you want to stare at something or someone, look at me because—"

He's staring at the ceiling, but I look at the floor, still ashamed for what I did.

"Seth, I'm so sorry for hitting you."

When he just keeps watching the lights, I plop on the sofa. I sure hope the doctors here in rehab can help him stop doing that.

I check Instagram and find comments about my ICU waiting room pic.

@SlimJimmyDude I know that waiting room. I even remember the smell.

@FetchinGretchenGal I was there ten years ago. It hasn't changed.

@Tinybiscuitlover You're good with the camera. Love your horses.

Two of the comments are from adults and one is a high schooler, but they all live in or near Scarboro. All of them tagged @Scarborostrong, but the two adults also tagged

@WATCH-US, the watchdog group. I follow them back, just to keep an eye out for anything my parents may need to know.

I'm excited about people responding to my post, but I'm even more fired up that I don't feel nervous or worried like I used to when people I don't know try to talk to me. Seth's going to be so proud of how I'm handling Shy Guy.

Jason comes in, startling me. "It's dinner time for Seth. Do you need anything? I've got soft drinks, popcorn, even cheese and crackers at the nurses' station. Want something?"

"I don't have my toothbrush and toothpaste. Any extras around here?"

"Let me see what I can find." He leaves but soon returns and hands me a bag. "Here's a patient kit with everything you'll need for an overnight stay. And I brought you a bag of popcorn, too. There's a microwave down the hall."

I stand and fist-bump him. "Thanks. I'll be right back."

By the time I make my popcorn and get back to Seth's room, Jason's there with two cans of milk. "This is not regular milk. It's specifically made for feeding tubes," he says.

I nod, rip open the hot bag, and stand next to him. But when he pulls back Seth's sheet, my knees buckle, the bag of popcorn slipping from my hands and spilling popcorn all over the floor.

"Are you okay?" Jason asks.

I'm still looking at the gadget on my brother's stomach, wondering what this place has done to him. Jason stops what he's doing. "Is this your first-time seeing Seth's feeding tube?"

I nod again, afraid that if I open my mouth, I may barf up lunch, and I don't even remember what that was. I stare at the round, plastic flip-top cap that looks more like something on a dish detergent bottle.

Jason walks with me to the sofa. "It's okay. Have a seat. I'll clean up the popcorn."

He comes back in with a broom, a dustpan, and a Sprite. He hands me the soft drink. "This will help your stomach calm down. Just relax. I got this."

After cleaning up the mess, Jason rewashes his hands and puts on clean gloves before feeding Seth. I watch even as my stomach grumbles. When he finishes, he cleans around Seth's feeding tube and closes the cap. "And that's it! You doing okay?"

I inhale and let it out slowly. "I think so."

He hands me a package of cheese and crackers, then sits next to me. "It's hard to watch at first, but I promise it doesn't hurt Seth, and it's giving him essential vitamins and nutrition."

"Thanks for helping us, Jason."

He smiles. "That's what I do."

Once we're alone, I step over to Seth's bed and whisper so no one can hear. "You've got to wake up so you can make decisions for yourself. You're always telling me to speak up. Now I'm telling you to practice what you preach before these doctors decide to cut on you again."

CHAPTER TWENTY-FIVE

All day Saturday, therapists and doctors come in and out of Seth's room to measure the length of his arms and legs, the circumference of his head, test his eyesight, even rotate his ankles. When the last person leaves, I'm hoping that's it, but then Zurie knocks on the open door.

I'm stuck in stupid, staring at her like I did when she showed up on the farm. Dad looks at her and then at me. I walk toward her, whispering. "What are you doing here?"

Zurie backs up, as if she walked into the wrong room. Snapsickles! I forgot to text her not to come and now she's fumbling as if she did something wrong.

"I . . . I waited for your answer, and then figured—I figured you'd gotten busy, so I didn't text again. I brought everything for us to get started on our project, but . . . I'm sorry, Ice."

"No, it's not your fault, it's mine. Come in," I say.

"Mom, Dad, this is Zurie. She's the editor of our yearbook, and a friend of mine."

Embarrassment creeps up my neck and heats my face as Dad gives me that *Ah sookie, sookie, now* grin he gets when he's dancing with Mom at the table. I turn to Zurie.

"Let's go find a place to work," I say, and walk toward the door.

She looks sad. "You're not going to introduce me to Seth?"

I want her to meet the strong, popular, funny Seth. This is the not-moving, not-talking, unaware-of-anything-or-anyone-around-him Seth. Dang it. I hate myself for thinking that way.

She follows me as I shuffle over to his bed. "Zurie, this is Seth. Seth, Zurie."

Her smile is as soft as her voice. "Hi. Nice to meet you."

I keep my eyes on Seth but can still see Zurie's face in my side vision. She's staring at him like he's an exhibit, and I can't take it. I'm about to say something when she beats me to it.

"I can tell Seth's fade was a lot nicer than yours."

My laugh has more relief in it than humor. "Girl, you must be new. My fade was legit, and a whole lot nicer than his. Let's go."

My parents laugh, and Zurie shares her smile with them before we leave. We find an empty waiting room down the hall, plug in our tablets, and Zurie takes over.

"On Tuesday in class, we learned about the three main

functions of the brain."

"Yeah, I read all that online. It needs to receive information, interpret the information, and then respond to the information."

"Exactly. I thought our project could explore how the brain and a computer are similar."

I sit back. "Snore! Everybody will do that. How can our project be different?"

Zurie grins and adjusts her glasses. "I'm glad you asked. While everyone else talks about how similar those two things are when they're working, we'll talk about what they both do when they break down."

I lean forward. "Now you've lost me."

She sighs. "Okay. Let's say you have a desktop computer at home, and you use a mouse for all the functions. What would you do if the mouse stopped working?"

"Probably switch all the commands over to my keyboard, maybe turn on voice commands until my mouse started working again or I got a new one."

She keeps smiling. "Exactly! Check this out. Is it okay if I use Seth as an example?"

I shrug. Her words put my guard up—but she's got my attention.

"Let's say when Seth wakes up, he can't walk. He's obviously walked before, but the part of his brain that would command his legs to move has stopped working. Sometimes when one part of the brain malfunctions, another part will take over, like switching from the mouse to the keyboard! Computers have backup plans, and our bodies do, too."

First of all, Seth's going to walk out of this hospital. That's what therapy and rehab is for. Second, I think Zurie's on to something because my thoughts travel back to when Seth taught me how to shoot free throws and told me how important it was to do things the same way over and over.

We talk about the information we want to include in our project, decide how we're going to divide the work, and even map out a schedule for deadlines. I pull the calendar up on my phone. "It's due the Friday before Thanksgiving, right?"

"Yep."

My phone pings.

Zurie leans over to see that I have a new follower. "By the way, I love all the pictures and reels you posted on IG, especially the ones of Dolly and Buster."

I try to keep a serious face. "They were, you know, just horsing around."

She scoots back. "And on that really corny joke, I'm out. You definitely need to be a vet because comedy is not your hustle. We can talk more about our project at school."

I'm still laughing as I walk her to the elevator. "Thanks, Zurie. See you Monday."

The clock on my phone shows eleven-thirty. Dang it! I missed Seth's morning therapy sessions! I can't miss the afternoon one because I have questions about retraining the brain.

As soon as I walk in, Mom and Dad leave to run errands. I'm watching television when a man and a woman dressed in blue scrubs knock and come in.

"I'm Katie, Seth's physical therapist. And this is David, Seth's occupational therapist."

"I'm Isaiah, Seth's brother."

Katie continues. "Hello, Isaiah. David and I are going to work together and do some stretching and circulation exercises on Seth's arms and legs."

I nod. "I've got some questions, and I'd like to record what you tell me. Is that okay?"

"Sure," says David. "Ask away!"

I tap the video button on my phone. "Thanks. Why is therapy important for Seth?"

Katie answers. "Therapy improves overall function of the mind and body."

"That includes memory, too, right?"

David nods. "Absolutely! Therapy is a key component in regaining memory."

"How can I help my brother with therapy?"

"We can show you exercises to do with Seth on your own. Would you like that?" asks David.

"For real? Yes! When should I do them with him?"

Katie shrugs. "You should do the exercises every day if you and Seth are up to it! Doing things over and over is what makes a difference and can spark recovery."

David signals me to join him. "I'll show you a few exercises right now!"

I'm getting hyped because this is exactly what I've been waiting for. "Perfect. Last question. Once we start these exercises, how long will it take for Seth to get back to the way he was before the accident? He leaves for college in January."

Katie and David share a look, then Katie shrugs again. "I don't know if anyone can answer that question, Isaiah. Therapy is not a guarantee of recovery. The key is to never give up. Sometimes it takes years to see a difference." My excitement fades away. Seth doesn't have years to get better. He's just a little over ninety days away from orientation at A&M. If I start working with him right away, maybe he won't lose his scholarship.

CHAPTER TWENTY-SIX

I text Zurie about what the therapists said.

That's fabulous news! Let me know if I can help.

When Mom and Dad come back to the hospital, I tell them, too. "Katie and David let me work with them today so that I can do therapy with Seth on my own, to help his recovery."

Dad fist-bumps me. "I can pick you up after school each day until I get a job. That way you can be here when the therapists come, even video them."

I love how we're working together, helping each other out. "Thanks, Dad."

Before I leave, I try a therapy session with Seth. At first I'm uncomfortable, but it doesn't take long for that to change. Lifting Seth's arms and legs, doing therapy with him for the first time, goes great—except he doesn't respond.

"Don't give up," says Mom. "Nothing good comes easy."

On Sunday, Katie and David let me help with therapy again.

"Can he have a later therapy time? I really want to learn how to help him."

Katie checks her schedule. "How about four?"

I grin. "That'll work!"

When it's time to go home, I hug Mom, then touch Seth's hand. "Heading back to school tomorrow, but I'll be here for your therapy."

I think about Seth all the way home, wondering if there's anything else I can do to help him. I wish I knew for sure that he understands because I'd apologize a thousand times for hitting him. What I really need, though, is for him to talk, because then maybe he'll forgive me.

Dad hangs up his keys, and I curl up on the sofa because I still refuse to sleep in my room until Seth's in there with me. But when my alarm goes off, I'm dragging. I manage to get the animals fed, then head down the road toward the bus. When Mr. Williams opens the door, I already know what he's going to ask.

"Hey, Isaiah. Missed you last week. How's Seth?"

"About the same" is all I say.

Seems like every place I go has problems. The hospital, the farm, and now I have to deal with Brandon again, after being Brandon-free for a whole week. At least he knows I'm not afraid of him now. Maybe that will change things.

I get off Mr. Williams's bus and get on the one to Brazos. As soon as I walk down the bus aisle, all talking stops. I sit next to Zurie.

She leans in and whispers. "Brandon's parents shipped him off to military school."

I guess his parents had enough of him, too. Maybe school, at least, is about to get better for me. I exhale Brandon out of my system. "You think military school will help him?"

Zurie's whispers get louder. "Who cares! The feeling around here is *Ding, dong, the witch is dead*, and everybody sees *you* as the hero!"

She's right because in advisory, in the halls, all day, my stress level is code calm. Everyone's talking, nodding, saying hello. Shy Guy's still around, but he must be getting weak because I nod back and even speak to other kids in the hall. Seth would be so proud.

By the end of the day, I'm still full of energy. Dad's waiting in his truck, and I climb in.

"Hey, how was your day? Mine was legit! How'd the interview go?"

He shrugs and shakes his head. "They said I was over-qualified."

Overqualified? Is that really a thing? Poor Dad. For the first time ever, I feel bad for feeling good, so I stay quiet until we get to the hospital. He drives slowly through the parking lot and surprises me when he parks near the emergency room. He glares at the reporters, then turns to me and says, "Isaiah, I've got something I have to do. Don't wait on me."

"Yes, sir."

As we get out of the truck, Dad points to the ER. "Get inside." Then he signals the reporters over to him. When I turn back to look, he's talking to Skyler Mills, the reporter from Channel 2, as other reporters listen in or hold tape recorders near his face. Dad looks my way and gives me a thumbs-up. I give him one back but hope he doesn't do anything that will get him in trouble, especially after what those reporters did to me when I went to get his phone. I head to Seth's room just in time to hug Mom and record Katie's and David's therapy session.

A doctor comes in to check Seth's feeding tube. Then two more doctors come in and ask Seth questions, and ask him to do stuff, and check his vision. Mom and I watch as they each type notes in his chart before leaving. The whole time, I'm worried about Dad.

Finally, he walks in and takes Mom and me to the cafeteria, where we sit at a table far away from anyone else.

"Dad, why did you talk to the reporters?"

"Trish emailed Skyler questions to ask me. There were some things I needed to get off my chest. It'll be on the news tonight."

I'm completely confused, but Dad seems to be in a better mood, so I don't ask any questions.

* * *

Later, Dad takes me home, and when the news comes on, we sit on the sofa and watch it together. It starts with Dad talking to Skyler in the parking lot with all the other reporters around them. Skyler asks, "Is Seth recovering from the accident?"

Dad answers. "Seth is still unable to talk or move. We're praying for a miracle."

My heart sinks. I didn't know we were totally relying on God to heal him.

"Mr. Abernathy, is it true that you were recently terminated by BMP?"

Dad nods. "BMP included me in their most recent layoffs. I'd been with them for over twenty years, and I'm the first supervisor in their history to receive a layoff notice."

"Do you think it's because of the lawsuit?"

"All I can say is, I've received annual awards, raises, and bonuses. There has never been a complaint filed against me by any employee I've managed or customer I've helped."

"Have you been able to find another job?"

Dad shakes his head. "I've been interviewing, but no luck."

"How can the community help you and your family?"

Dad looks right into the camera. "I'm not asking for charity. But I would like to do a trade-off if anyone is interested—a couple of my boars, or maybe a sow, in exchange for feed for my other animals. I've got chickens, horses, and pigs."

He's giving away two of our pigs? My heart sinks, even

though I know he wouldn't do it if he had any other choice. The news has barely stopped for a commercial when Dad's phone buzzes.

"Hello? Yes, this is Ray Abernathy. They weigh around two hundred and fifty pounds each. Sure, that sounds fair. Yes, I'll meet you at your store. Thank you."

He hangs up and smiles. "A feed store owner just saw the interview and got my telephone number from the news station. We're meeting in the morning, and he'll send a worker to pick up two boars. That's all I could do."

I smile the best I can. "I know. Thanks, Dad."

I hurt for the two puddle-waddling friends I'm about to lose, but I'm happy Dad figured out a way to feed the rest of the animals. He leans over and hugs me.

"Abernathys don't quit. We always figure out a way to get things done, right?"

I hug him back. "Right."

CHAPTER TWENTY-SEVEN

When the end of September hits, I can't believe it. Seth's been in the hospital for nearly three weeks, two of those on the rehab floor. Even though I haven't seen any changes in him, I feel like I'm helping by doing the extra therapy. But this busy schedule is breaking me down.

Every morning, I'm up early to feed the animals, then I sit in class for six hours, before rushing to the hospital, where I video the therapists, finish my homework, do an extra therapy session with Seth, and then leave with Dad. When I get home, I fall asleep on the sofa and wake up in the morning, still tired. It's been a long minute since I took pictures or hung out with the animals. I miss it, but helping Seth is more important.

The only real "me" time I have is during lunch in the school courtyard. I'm thinking about taking a nap when my phone buzzes.

**Can't pick you up after school. You'll have to walk.
See you at the hospital.**

I don't even have time to be upset before someone says, "Hey, Abernathy, can I talk with you a minute?"

Rhino's voice puts me on red alert. I brace for something petty until it dawns on me—he didn't call me Ice Cream. I nod, and he spreads his lunch out on the table.

"Last night, Unc and I saw a picture of Seth on the news. How's he doing?"

I glare at him. "What do you want? Brandon's gone. You running your own bully show now?"

Rhino unwraps his sandwich. "Everything isn't always as it seems. Brandon bullied me, too, and I took it—until he started bullying Unc."

I wasn't expecting to hear that, so I unwrap my sandwich and eat while Rhino says what's on his mind.

"Brandon used to tell Unc he looked like a monster. Unc would cry and believed that's why people stared at him—he thought he was scaring them. Brandon got a big laugh out of that."

As much as I want to say something, I don't, because thinking about Brandon hating on Uncle Jerry stirs up old anger.

"So I made a deal with Brandon. If he'd leave Unc alone, I'd have his back no matter what. The price I paid was knowing people hated me."

Rhino crunches through a bag of chips. "But when he didn't honor the bet you two made, and kept on calling

171

you Ice Cream, I realized he could do the same to me. So last week when you took him down, it was a good day for a lot of us."

I look away. "It wasn't a good day for me. I don't like fighting. It's not who I am."

He finishes his lunch and grabs his trash. "Hanging with Brandon wasn't who I am, either. That's why I'm apologizing to every person I helped Brandon bully. I'm sorry, Abernathy. I hope we can be friends again."

"Me, too. My bad for judging you, Rhino. Seth's still working hard to recover."

"Unc and I will keep praying for him. All right, then."

I swallow the knot in my throat. "All right, then."

I've hated Rhino as much as I hated Brandon, and had no idea he hated Brandon, too. I judged him, just like people have judged me—but now I know how both sides feel. Judging and being judged hurt the same.

Maybe if I had talked to Rhino more, I would've known what he was going through.

After school, when I step inside Seth's room, I stop when I notice he's not in his bed. He's sitting in a wheelchair with light blue Velcro belts wrapped around his feet, waist, chest, and head. He's even wearing a seatbelt.

Mom's sitting on the sofa as Katie and David demonstrate different features of Seth's new chair. Dad's scrolling through his phone, blinking hard and looking angry.

I swallow the cry in my throat. "I thought therapy was at four. And why is Seth strapped down like a criminal?"

Katie answers. "There was a scheduling issue, so we had to see Seth at three today. The straps keep him safe in the wheelchair until he can build up muscle strength. He's extremely weak."

David signals me to come stand by him. "Seth's overall health and well-being should improve now that he's out of bed."

I close my eyes. *Seth, please say something, do something, move, anything! I'm sending you some of my strength—use it, and make a move.*

I'm still talking to Seth in my head when Dr. Ramirez comes in. "Good afternoon. I'm delighted to see Seth out of bed and in his wheelchair. I've looked over all the notes from Seth's rehab team, and we're prepared to have a meeting with the family tomorrow afternoon at two in the conference room. We'll talk about progress, prognosis, and Seth's needs in the future."

Dad smiles. "We'll be there. So, Dr. Ramirez, how much longer do you think Seth will be here in rehab?"

"I've started the paperwork to discharge him, but we can talk about that more tomorrow during the meeting."

The looks on Mom's and Dad's faces don't need words. I can feel what they're thinking. How are we going to take care of Seth at home? One wrong move, one wrong medication, one wrong dosage could kill him. He can't walk, or talk, or wash himself. Not to mention feed himself, dress himself, go to the bathroom—even brush his own teeth.

I plop onto the sofa, glance at my brother, and rewind all the memories I have of him chasing and tickling me until I begged him to stop, trips to Sir Smoothie, laughing at dinner with Mom and Dad, taking pics of him as he broke the tape at his cross-country meets. Those days can't be over.

Mom must've read my mind. "With God's help, we'll be just fine."

As my parents talk to Dr. Ramirez, I step over to the window, and even though I'm nowhere close to the farm, I lift my eyes to the sky and hope my thoughts are heard.

Wish granter, Seth's coming home. I'll give you points for making that happen, but don't forget that I also asked that he make it to college, that he knows I still believe in "between brothers," and that he forgives me for hitting him.

Once Dr. Ramirez leaves, Dad sighs. "We've got our work cut out for us, don't we?"

Mom nods. "Yes, but we've seen progress in Seth, and that's all the motivation I need. He opened his eyes, got off the breathing machine, and now he's sitting in a wheelchair."

"Well, that's true, you've got a good point, we have to believe," says Dad.

Mom keeps talking. "And tomorrow the doctors will give us the plan for Seth's recovery. Maybe home is where the biggest parts of his improvement are going to happen, right?"

"Right!" I say. "It wouldn't surprise me one bit if Seth gets home and starts talking right away. I'm glad he's leaving the hospital. The sooner, the better."

CHAPTER TWENTY-EIGHT

The next afternoon, Dad doesn't show up at school to pick me up, so I send a text to let him know I'll catch a metro bus and not to worry. But when I get to Seth's room, Dad isn't there, either. Dr. Parker and Mom are sitting on the sofa. Mom's eyes are swollen, and she's holding a box of tissues. What happened? Seth's eyes are closed, and my eyes immediately dart to his chest. It's moving up and down. Thank goodness he's still breathing.

Dr. Parker stands. "Hello, Isaiah. Seth's team of doctors met with your parents today, and your mom asked me to summarize the meeting for you."

My eyes bounce from Dr. Parker to Mom, and back to Dr. Parker again. "Where's Dad?"

Mom shakes her head. "He . . . needs some time, but you need to hear this."

I know a clue when I hear one. Dr. Parker must be

droppin' bad-news bombs. Mom takes my hand like I'm five, and I don't pull away because, right now, I *feel* like I'm five as we walk down the hall to the break room. Dr. Parker shuts the door behind us, and I take a seat at the table. My heart pounds and my knee jumps as Dr. Parker sits close to me and opens a folder. She doesn't waste any time getting started.

"Isaiah, when Seth was brought into the trauma center the morning of September tenth, he'd been in a bad accident. Upon examination, we noticed his brain was swelling. We needed the swelling to go down before we could find out what was going on in his brain, remember?"

"Yes."

"Good. After the swelling went down, our neurologist ran tests on Seth's brain and determined that it had obtained a significant injury from the accident."

"How significant?"

Mom turns away as Dr. Parker zones in on my face. She looks back at her notes, and in my mind, I visualize an enemy plane, loaded with gigantic bombs, ready to fall.

"The injury is catastrophic. Even though Seth looks the same, he's not."

BOOM! Direct hit.

The inside of my stomach gets hot. My jaw clamps, and Dr. Parker takes my hand as she talks. "Because of the brain injury, some of the things he could do before the accident, he's now unable to do. For example, Seth used to eat with a knife and fork. Now he is unable to chew or swallow properly. That's why we placed a feeding tube in his stomach."

"But that's just for now, right? You'll take it out later?"

Her lips tighten, and she blinks slowly. "We believe the feeding tube is permanent."

BOOM! Structural damage.

Then she drops something I wasn't expecting. "Seth's rehab team gave their opinions on Seth's future. It is believed that his brain injury may have affected his memory."

My eyes widen. "His memory of what? Everything? Even me?"

Dr. Parker squeezes my hand. "I'm afraid so, Isaiah. We don't believe Seth will ever walk, talk, or do anything else independently again. He is unable to follow simple commands, and we don't think he ever will because he now functions at a much younger age."

I wait for her to finish, but she leaves me hanging. I want to know, but my brain screams at me, *Don't ask! You'll regret it!*

I ask anyway. "What age is he functioning at now? Fourteen? Fifteen?"

She's taking too long to answer—I should've kept my mouth shut. Before I can say, "Never mind," she releases the last bomb, and it's nuclear.

"Seth's abilities are the same as those of a seven-month-old infant."

BOOM! It's all over.

I'm covered in shrapnel, totally defeated and furious that I was misled. I pull my hand away and grab the sides of my head. "You're lying! I knew it was going to take time for him to recover, but you made me believe he would get better once his brain stopped swelling!"

Dr. Parker shakes her head. "No, Isaiah. I said we wouldn't be able to know what's going on inside his head until the swelling went down. I'm sorry to give you this news."

She wipes tears from the corners of her eyes, as Mom slides down the wall until she's on the floor, crying so hard that it hurts to watch. I stand, knocking over my chair.

"What are we supposed to do now?"

Dr. Parker wipes her eyes again. "Do the best you can, and everything you can. That's all you can do. I completely understand how you're feeling right now."

I hold my head and scream at her. "Shut up! Just . . . stop talking to me! How could you possibly know how I feel? You don't understand anything!"

She reaches for my hand again. "Isaiah, please wait."

I run out of the room, dodging people and medical equipment. I duck inside the conference room, and that's where I spot Dad, sitting alone in a corner, crying with no sound, rocking without a chair. I can't handle it, so I take off again, hoping to outrun what I just heard. I turn the corner and bulldoze right into Juan Carlos.

He quickly helps me up. "What happened? Ice Pic, talk to me!"

I grab his shirt, crying through my words. "The doctors said Seth won't get better, and they're kicking him out of here. He's going to be like a baby for the rest of his life. He won't even remember me."

Juan Carlos hugs me as he speaks truth in my ear. "Don't let them steal your hope. The doctors don't know Seth like we do. He's got you on lock in his brain. You're in there!"

I hope he's right because the secret *I* have on lock hurts worse than ever right now.

He pulls away and paces, then nods at me. "Okay, until Seth gets back, you can count on me, understand? And he *is* coming back, do you believe me?"

I wipe my eyes. "Yes."

"Say it!"

"Seth's coming back."

Juan Carlos grips my shoulders. His eyes demand my attention, so I stop crying and listen. "They can't control Seth with some jacked-up report. You and me, we're going to help our boy find his way back. Do you know why people use a compass?"

"Yeah, for direction when they're lost. Do I need to get one for Seth?"

"No. We need to *be* one for him. Are you with me?"

I wipe tears from my face. "Yeah, I'm with you."

"Good. Let the doctors do their thing. And then we'll do ours."

He puts his arm around my shoulder, and we walk back to Seth's room. Dad still hasn't made it back, but Mom has, and she's pacing. Juan Carlos and I sit on the sofa, staring at Seth, staying quiet until Mom stands in front of us like a war general and gets our minds right.

"This is very painful, but we will *not* crumble. Let's go."

Juan Carlos and I follow her like soldiers to the conference room. Dad's now leaning against a wall, and he shakes his head when Mom asks him to join us. There's pain in this room, all mixed together like some busted science formula: Angry air plus sad air minus hopeful air equals *this* air. Mom clears her throat and brings me out of my hate fest.

"If my father were here, he'd say, 'Sandra, plan your work, and then work your plan.' Let's plan in here because we're not taking their message of hopelessness back into Seth's room. The air he breathes needs to be full of faith, healing, and love." Mom rubs her face. "What's today's date?"

Dad mumbles from across the room, "Wednesday the twenty-ninth."

"Okay, then on Friday, October first, Seth comes home. The house needs to be ready."

I shrug. "What does that even mean?"

Dad leans back. "We need to clear space for a hospital bed, a wheelchair, milk, medications, diapers, feeding tubes, and a bunch of other things I can't even think of right now."

"I can move into the study. All I need is my bed and my dresser. If Seth is going to work with Mom in the mornings, then I won't be waking him up when I shower, right?"

Mom combs her fingers through her hair. "I don't even know what I don't know. That's what worries me. And I only have two days to ask questions and learn."

I sniffle. "It'll be okay, Mom. I'll type notes on my phone and then text them to you."

Juan Carlos nods. "Everything's going to be all right. Seth's coming back to us."

A spark of hope makes me speak up. "That's truth, Mom, because me and Juan Carlos, we're going to help him."

CHAPTER TWENTY-NINE

We're still in the conference room when Dad steps out to take a call. Minutes later, he rejoins us. "I have an interview tomorrow morning."

"Good for you," I say, and try to smile, but the edges of my mouth won't curve up.

"Good luck, Mr. Abernathy," says Juan Carlos.

Mom gives Dad a huge hug. "Maybe this is the one! Ray, you've got so much on your plate with Seth, trying to find a job, and keeping the bills paid. I see you, honey. Thank you."

I hadn't thought about everything he's going through. Mom's right for calling him out.

Dad still looks beat down, but he takes Mom's hand. "After I set up my interview, I called Trish about this morning's meeting. She wants to talk with us, so I told her we'd be there in an hour."

"I'll stay with Seth," I say.

"Thanks, Isaiah," says Dad.

Mom starts walking and talking about everything on her mind that she needs to buy, or learn, or research, or pray about. When she finishes, she looks my way. "Did you get all that?"

"I did. Here's what we got." I read out the list.

1. Get trained on how to clean Seth's feeding tube.

2. Get trained on how to feed Seth his milk and add his medications in it.

3. Get trained on how to record his vital signs.

4. Who is his doctor now, and when (and how often) does he need an appointment?

5. Is there a twenty-four-hour number in case we need help or have questions?

6. What things should we be most concerned about?

7. How will we know if he's in pain?

8. How will we know if he doesn't feel well?

9. Find out where Seth's therapy is going to be, and what time.

10. Call the church and tell them I'll start work at the daycare on Monday.

11. Ray has an interview tomorrow at Kurt's Butcher Shop. Pray about that.

12. Will we need any special electrical outlets for Seth's equipment?

Dad points at my phone. "Send that list to both of us. Sandra, we've got to get to our meeting with Trish. Isaiah, here's ten bucks for dinner. We'll be back in a couple of hours."

Once they're gone, Juan Carlos and I walk to Seth's room. Juan Carlos takes the seat next to the bed. "All right, we've listened to everybody else's plan. What about ours? Any ideas?"

I clear my head of all the lip service from Dr. Parker and those other docs. I have to go with what I know—and I know Seth. I empty out my thoughts.

"In science, we use thinking skills to recognize a problem that needs a solution. For Seth, his problem is his brain injury. How can we help him heal?"

Juan Carlos nods. "Keep going, I'm listening."

"Seth's therapists told me doing therapy over and over will help."

Juan Carlos looks surprised. "Repetitive exercise is a thing for brain injuries?"

I shrug. "That's what they said. I'll talk to a friend about it tomorrow."

He nods. "Speaking of talking, you seem to be doing better with that shyness."

I stand stronger. "Things are different now. I'm not just speaking for myself."

"Truth," he says.

"And posting on Instagram has helped. You should follow me."

Juan Carlos opens his phone. "Is it under Isaiah Abernathy?"

I smile. "Nope. It's under IcePicAbernathy."

Juan Carlos grins. "There you are. I just followed you. Nice pictures! I really loved the ones you took in front of Redd's. Are you still doing your thing?"

I look out the window. "No time, and I'm too tired. Helping Seth is more important."

Juan Carlos puts an arm around my shoulders. "We'll help Seth find his way, but you can't lose yours, you feel me?"

I lost my way weeks ago when I hit Seth. Then I got kicked out of the hospital and out of school. And now the doctors are kicking Seth out of the hospital as if he doesn't matter, either.

But maybe if I can help him get better, my life will get better, too. If Seth can't understand me saying I'm sorry, I'll just have to find a way to *show* him how sorry I am.

Juan Carlos strolls over to Seth's bed, hugs him, and whispers something before heading to the door. "Stay strong, Ice Pic. And text me if you need me."

"Okay. Thanks, for everything."

I'm alone again with Seth, but it feels different now. As I look at his unmoving body, I vow that it won't stay that way—not if I can help it. I'll do everything I can to help him, no matter what.

When my parents come back, Dad takes me home and as I lie on the sofa I talk to the wish granter again, but this time ask for extra strength to help my brother.

* * *

Thursday morning, I feed the animals and then get dressed for school. Dad steps out of his room in a suit. "I'll drop you off on the way to my interview."

"You look nice," I say, grabbing my backpack. And when he pulls up to my school, I give him the best smile I've got. "Do your thing, Dad. I'll be rooting for you."

"Thanks. We're going to be okay. I promise."

"Yes, sir."

I'm still off my game after yesterday's bombshells about Seth. I feel like I'm on autopilot as I lift my hand to wave, put it down, keep walking, left foot, right foot, sit in advisory. Now to yearbook. But Mr. Whitaker stops me at the door.

"Are you okay?"

Even my words sound mechanical. "Seth's coming home tomorrow."

His eyes widen. "That's wonderful news! He must be doing better!"

Sometimes it hurts telling the truth. "Other than opening his eyes, nothing's changed."

Now he looks like I feel. "I'm so sorry, Isaiah."

"I won't be able to stay after school for a while. I need to help take care of Seth."

"No worries, I completely understand."

"Okay."

I take my seat, and Zurie plops down next to me. "How's it going?"

I stare at the floor. "Seth's coming home tomorrow."

She takes off her glasses. "I didn't see that coming."

"Neither did we."

I tell her what Dr. Parker said, and how it rocked me.

She lets out a sigh. "How's your mom?"

"Scared, but she won't admit it."

"I can't blame her. What can I do to help?"

I look at her, so glad she's asking me instead of me having to ask her. "Can you meet me for lunch out in the courtyard? If you really want to help, I've got an idea."

"Of course! I'll be there."

Mom said we needed to prepare for Seth to come home. I'm getting ready, too, but in a different way. I'm designing a plan to prove the doctors wrong. Seth just needs to do one thing they said he never would do again. But first I need a crew.

CHAPTER THIRTY

As Zurie unrolls her sack lunch and sets everything out on the table, I get right to the point. "I want to test a theory for our project."

"Okay. I'm listening," she says.

"Technology shows us that if our computer mouse malfunctions, we can rewire the computer to use the keyboard to do the same things, right? But what about rewiring the brain after it malfunctions? You used the example of teaching Seth how to walk again by making something else in the brain take over. Can that really happen?"

Zurie takes a bite of her sandwich. "I don't know, can it?"

"I don't know, either, but what if we *did* use Seth in our project like you talked about at the hospital? What if we can prove that rewiring the brain is possible?"

Zurie closes her eyes. "I've been meaning to apologize

for that. I didn't even ask if you were okay with me using Seth in my example. And now, after yesterday's news—"

"I think it was unintentionally . . . intentional. Does that sound weird?"

A half smile brightens her face. "No. It kind of sounds like fate! And now I've got chill bumps. But what if—what if we can't help Seth rewire?"

We go quiet, letting that question sit in the air while we eat, until Zurie speaks up.

"I'm not being negative, but our report is due the Friday before Thanksgiving. What if Seth needs more time than that? What's the backup plan?"

"Don't have one. He got two weeks of outpatient therapy, so hopefully—"

Zurie's eyes widen, and her voice rises. "Two weeks? You do realize that's really only ten therapy days, right? Clinics are closed on the weekends. And Seth's had in-the-hospital therapy already. What's going to be different with this?"

"I don't know. All I can say is there's going to be a difference between in-the-hospital therapy and at-the-house therapy. Okay, how about—if we don't see a change in Seth during those ten days, then we can do something else for our report. Can we just roll with that?"

"Sure. Have you done any research or read any articles that support our theory?"

I lean back. "No, but I did read this story once about a dog that got retrained to walk after it got hit by a car. I believe retraining can happen for people, too."

Zurie bumps fists with me. "I'm with you, Ice. Your brother deserves a chance. And if he doesn't change in those ten days of outpatient therapy, that doesn't mean we stop. We'll do something different for the science project but keep helping Seth."

"Juan Carlos is in, too."

She smiles. "When do we start?"

"I've already started. Whatever the therapists do with him in the afternoon, I do those same exercises again with him in the evening before I go home."

"Fine, but you have to write everything down—therapies, meals, I mean everything—and send me a report."

I lower my head. "Okay, but not bathroom stuff."

I hope Zurie understands. I don't want to tell her that my older brother wears diapers.

"That's not necessary for the project," she says. "Mostly just the therapy, and any changes in Seth."

The five-minute bell rings, and Zurie picks up her tray. "It would be a good idea to write down your first goal, and then work on that."

"I already know what that is. I need him to talk again because . . . see, I—"

Zurie puts her hand on mine. "I know. You don't have to explain it to me again."

A sprinkle of hope makes me smile. Now I'm ready for Seth to come home.

After school, I've got pep in my step on the way to the hospital. No reporters hassle me—I guess the church calvary must have set them straight. When I walk inside Seth's room, Mom and Dad are smiling for once, but I'm suspicious.

"What happened?" I ask.

Dad stands and puffs his chest. "I got a job! That's what happened!"

I drop my backpack and rush to him. "For real?"

"You're talking to the new supervisor at Kurt's Butcher Shop! Monday through Saturday, baby! Nine to six. I start on Saturday!"

I hug him, and I'm not sure who's holding who tighter.

"Okay, now let's talk about Seth coming home," he says, "Two trucks made drop-offs at the house today. One brought his hospital bed, a feeding table, and a bath chair. The other truck brought milk, wipes, diapers, disposable bed pads, stuff like that."

Mom gets her purse. "I hate to leave Seth, but Jason promised he would take care of him. We only have tonight left to get things done, so let's get a move on it."

While Mom and Dad talk in the front seat, I'm in the back, tightening up my own plan. I need to ask Seth questions about things, keep it rolling until something inside his brain rewires. If he can talk, then he can tell me what he needs. And he can forgive me.

Once we're home, Dad and I start moving things around. We push my bed away from the wall, and just before we lift it to bring it to the study, something shiny catches my eye.

Seth's necklace.

Dad pushes his end away and then grabs the bottom of the headboard.

"On three," he says. "One, two . . ."

"Dad, wait!"

I pick up the necklace, blow the dust off, then rub it across my shirt to make it shine again.

Dad's watching me, and he clears his throat. "I need a water. I'll be back in a few."

I sit on the edge of my bed and close my eyes as I'm hit with the memory of me in the living room with Seth and Dad, saying the worst thing ever.

What's between brothers? I guess nothing.

I open my eyes and look at the necklace. It's been on the floor for almost a month, and I hadn't even thought about it—as if what I told Seth was true. I stand and tuck the necklace in the top drawer of my dresser. It hurts too much to look at it.

Dad walks back in. "Come on, let's finish up."

I hide my pain from him by smiling. "Yes, sir."

Mom, Dad, and I clean the house from one end to the other until we all crash around ten. But at midnight, I'm still wide awake, staring into the darkness. I'm not used to sleeping in Dad's study, so I use my hand to feel my way to my dresser to get Seth's necklace. Holding it makes me miss him more, and his face and voice fill my mind.

"It's not just a pair of shoes on a chain. It's who I am. But I'm giving it to you. Between brothers. I won't be gone

forever—I promise I'll be back."

I fasten the chain around my neck, feeling calmer than I've been in a long time. I'm no fortune teller, but I think this has to be a sign from Seth letting me know he's still here and that he hasn't gone away like the doctors think he has. He's just lost in a place that's as dark as this study, and he can't find his way. But it's okay because I'm going to be his compass, his light in that dark place. I'm going to lead him back home.

CHAPTER THIRTY-ONE

When my alarm goes off, I'm still sleepy, but as I swing my feet from under the covers and sit on the edge of the bed, Seth's necklace dangles from my neck. That's all I need to see. It's time to get gone.

My brother's coming home today, and it'll be his first big step toward breaking free of whatever has him tied down. Smelling the good farm smells and being back in our room will help him find his way. I grab a pen and a piece of paper from Dad's desk.

Friday, October 1st. Seth's coming home. Goal: Talking

At breakfast, Dad prays longer than normal, asking God to help us take care of Seth. As we eat, we don't talk like we normally do, but I can't think of anything to say, either.

Afterward, Mom and I get in the back seat of Dad's

truck. Seth's going to sit up front, so we stocked it with pillows and blankets for him. On the way, Mom shares her checklist of things to ask at the hospital, but as we pull into the parking lot, reporters surround us again.

"I can't wait for all this to be over," Dad says before getting out of the truck and slamming his door. He walks right up to the reporters. "Can I please just have this day? It's special to me and my family, and I shouldn't have to share it with the world."

A reporter answers. "We understand, Mr. Abernathy, but we've been waiting on this day, too. We're all happy for Seth, and we want to see him."

Dad comes back to Mom and me. "They want to see Seth. Let's go get him."

What?

Mom gets out on one side, and I get out on the other, rushing to catch up with Dad.

"Wait! Dad, hold on a minute!"

He's power walking to the hospital doors. Mom shakes her head at me, so I leave him alone until we get on the elevators before I go off.

"They don't care about Seth! All they want to do is stare at him, snap pictures, and then blast them all over the internet! We should've parked in the garage and brought Seth out a back door or something, away from the reporters. What are you doing, Dad?"

"I didn't do anything—BMP did! I've worked hard to control my anger until now. When I wheel Seth out for their cameras, let's see how well these reporters control theirs."

As soon as the elevator doors open, I'm the first one on. We ride in silence to the fifth floor, but the air is full of Mom's stress and Dad's frustration. I'm hoping they leave both those emotions in the elevator because they won't help anything. When we walk into Seth's room, he's strapped in his wheelchair, just like he was on Wednesday. Jason smiles when he sees us.

"Yay for Seth!" he says until he notices our expressions. "Everything okay?"

"Reporters," says Dad.

Jason grabs a stack of papers and a pen. "Well, we're going to be here for a while. I can make it take longer if you want—maybe they'll get tired and leave. Mr. Abernathy, you start on the paperwork while I show Mrs. Abernathy how to feed Seth and give him his meds. I'll unfasten his seatbelt so we can lift his shirt and attach the tubing to feed him his milk."

Mom washes her hands, but I can tell by her slow walk that she's nervous. Jason must notice because he says, "It's so much easier than it looks, Mrs. Abernathy. You're going to do great. Isaiah, why don't you record this? That way you'll have it as a reference."

"Good idea," I say.

Mom puts on disposable gloves, attaches the tubing, and then measures Seth's milk, checking it three times before she's comfortable that it's right. But when she tries to pour it into the tubing, she freezes.

"You're doing great, Mrs. Abernathy. Be sure you clamp off the tubing before pouring the milk so you can control how much he's getting at one time."

Mom nods. "Okay."

Her hands tremble, and milk spills on the table. "I don't know if I can do this," she says, tearing up.

Jason assures her. "You can. The first time is always the hardest, but you've already done better than most other people. Don't give up."

"We're not quitters, Mom. You can do it," I say.

Jason shows Mom how to add Seth's medications to his milk, and how to finish by cleaning around his feeding tube with an alcohol wipe, and then making sure it's closed. When they finish, Jason refastens Seth's seatbelt.

"Here's a list of recommendations for soaps, lotions, and other products that will be less irritating to his skin. I've also listed the brand of milk we use here, and the name of a medical supply company that delivers."

Mom looks over the paper. "This is a lot, but thank you, Jason."

Jason smiles. "We're not even halfway finished. Have a seat so we can go over his medications. There's quite a few."

I record everything Jason says, just in case Mom needs it. When he finishes, Jason hands Mom another paper. "Seth's therapy will begin on Monday at Scarboro Rehab Clinic on Center Street—a two-minute walk from the church that held his special prayer service. I was there."

"That's our church. Center Street Baptist," I say.

"Awesome. Seth needs to be at the clinic at four thirty on Monday for his evaluation. After that, you can work with the therapists to create his schedule. Okay, are we ready?"

"Can I push his wheelchair?" I ask.

"Until we get to the emergency room doors. Then I'll need to take him," says Dad.

As the elevator takes us to the first floor, my insides flip. When the elevator opens, people stop and watch us.

"Good luck, Seth," says a man in a hospital gown.

"We're rooting for you," says someone else in the emergency room waiting area.

Dad thanks them as we walk toward the exit doors. Then he stops me.

"I need to roll Seth to the truck, just in case these reporters get rowdy. Sandra, here's the keys—open the truck and turn on the AC. You and Isaiah get in and stay put. Jason, stay close to me, okay?"

"All right," says Mom.

"Will do," Jason says.

Dad takes a deep breath and lets it out. "Here we go."

Outside, reporters rush toward us, talking and filming, but when they see Seth heavily strapped to his wheelchair, everyone freezes. The lights on the news camera switch from green to red. Not one reporter pushes a microphone toward Dad. He hits the alarm, and a reporter rushes to pull down the truck bed, and open the doors for Mom and me. A camerawoman puts her equipment down and holds the passenger door for Seth.

Dad wheels Seth to the truck with Jason behind him. Then he lifts Seth onto the passenger seat and belts him in. Another cameraman lifts Seth's chair into the truck bed while other reporters help Jason unload the cart. Dad thanks everyone, and Jason wishes us well.

We roll slowly out of the parking lot, and it feels like part of this nightmare is over. I look out the back window. Dad was right about letting the reporters see Seth. They're still standing statue-still, watching our truck, their faces filled with a mix of sadness, sympathy, and anger.

CHAPTER THIRTY-TWO

The whole way home, Dad stays in the slow lane with his flashers on, but people don't honk or go around him—it's as if they know Seth's in the truck. Once he gets on the gravel road, he goes even slower. At home, he lifts Seth out and carries him to his bed as Mom reorganizes the shelves.

"Sandra, what are we going to do about Seth's therapy schedule on Monday? I don't get off until six, and you have to work, too. Can someone from the church help?"

Mom's arms fall to her sides. "I hate to keep asking them for help."

"What about me?" I say. "It's just down the street from the church. If his therapy is in the afternoon, I can take him. I really want to."

Dad winks at me. "Sandra, let's give him a chance. I can take you and Seth to the church in the mornings, then pick everybody up in the afternoons."

She nods, and I high-five Dad and hug Mom. "You won't regret it."

Once they step out of Seth's room, I write up a sheet for today just like Jason did.

MY NAME IS SETH ABERNATHY
TODAY IS FRIDAY, OCTOBER 1

I wish I could tack another note for him to read that says *I'm sorry. Please forgive me*, but that would bring unnecessary drama from Mom and Dad. An hour later, Mom comes in and grabs milk, tubing, and a big diaper from the shelf.

"It's time for me to feed Seth and change his, um—clothes."

I can't imagine how embarrassed my brother is right now. The last thing I'd want is for Mom to see parts of me that she ain't got no business seeing after I'm grown. I shuffle out to the sofa and sit next to Dad, who's watching football. But only minutes after taking a seat—

Crash!

We rush to Seth's room but brake at the door. Milk runs in all directions across the floor. Seth's staring at the ceiling, and Mom's crying. "I should've changed his diaper first."

"It's okay, Honey. I'll clean him up," says Dad.

The room smells horrible. I get the mop, broom, and dustpan and bring them back to Dad.

"Thanks, now step out for a minute and close the door behind you."

"But, Dad, let me . . ."

He points to the door, holding the mop and broom. "Now, Isaiah!"

I shuffle to the living room and soon hear water running. I could've mopped the floor for them. I want to help with something! What can I do? I guess I could call Juan Carlos and let him know Seth's home. Or I could call Scarboro High School and give them an update. I step outside, over to the apple tree, and sit in the grass. As I sit there, a fresh idea pops in my head. I tap the reel button on Instagram.

"This is Icepi— This is Isaiah Abernathy. Seth's finally home. Please send him good thoughts. I'll keep you posted."

I upload my reel and post it, then go back in the house. Suddenly, my phone pings. And then pings again. Comments are coming in, thanking me for the update on Seth. My phone pings again, so I put it on silent since Dad's back on the sofa now, and the front of his shirt is soaked.

"Seth's been home less than two hours, and your mom and I are already exhausted. I had to put him in the tub because he pooped, and it got all over him. That is not something I ever imagined doing for my grown son.

What's going to happen when I go to work tomorrow?"

"I'll be here."

When he doesn't answer, I glance over. He's asleep. I look in Seth's room and Mom's nodding, too, but keeps waking up every few seconds to check on him. All day, Mom and Dad tag-team on taking care of Seth. At seven, I make sandwiches for dinner because I'm starving, Mom won't leave Seth's room, and Dad's napping on the sofa again.

Around ten, Mom curls up with a blanket in the recliner near Seth. Dad drags to his room, and I go to the study and listen to the silence that seems so loud. Lying in bed, I grab my phone and pull up Instagram. I spring up like I'm running late for school when I see that I have 214 followers.

There are so many supportive comments—not just from friends, but even people I don't know.

> @MrWhitakerwrites We're with you. Let us know how we can help.
>
> @CenterStreetBaptistChurchScarboro Prayer changes things.
>
> @Scarborostrong We got your back.
>
> @LadyZurieM You are not alone, Ice.

I doze off in the middle of reading all the support, but at four, I'm wide awake again. I tiptoe in to check on Seth. Mom's reading her Bible, and Seth's staring at the ceiling.

"He's been awake since two. I think he's got his nights and days mixed up."

So do I, but I'm still reminded of what Dr. Parker said

about Seth functioning like he's seven months old. Her words discouraged me then, but I've got a plan to flip that.

I stay with Seth and Mom for an hour, then I go eat breakfast and feed the animals. Soon Dad walks in and asks me to leave again while he helps Mom wash and dress Seth. I stand outside the room, as if I'm back at the hospital. I hate this, but it drives me even more to stick with my plan. Wait a minute—why is Dad up three hours before he has to be at work?

Snapsickles. All of us have our days and nights mixed up.

As soon as the front door closes and Dad drives off, I change my mood, my focus, and my mind. "Mom, you should go lie down, and I'll do therapy with Seth."

"Maybe for an hour or two."

Just as she steps out, Latin rap thumps outside my bedroom window. Juan Carlos climbs out of his Jeep and straps a backpack to his shoulders. I open the back door and whisper.

"Mom's taking a nap. She's been up all night with Seth."

He nods and drops his backpack on the recliner. "Let her sleep. What's the plan today?"

"Figure out what we can do to get him to talk?"

Juan Carlos unzips his backpack and pulls out a DVD. "That's a good idea. Put this in your game console. It's video of a cross-country meet back when Seth was a sophomore and I was a freshman. I brought a playlist, too."

I shrug. "It's a toss-up whether he's really seeing or hearing anything."

He frowns. "We know that. Our job is to get him unstuck. Get your mind right."

I tap my head. "Right, my bad."

While Seth watches the video I show Juan Carlos the exercises I learned from Katie and David. At noon, Mom comes in with two plates. "What a great nap! It's time to feed Seth and give him his meds. I made you boys grilled cheese sandwiches for lunch."

"Thank you, Momma Abernathy," Juan Carlos says. "And I can help with Seth. I assist my aunt with my uncle's care all the time."

Mom hugs him. "You're a gem."

We're chowing down on our lunch as Mom feeds Seth. Around three, the delicious aroma of food drifts in again, and Juan Carlos take in a big whiff of Mom's cooking as I write down everything we did so I can send it to Zurie.

"You know what that smell is?" asks Juan Carlos.

I'm too busy writing to look up. "Of course. It's pork chops."

"It's more than that, Ice Pic. It's the smell of things getting back to normal. I've got to go, but I'll be back soon."

He heads to the kitchen to hug Mom, and then leaves.

At five-thirty, when Dad pulls up, I open my bedroom window and wave. He gets out and grins. "You're not going to believe what happened. My friend Deacon from BMP stopped by Kurt's—said he'd heard I was working there and just came by to put something in the back of my truck to use as long as I needed it."

Dad opens the back of his truck. It's a wheelchair ramp.

CHAPTER THIRTY-THREE

On Sunday morning, Mom and Dad nod off in the middle of watching a church service on television. I got a pass because I'm doing therapy with Seth. Once I finish, I send all my notes, charts, and observations to Zurie for our project. I wonder what tomorrow is going to be like when I wheel Seth to therapy. Will people stare?

Even though today is Jesus Jail, it feels different. It's supposed to be a family day, but there's only three of us at the dining room table, and the only sounds come from forks hitting the plate. At ten o'clock, Mom sends me to bed, but I can hear her in Seth's room, going over the list of things she's already packed, making sure she didn't forget anything.

How are we going to make it through this? I'm worried that it's too much for us to handle. But I know there's no other way.

I don't want to cry myself to sleep, but I do. And when Monday comes, the sadness is still on me as I watch my parents check, then double-check, to make sure they have everything for Seth. Finally, Dad carries Seth while I carefully load the wheelchair into the truck. I wave at Seth in the front seat.

Once they leave, I grab a muffin off the table and eat it as I feed the animals, get ready for school, then walk to the mailbox. When Mr. Williams stops and opens the door, I climb the steps, and he nods my way.

"Mornin', Isaiah."

"Mornin'."

He closes the bus door and drives off without asking me about Seth. Even before the accident, he always asked about my brother. I don't know what's up with that, but as soon as I take a seat, one of the high school riders comes and sits with me.

"Hey, my name's Bruce. I don't really know Seth—he's a senior, and I'm just a sophomore. But I wanted to say I'm sorry about what happened to him."

"Thanks. Call me Ice," I say.

"I saw your post on Instagram. Thanks for letting us know Seth was finally home. And my family signed that online petition not to buy anything from BMP."

"What petition?"

He takes his phone from his pocket. "I can't believe you don't know about this! It made the news!" He's scrolling and talking at the same time. "Remember the group that organized the huge protest march to BMP?"

"Yeah, what about 'em?"

"They did an interview on Channel Two and showed pics of your brother. One is a photo from last year of him signing his letter to run cross-country at A&M. The other is a shot somebody took on their cellphone of Seth leaving the hospital last week, strapped down in his wheelchair."

Bruce shows me the two pictures of Seth, side by side. I swallow hard, hoping I don't break down right there on the bus. He looks at my face and lowers his phone. "I'm sorry, Ice."

He types something else. "This is the 'Boycott BMP' website. Yesterday morning, there were over thirty-two thousand signatures. Look at it now."

Fifty thousand signatures! I text Dad.

Did you know about the boycott of BMP?

He answers quickly.

Yes. Stay focused. I got this.

I bet that's why Mr. Williams didn't ask about Seth. He saw the pictures.

I bump fists with Bruce. "Thanks for telling me."

"Sure. My family is praying for Seth. And I brought my lunch today."

I'm not sure why he's telling me about his lunch, but I smile anyway. "'preciate it."

As I get on the Brazos bus, everybody stops talking. Zurie moves her books, and I quickly take a seat.

She leans in and whispers. "Are you okay?"

"Why didn't you tell me about the boycott?"

"I thought you knew! All the meat in our school district comes from BMP. Lunchtime is about to get interesting."

"Nobody's going to stop eating meat in the cafeteria," I say, and roll my eyes.

She holds up a brown sack. "Peanut butter and jelly, carrots, and a granola bar. BMP's in for a beatdown that doesn't involved fists."

Her words make me think of Brandon—just like he thought I was soft, BMP must've thought that same thing about their customers. But like me, when something pushes you hard enough, you order a combo meal. And BMP's combo meal comes with no meat.

"Seth starts therapy today, right?" she asks.

I nod. "I'm kind of nervous."

"Want me to come with you? I can ask my parents."

Our bus pulls up to the school. "That would help. Thanks, Zurie."

As I walk down the hall, teachers and students hold up their sack lunches to me and also to each other like a new form of saying good morning.

When lunchtime comes, there's brown paper bags everywhere! Cafeteria workers hold clean serving utensils, while stacks of chicken, burgers, and hot dogs sit untouched. I walk to the courtyard, and Zurie's already there. She gives me half her sandwich. Peanut butter and jelly have never tasted so good.

"This protest thing is serious business," I say.

"I love that we're taking a stand together, as a school, as a community. Oh, and I got permission to meet you at the therapy clinic." Her face has concern all over it. "You told me Seth's got ten days of therapy, right? Are you planning on asking for more?"

"Of course! He's going to need lots of it."

Zurie's eyes droop. "I spoke with my parents. The only way Seth can get more therapy time, beyond those two weeks, is if he improves. If he doesn't, he'll get released."

Her words hit hard. "But ten days is nothing! He'll need more time than that."

"I know. What do they plan to do for Seth in therapy? Do you remember?"

"No, but if they only give him ten days, it's not just the science project that's on the line. It's Seth's life."

CHAPTER THIRTY-FOUR

As soon as I get to Center Street Baptist Church, I'm ready to take Seth to therapy.

"Everything's in his backpack," Mom says. "I've already taken care of the paperwork for you to be with Seth during therapy. Promise me you'll be extra careful."

"I promise, Mom."

She makes sure his seatbelt is fastened then opens the door, and I'm in super-slow mode as I wheel him down the ramp and across the street. Cars slow down and people point at Seth. I wish I could run, but I don't want to accidentally flip Seth's chair.

"Hey, Abernathy! Where are you guys heading?"

It's Rhino and Uncle Jerry. Rhino takes a long look at Seth before bumping fists with me.

"Scarboro Rehab Clinic. Seth starts therapy today."

"That's where we're going! Unc's training for the

Woodbridge Turkey Trot next month. You should think about entering with Seth, if he's not back to walking on his own by then."

It feels good to hear someone talk positive about my brother, but the Turkey Trot is for runners, and Seth's not even walking yet. "Thanks for telling me about it."

Inside the clinic, I sign us in. The waiting area is full of people on walkers, in wheelchairs, wearing casts, leg or arm braces, even helmets. Zurie waves and points to a seat she saved for me, so I park Seth near her. I know she's staring at all those Velcro straps but I did, too. After a few minutes, a door opens and a woman calls out, "Seth Abernathy?"

I look at Zurie and breathe out my anxiety. "We're up."

I push Seth's wheelchair to a smiling young woman wearing scrubs with superhero characters all over them.

"I'm Nicole, Seth's physical therapist."

"I'm Isaiah, Seth's brother. This is Seth. And this is . . . my best friend, Zurie."

I didn't mean to make Zurie blush, but she does. "Hi."

Nicole's still smiling. "Nice to meet all of you. Isaiah, you said?"

"Call me Ice."

"You're a big guy! That's good for Seth because you'll be able to assist him in his recovery efforts. Would you and Zurie like to come watch his therapy?"

"Sure!" Finally, someone who recognizes that tall

people can do more than play sports.

The room is huge, and packed with patients lying on long, mat tables, working hard to lift their arms or legs or to turn over as therapists watch and help.

A young Asian woman with short black hair walks toward us. Her smile is full of neon pink dental braces, and I can't help but smile back. "Hi. I'm Trinh, and I'll be Seth's occupational therapist."

"Hi," I say.

Nicole explains that she and Trinh will do their initial evaluation together. I watch closely as they introduce themselves to Seth and explain what they're going to do. Very slowly, they unstrap and unbuckle him from his chair and transfer him together onto a low, padded table that's big enough for all of us to sit around him.

They measure and chart the length of his arms and legs before testing how much they're able to bend his knees, close his fingers into a fist, and move his head from side to side. The whole time they're evaluating Seth, Nicole and Trinh ask Zurie and me about school and our hobbies.

But now I've got a question for them. "The doctors say my brother's trapped inside his own body. But he was only given two weeks of therapy. How can he improve if we don't do something to help him?"

Trinh smiles. "Exactly!"

I'm confused by her answer, but also locked in, waiting for an explanation.

"It's important that we look for and see change. Right now, Seth is in what we call an altered level of consciousness. Our job is to motivate him to become alert, aware—even angry."

Nicole adds, "We'll follow Dr. Ramirez's orders, but we're also going to do aggressive therapy to see if we can't help wake him up. Dr. Ramirez requested approval from your family's insurance carrier for Seth to have physical and occupational therapy. The insurance company approved two weeks. If Seth shows improvement during those two weeks, we can request another block of therapy time based on progress toward his goals, and he can be approved for more. But if Seth doesn't improve, we'll have to release him."

The sound of a ticking clock begins inside my head. I feel as if I'm wasting time just standing here. "Will you teach me exercises I can do with him at home?"

Trinh nods. "We'd love to! If you record our sessions, you can refer to the videos when you work with him."

Nicole agrees. "And take pictures! Then you can show everything to your parents. I'll send them updates every few days, and the pictures will help them see what's going on."

"Just make sure Seth is the only patient you record. You've videoed before, right?"

I puff my chest. "You're talking to the yearbook photographers for Brazos Bayou Middle School. Recordings and pictures are what we do."

Nicole and Trinh give thumbs-up as Zurie and I fist-bump.

"Let's get started! Who's filming?" asks Trinh.

Zurie takes my phone so I can watch and listen. Trinh and Nicole gently move Seth from the mat back into his wheelchair before Trinh gives me specific instructions.

"At home, try to work on waking up his senses. Help him touch things, smell things, hear things, see things. Put things in his hands, and as you do, tell him what they are. It sounds simple, but simple works, okay?"

"Okay. What can I do to help him talk again?"

She unstraps Seth's head from the wheelchair and holds it steady. "His neck muscles are weak. That can make talking difficult. I'll do neck exercises here to help him strengthen them—but don't try these at home."

"Okay. Thank you, Trinh."

Nicole moves closer to Seth. "Always be on the lookout for change. Sometimes rewiring can take a while, under-stand?"

I nod.

"Good. Now here's a few fun things you and Seth can do together for therapy." Nicole shows me games for his feet and legs called "press the gas pedal" and "Kick the rubber ball."

"Thanks. I'll start tonight and do things exactly the way you and Trinh show me."

"You're welcome. See you tomorrow," says Nicole.

Zurie stops filming. "Not only did they map out a plan for Seth's therapy, Trinh and Nicole just gave us our outline—our strategy for the science project. And it's all on video."

CHAPTER THIRTY-FIVE

Zurie's cousin picks her up, and while Seth and I wait for Dad, I check out the bulletin board in the reception area. There's all kinds of ads for wheelchairs, hospital beds, and other medical equipment for sale. One person is looking for live-in help.

In the center of the bulletin board is a flyer about the race Uncle Jerry's training for.

**WOODBRIDGE COMMUNITY CENTER'S
ANNUAL 5K THANKSGIVING TURKEY TROT
COME FOR THE RUN, STAY FOR THE FUN!
THANKSGIVING MORNING 7:00 A.M.**

Where: Woodbridge Community
Campus, Scarboro, Texas

Entry Fee: $5

All participants will receive:

1. T-shirt and participation ribbon
2. Assistance if needed
3. All abilities welcome!
Trophies for: First place special-needs
adults (with and without assistance)

What does *all abilities* mean? I wish Seth was walking. Rhino was right. He'd be all over this! I point my camera at the flyer. *Click*.

When Dad pulls up, Mom's already in the back, holding a pan of lasagna one of the church members made for us. Dad and I get Seth buckled in, and then I join Mom in the back.

"The boycott is real," I tell them. "Nobody touched the meat in the cafeteria, not even the teachers. Everybody brought their lunch—which reminds me that I need to take mine from now on."

Dad agrees. "The butcher ran out of meat today because Kurt's joined the boycott. We paid for overnight service from a different meat packing company to deliver to us in the morning."

"It's not just Scarboro. People from all over have joined," says Mom.

"Trish had her hands in this. She helped organize it with

that watchdog group, and she said there were more vol-unteers than she's ever had," Dad says. "Scarboro strong."

"Wait. Scarboro strong? That's a hashtag on Instagram!"

"Is that like corned beef hash? I love me some corned beef," says Dad.

"No, Ray," says Mom. "it's just another name for the pound sign on the phone."

I shake my head. "Y'all need a class in social media."

We're home by six thirty, and Dad warms up dinner while Mom feeds Seth in his room. I'm killin' this lasagna when I notice Dad's plate is empty.

"You're not hungry?"

"I'm waiting on your mom. Listen."

I stop chewing. "I don't hear anything."

"Exactly! She's getting better at feeding Seth! I'm going to wait and eat with her."

It's cool that Dad noticed that, so once I finish, I let Mom know Dad's waiting.

"You can't do therapy yet. Seth just finished eating," she says.

"I just wanted to show you the evening therapy sched-ule I created for after dinner."

	MON	TUE	WED	THURS	FRI	SAT	SUN
7:30	Music						
8:00	Talk/Read						
8:30	Videos						
9:30	Legs and Arms Therapy						
Notes							

Mom hugs me. "You're a good brother, Isaiah."

I hold my smile until she leaves because Mom doesn't know my other reason for wanting Seth to get better, and especially for him to talk. Even though I can't see the scar on his lip anymore, it's still bleeding in my mind.

I do the leg and arm exercises Trinh and Nicole showed me. Then while Seth watches the video Juan Carlos left here on Saturday, I do my homework and send Zurie all the notes from the evening therapy schedule. Filling in the notes section hurts: *No change*.

I rub my eyes. "Dude, you wore me out. See you in the morning."

By the time I get to the study, I'm almost sleepwalking, so I kick off my shoes, set my alarm, and lie down without getting undressed. I must fall asleep right away, because next thing I know, the alarm goes off. How can it be morning already? Feeding the animals used to take thirty minutes because I'd talk to them, pet them, make them feel special. Now it only takes me ten because I don't have time to give them extra love. Mom needs me.

I can feel Mom staring at me. She rolls down the back window of Dad's truck.

"You look tired, Isaiah."

I step closer and rest my head on the window. "So do you, Mom."

"Maybe you should cut down to only three days a week of therapy. I can make a call."

Dang it. Now I'm mad at myself for looking weak. "Please don't do that. I feel great! Anyway, Seth can't miss any days of therapy, and yesterday was just a long first day. Once I get used to the new schedule, I'll be fine."

But when Mr. Williams picks me up, I nod off on the bus, and he has to wake me when it's time to switch buses. I do the same thing on my next bus, so Zurie wakes me when we get to school. After advisory I shuffle into yearbook and put my head down on our photography table.

Zurie's voice startles me. "You look worn out. Are you okay?"

I yawn. "It's this new schedule with Seth, that's all. Still getting used to it."

Once the bell rings, Mr. Whitaker make an announcement. "On Saturday, October twenty-third, Brazos will host the Harvest Holiday Dance. Zurie, you've got photography duty. Savannah and Rashad, interviews. The rest of you can take notes for the captions and help out wherever you're needed. It's a costume party, but not for us. Isaiah, it would be ideal if you could help Zurie, but there's no pressure."

I shrug. "I'll let you know if I can."

Mr. Whitaker smiles and winks. "Good enough."

I've never been to a school dance, and the thought of it makes my knee jump in a good way. But Seth is in a race against time, and his recovery is way more important.

CHAPTER THIRTY-SIX

On Wednesday, Juan Carlos comes to help me, dressed in a Texas Rangers baseball jersey and jeans. I'm glad to see him because Mom and Dad are heading to Bible study, and these last few days have me wiped out. I've done everything Trinh and Nicole told me to do, but it's not working. Seth still hasn't changed.

"Take a load off your feet and let me handle therapy today," Juan Carlos says as he unzips his backpack and pulls out another cross-country DVD. "Seth crushed everybody in this one."

I show Juan Carlos the schedule. "You have to do everything in this order because we need to do the same things over and over, the same way."

"What if we do the same things but switch up the order? I always switch up my routine in the weight room so my body doesn't get used to one way of doing things."

My body tightens. "No! I've done research and—"

Juan Carlos smiles. "Look, I agree with you that we should keep doing these exercises. I'm just saying the order doesn't matter."

"I know what I'm talking about! After this week, we only have one more week to get Seth to do something or else he's going to get kicked out of therapy!"

Juan Carlos gets in my face. "I understand, but order is not a big deal!"

I get right back in his. "Yes, it is! You're wrong!"

It's a nasty standoff, and I don't know how to compromise.

Juan Carlos sighs. "Relax. We both want what's best for Seth. I'm just trying to help."

I'm too tired for this. "But you're messing everything up!"

He holds up his palms like stop signs. "Fine. We'll keep doing it your way. But tomorrow, ask a real therapist about it, okay?"

Maybe Juan Carlos isn't the right person to help me with Seth after all. To begin with, he wears baseball clothes but runs cross-country—and now he doesn't even know how to follow instructions.

After finishing therapy with Seth, Juan Carlos leaves without saying goodbye. Well, he's going to be even quieter tomorrow when he hears what Nicole and Trinh have to say. Moments later, keys jiggle in the door, and Mom and Dad come in, so I head to the study for bed. It takes all the energy I have left just to get my pajamas on before I lie down.

Thursday feels just like Wednesday, except for one thing. In therapy, when I ask Trinh and Nicole about the order of the exercises, I press record on my phone so Juan Carlos can hear it, see it, and apologize for not believing me.

"So, Trinh, I was trying to explain to someone that we have to do therapy in the same order, the same way every day and—"

"That's actually not true," she says, "but continue with what you were going to say."

Snapsickles. "Never mind."

Now I can add Juan Carlos to the list of people I need to apologize to.

Nicole comes over to me. "Seth's birthday is next week!"

I nod and yawn. "Yep. He'll be eighteen on October fourteenth."

"Did you have anything special planned?"

I shrug. "Like what? I'm not even sure he'll know it's his birthday."

Nicole sits next to me. "Does that mean he doesn't deserve to be honored on his day? If you don't see him as worthy of being celebrated, how will others?"

What's wrong with me? My brain must be as tired as the rest of my body. I would never not celebrate Seth's birthday. I turn to my brother. "We'll do something special, I promise."

226

Nicole pats my knee. "And get some rest. You need it."

If I could get more sleep, I would, but it's just not that simple. I've got chores in the morning, then school, and then therapy with Seth. My parents work all day, and then they're up at all hours of the night to help Seth. It's as if we're all working two jobs.

After Seth's evening therapy on Friday, I try to follow Nicole's advice and go to bed early. Since it's the weekend, I can sleep a little later in the morning. I crawl between the sheets and rest my head on my soft pillow. It feels so good. Maybe I should make a quick Instagram reel about Seth finishing his first week of therapy. But I can't. I'm too tired.

And that's the last thing I remember until light shines on my face. I squint before opening my eyes, but then jump up and grab my phone to check the time. Dang it! It's nine o'clock!

I rush out in my pajamas to feed the animals, then hurry to change Seth's info sheet.

MY NAME IS SETH ABERNATHY
TODAY IS SATURDAY, OCTOBER 9

Seth's still asleep, but I need to start his therapy. I take his hand to begin, and his eyes open.

"Dude, did you feel that? Is that why you opened your eyes? Because you know I touched you?"

I let go of his hand and pump my fist. That's change, baby!

Okay, Nicole and Trinh said I need to wake up his senses. That would be sight, sound, touch, taste, and smell. I can't feed him, so taste isn't happening. What if I worked on the other senses, one at a time? The answer comes so fast that it's as if Mr. Whitaker was standing here with me. *What makes the perfect collage?*

I grab Dad's truck keys, an orange, the remote for the television, a spoon, and Seth's phone. I get Mom's hair clippers, Seth's cologne, and his hairbrush. On my tablet, I pull up a YouTube video with farm animal sounds.

Once I've got everything piled high in the recliner, I separate them into groups of things for sight, things for sound, things to touch, and things to smell. It's fun making real life collages for Seth's senses, and I've got Mr. Whitaker to thank for that. He opened up my mind to the possibilities, and now I'm trying to reopen Seth's.

"Dude, Trinh said we need to work on waking up your senses. We'll start with touch."

Dad helps me get Seth in his wheelchair, but I leave the Velcro straps for his arms and wrists on his bed. I put Dad's keys in Seth's hand and close his fingers around them.

"Keys." I lift his hand so he can see himself holding them. Then I do the same thing with the remote, the spoon, and his phone. Next, I switch things up and plug in the clippers.

"Barbershop clippers. Jeremiah uses these to cut hair at

Redd's. Feel that vibration?" I do this same exercise three times before switching things up again. "Okay. It's time to go outside."

I put Seth's sunglasses on him and take him outside, using the ramp. At the pasture, Dolly and Buster trot over to us. I slowly hold up Seth's hand so Dolly can see and smell us before we touch her. "Horse. This is Dolly." I help him pet her, and then we switch to Buster.

It's time for Seth to rest, but instead of going inside, I roll his chair onto the grass, tilt it back until he can see the sky, and then lie in the grass next to him. "Dude, there's so many things I miss doing with you. But most of all, I miss your voice—I miss hearing you talk to me."

Later, in my notes to Zurie, I'll write that Seth opened his eyes when I touched him, and then we worked on the sense of touch. But right now, I'm just enjoying having my brother with me again in our favorite spot, under the apple tree.

CHAPTER THIRTY-SEVEN

On Sunday, Juan Carlos comes over again. "What's up, Ice Pic? You in Jesus Jail?"

He's laughing, but it makes me feel even worse that he's joking around and being nice when I was a jerk to him. So I come clean.

"I talked to Seth's therapist, and you were right. Order doesn't matter. My bad."

He holds out his fist, and I bump it. "Forget about it."

I nod at his baseball shirt. "Why do you wear so much baseball gear?"

He chuckles. "Baseball is my first love. My dad played in the Dominican, where it doesn't matter if you have a bat and ball or bottle caps and a stick. He taught me how to play the game. I only run cross-country to stay in shape in the offseason. That's how I met Seth."

I never knew that! Now his baseball gear makes total sense.

"The day you were at Redd's for the first time was the same day I got my official invitation to visit Blinn College from their baseball coach. I might get a scholarship to play ball! Seth and I were making plans."

As I lift my eyes to look at Juan Carlos, it hits me that Seth was a best friend *and* brother to both of us. "I hope you get a scholarship and make it to the big leagues," I say.

He smiles. "Thanks. That would be sweet. So how are you doing?"

"I feel like I'm drowning in stuff to do. And the things I want to do, like take pictures, go to the school dance, stuff like that, I don't have time for. Seth's therapy is more important."

Juan Carlos stops smiling. "I noticed you haven't posted anything on Instagram since the day Seth came home. And why didn't you tell me about the school dance?"

I shrug. "I'm not going. I mean, I want to, but I don't have time."

"I told you—as we help Seth find his way, you can't lose yours. When's the dance?"

"It's on the twenty-third. I was going to take pictures for the yearbook."

"And you still are." Juan Carlos looks at his phone. "The twenty-third is a Saturday."

I watch him add the dance to his calendar, and then he

puts his arm around my neck. "This means I get an extra day doing therapy with my boy while you do your thing."

I can't believe I'm going to the dance! "Thanks, Juan Carlos."

"Okay, it's therapy time. Let's get busy. Any changes?"

"Yesterday, he opened his eyes when I touched his hand. Maybe that's something. I wrote it in the notes of his chart just in case."

Juan Carlos nods. "We're going to count it."

The three of us hang out in Seth's room, listening to music, watching videos, and doing lots of therapy. When we finish, I send the data to Zurie, except today I had to write *no change* again in the notes section. Maybe yesterday was just a coincidence.

I'm still thinking about how to jump-start changes in Seth when Mom calls us to dinner. Juan Carlos joins us.

"Are we going to do something for Seth's birthday on Thursday?" I ask.

Mom looks toward the ceiling. "We can definitely sing 'Happy Birthday' to him."

Singing is so . . . basic. I want to do something awesome for him.

Juan Carlos fist-bumps me on the way out. "Let me know if you go all out for my boy's birthday."

I promise, and after he leaves, I step inside Seth's room and ask him. "What do you want for your birthday?"

I don't expect him to answer. I was just hoping an idea would pop in my head.

Monday morning, I sit with Zurie on the bus. She's talking nonstop. "Keep the therapy data coming. It's good that he opened his eyes when you touched him, but we need more."

I nod. "I know, but I guess it's better than nothin'. Oh! I've got good news. I'm going to the dance. Juan Carlos is going to do Seth's therapy for me that night."

"Perfect!"

"Yeah, maybe. Seth's birthday is on Thursday. If he doesn't show signs of improvement this week, his last day of therapy will be Friday. If that happens, I'll probably skip the dance."

She nods. "I totally get it, and Mr. Whitaker will, too."

Things are happening so quickly, and I've got so much to do that I'm losing track of the days. It's already Wednesday, and I still have no idea what to do for Seth's birthday tomorrow. I want to make his birthday just as amazing as he made mine. I feel a thought trying to creep into my mind, so I sit still and let it finish. Snapsickles! I know exactly how we can celebrate!

After school, I let Mom in on my plan. "Seth needs to look super nice tomorrow, okay?"

She takes Seth's hand. "I wish he had more clothes choices."

I hug her. "I know. Just—whatever you can do. Thanks, Mom."

* * *

For the first time in a while, I'm pumped about waking up to a new day. I rush through my morning chores so I can sing "Happy Birthday" to Seth, but when I see him, he's dressed in extra baggy clothes like he always is, and it sucks some of the excitement out of me.

"It's the best I could do," Mom says with watery eyes.

I'm disappointed in myself as I realize my expression may have hurt her. So I try to clean that up. "He looks great! Blue is his favorite color. You picked the perfect out-fit, Mom."

I change his information sheet and draw balloons all over it.

MY NAME IS SETH ABERNATHY
TODAY IS MY BIRTHDAY! THURSDAY, OCTOBER 14TH!

I spray cologne on his baggy shirt. "Happy eighteenth! Whoop-whoop!" I lean in and whisper so Mom can't hear me. "I've got a special surprise for you today!"

When I tell Zurie my plan, she's excited to help.

"Can you pick up his surprise at the store?" I ask.

"Of course! I'll bring it to therapy."

"Thanks, Zurie."

After the fifth-period bell rings, I slow-walk into his-tory class, holding my stomach.

"I think I need to go home. I'm not feeling good."

My teacher writes me a pass, and I burn off to catch a metro bus. Mom's surprised to see me a whole hour early, but I avoid answering her questions and instead change the subject.

"Since it's Seth's birthday, can I take him for a walk down the street?"

"He'd like that! Don't be late to therapy, though. Have fun!"

Once Mom goes back inside, we cut a right on Pine Street, toward Lexington Avenue. When "Don't Walk" changes to "Walk," the cars on both sides stop. Even the headlights seem to stare as we cross the busy street. I grip the handlebars and look straight ahead.

"Don't pay any attention to them," I whisper.

When we get to where we're going, I stop short. Dang it. I forgot they don't have a ramp. It's as if people in wheelchairs aren't welcome.

"Sorry, Seth. This was supposed to be a surprise for your birthday."

As we turn around to leave, someone calls out. "Ice, is that you?"

I look over my shoulder. "Yes, but you guys need a ramp."

Jeremiah nods. "You're right. I'll work on that. Come on, I'll help you."

Together, we pull Seth's chair over each step, and Jeremiah rolls him to his station. I lock the brakes on his wheelchair, and then wipe the sweat from my face.

"Seth brought me here for my birthday, so I'm bringing him here for his. Do you have a birthday discount?

I've only got eight bucks. Or could you just give him an edge-up?"

I gently remove Seth's sunglasses and head strap, keeping my hand on his forehead—just like I do for Dolly—so he'll know I'm still there. Slowly I allow his head to droop until his chin touches his chest. For a moment there's sadness on Jeremiah's face, but then he smiles.

"We just started a new policy. Birthday cuts are free," he says.

I bend until I can see Seth's face. His eyes are open. "Happy birthday, bruh! Your barber's going to hook you up for free!" I turn back to Jeremiah. "He has therapy in forty minutes, and it'll take me ten to get him there. That's enough time, isn't it?"

Jeremiah grins and wraps a black cape around Seth. "That's plenty of time. And today is my two-for-one Thursday throwback special. I'm going to hook you up for free, too."

I don't know if that's true, but it feels good that Seth and I are doing something together again. Jeremiah takes his time and talks to Seth while I hold Seth's head still for the edge-up. Once Jeremiah finishes with mine, I turn Seth toward the mirror, hold his chin, and lift his head.

"Like you told me—it's mandatory for a guy's fade to be super fly on his birthday!"

Jeremiah smiles and gives me his card as I strap Seth back to his chair. "Call me anytime. I'll come to your house and hook you and Seth up if you need me to."

"Thanks, Jeremiah—for everything."

When we get to therapy, Zurie hands me a small bag and smiles at Seth. "Happy birthday! Did you just come from the barbershop? Nice cuts!"

Before I can answer, Nicole calls up. "So is the birthday guy ready for therapy?"

I'm fired up as I turn to Zurie. "I sure hope this works!"

CHAPTER THIRTY-EIGHT

I give Zurie my phone, and she records Nicole working with Seth on a mat, gently rotating his feet and ankles, bending and straightening his legs. Nicole shows me some new exercises to do with him at home. Then Trinh joins us, and they sing a horrible version of "Happy Birthday." Zurie and I join in along with other therapists and patients, and everyone claps.

When Nicole leaves, Trinh and I sit on a stool in front of Seth, still lying on the mat. Zurie keeps filming as I reach inside the grocery bag and pull out a bottle of chocolate syrup.

"Since it's his birthday, we can mix it with his milk. And when he belches, he'll taste chocolate!" I say.

Trinh's not smiling anymore. "That's such a sweet idea, but it could make him sick."

My shoulders droop as I put the bottle back in his bag.

Seth can't have Mom's pork chops, or her meat loaf, or anything awesome like that, and now he can't have chocolate syrup, either? Trinh touches my arm and smiles.

"There *are* assorted flavors of milk available for feeding tubes. And there's definitely chocolate. Check online."

"Okay."

She keeps smiling, and her voice has a lot of happy in it. "I'm glad you're filming today. I'm going to take this head strap off and allow Seth to watch what I do with his fingers and wrists. Isaiah, I want you to watch, too, so come sit over here closer to Seth and me."

Zurie's already filming, and as I walk around her, my foot catches on a rug, and I trip.

"Augh!"

Trinh rushes over. "Are you okay?"

I quickly get up. "I'm fine."

Trinh's making sure I'm okay when Zurie gasps. "Ice, Trinh, come here. You have to see this."

Widening the screen, she restarts the video from me holding the chocolate syrup.

I'm getting an attitude. "You think it's funny that I fell? You going to post it on social—"

She cuts me off. "Keep your eyes on Seth."

I zone in on his face as I put the chocolate syrup back in the bag, and Trinh talks about what she's going to do with Seth today. Next comes the fall and the holler. I'm about to look away but then Zurie zooms in on Seth's face. His head trembles as he struggles to lift it, then turns to watch me.

My breath catches, and without thinking, I take my phone from Zurie, rewind the recording, zooming in on Seth. Once I say, "I'm fine," his head slowly drops back down, and the recording stops.

Trinh touches my arm. "Can we watch it again with you?"

I give her my phone, then I rush over to my brother and drop to my knees so I can look into his eyes. "Thanks for always looking out for me. I love you, bruh. Between brothers."

If Trinh wasn't here, I'd apologize right now for hitting him. She comes over and takes a seat. "That was incredible. I'm going to request another block of therapy time."

She asks Seth to lift his head, but he doesn't move. I get an idea.

"Let me try something."

I take a few steps, and then fake another fall, crumpling to the floor. "Whoa! I just fell!" Seth looks my way and then slowly drops his head.

Trinh types on a tablet as she talks. "Well, Seth, now that I've seen you raise your head and control it, Nicole and I are going to upgrade your therapy plan! If you're trying to break free, we're going to help you."

I'm so excited. "When do you think he'll start talking?"

Trinh shrugs. "Nobody knows. It's just like how we didn't know he was going to raise his head—changes happen quickly, and we need to be watching for them, but we can't predict what we'll see. We should talk with Kris, our speech therapist. I'll be right back."

Nicole returns with Trinh, who's carrying a board in her hand. "Kris is with a patient but gave permission for you to borrow this voice board—it's like an iPad with pictures on it. Let's see if he'll use his hands to touch one of the pictures. I need to upload a picture of you to the board. This will help him figure out how to communicate again."

"Okay," I say, not sure if I'm supposed to smile or just stand there.

Click.

It doesn't take long for Nicole and Trinh to program the voice board and explain how it works. Seth's head is down, and Nicole squats so she can see his eyes.

"Seth, any time you want to communicate, press one of these pictures. Like this one with a thumbs-up. If you press it, a voice will say 'Yes.' The thumbs-down is for 'No.' If you press the picture of your brother, it will call his name. Understand?"

He stares at the board in silence.

"I also put some fun pictures on the board—things like tire, shoe, ocean, cookies—for games we can play later, if you feel up to it."

Trinh and Nicole continue to teach me about the voice board. "Here's the manual. Take it and the board home tonight. Try to get him to respond. You can change the voice to yours if you want, get more pictures from their website, even upload your own," says Nicole.

"You mean pics from my phone?"

Trinh smiles and nods. "Get creative!"

"The website address is on the back of the board if you need ideas," says Nicole.

I don't need their website for ideas. I'm going to use the board to create collages of his life.

When therapy's over, Zurie and I find seats in the reception area and watch out the window for our rides. We can't stop grinning at Seth, or at each other.

"And you know what else?" she says, "with all the data and research you gave to me, and what happened in therapy today, we're close to finishing our science project. We just need more data showing Seth's success at rewiring, and we'll be on our way to a solid A plus!"

I let out a sigh that feels as if it's been inside me for a long time. "Thanks for being here again today. It would've been completely different if you hadn't come."

"You're welcome. I'll come join you when I can. I meant it when I said I wanted to help." She stands. "I'll see you at school tomorrow. Bye, Seth."

I'm so glad Zurie's our friend. She's been with me through this whole thing with Seth, helping me to stay focused and not get too overwhelmed. People got it twisted—to me, she's not Zurie Fury. She's more like No-Worry Zurie.

When Dad pulls up, I roll Seth to the door. "Wait until Mom and Dad see the video," I tell him.

Dad lifts Seth into the passenger seat and then helps me tie down his wheelchair in the back of the truck. "Looks like you had a good day. Nice haircuts," he says.

I grin. "I've got something to show you that's even more fly than our fades."

Once we're all in the truck, I go for the drama. "I fell today."

Mom's eyes widen. "What? Are you okay?"

Dad chuckles. "And that's why your day was good?"

"Yes, sir. I want you to watch this video and keep your eyes on Seth."

I make my screen bigger so they can see everything. I watch their faces when Seth raises his head. Dad looks at Mom, who covers her mouth, but her cry seeps out anyway. Dad's voice cracks as he stares at the screen.

"Play it again," he says.

I do, and Mom puts her arm around me. "Your father and I raised you and Seth to watch out for each other. And you still do, even in the roughest times. We're so proud."

"Thanks, Mom. The therapists gave Seth a board that talks when he presses the buttons. I have to program it, but that's not a big deal—I'll let Seth help me. And I think Seth should eat at the table with us again. He shouldn't have to stay in his room."

When we get into the house, I roll Seth to the table. As I'm talking to Dad and Seth, Mom slides a meat loaf onto the table, and for a minute I forget what I was talking about. We bow our heads, and Dad thanks God for all of us being at the table again. His voice quivers, and I tighten my jaw to keep from crying as Mom sniffles and whispers 'Thank you' to God.

Dad chews a chunk of meat loaf, then closes his eyes, pushes away from the table, and reaches for Mom. I immediately grab Seth's handlebars and turn his chair so he can watch.

"Honey, this meat loaf makes a king want to dance with his queen."

I've got the video rolling as Dad sings some busted song in Mom's ear and they dance. It feels like old times as I whisper to Seth. "Check it out. It's back to dinner and dancing with the Abernathys."

CHAPTER THIRTY-NINE

Friday morning, Dad comes into the study. "Tomorrow your mom and I are going to be gone all day listening to depositions at Trish's office. Those are question-and-answer sessions, under oath, from people involved in our lawsuit, and Saturday was the only day everyone could be available." He looks at me. "One of the people being deposed is Johnny Earl."

Just hearing his name makes me lose my appetite. "You're going to see him?"

He nods. "First time since before the accident. I don't know what I'm going to do."

I'm so glad I won't be there. Seeing Johnny Earl would stir up a lot of anger—and if I'm feeling that way, I can't imagine how Dad must feel.

"Would you like me to call someone from the church to come sit with you and Seth?"

"Hold on," I say, and send a text asking for help. In seconds, I get a reply.

See you at 8 sharp.

I grab my backpack. "Juan Carlos said he'll be here at eight tomorrow morning."

"He's an excellent choice," says Dad. "We'll come home for lunch so we can feed Seth and give him his meds. Then we'll go back."

"So does this mean the lawsuit's almost over?" I ask.

Mom removes the tubing from Seth's stomach and closes the opening. "This lawsuit was over before it started. My prayer group prayed about that."

I've seen strange things happen after Mom's prayer group got busy, so I'm not going to hate. But my crew of Juan Carlos, Zurie, Nicole, Trinh, and the wish granter know how to make things happen, too! And after seeing what Seth did yesterday, I believe more changes are coming, and I'm not alone. On the Brazos bus, Zurie talks nonstop about the video, and later, Nicole and Trinh start new therapy routines with Seth. Tomorrow, I'll show Juan Carlos everything. I can't wait to see his face.

Before Juan Carlos comes, I change Seth's information sheet.

MY NAME IS SETH ABERNATHY
TODAY IS SATURDAY, OCTOBER 16TH

At eight, Juan Carlos walks in, and my parents thank him as they leave. Even though they're dressed up in church clothes, I'm worried about Dad and what he's going to do when he sees Johnny Earl. I sure hope Mom and Trish can keep him calm.

Juan Carlos is in the dining room eating the breakfast Mom left for him. I pull up a chair.

"On Thursday, at therapy, I tripped over a rug and fell."

He scans me from head to toe. "You don't look like you broke anything."

I hand him my phone. "I didn't. But I got this video. Keep your eyes on Seth."

I can tell when he sees Seth raise his head because he stops chewing. When the video ends, I reach for my phone, but he holds it away from me, wiping his eyes. "One more time."

After watching the second time, he's fired up. "I told you! Those doctors don't know jack about our boy! It's *our* therapy, Ice—we're helping him get back home. Now it's time to step up our therapy game."

"I was hoping you'd say that! Let me show you something else."

I get the voice board. "Check it out."

I touch pictures, and each time a voice says the word for what I touched. "We can fill this board with things Seth knows, and I'll change the voice to mine."

Juan Carlos strolls to Seth's room. "Here we go! Let's get

him dressed and out of bed!"

Once Seth's ready, Juan Carlos and I transfer him to his wheelchair. I slide his sunglasses over his eyes before Juan Carlos takes his wheelchair down the ramp. He points to the barn.

"Seth and I used to hang out in there with Gramps while he worked on stuff. Gramps talked to us about life and about being a good person. I'll roll Seth in, and you snap the pic."

Click.

Next, I stop in front of the apple tree, unstrap Seth, and pick him up. Juan Carlos rushes over, "Be careful! Don't drop him, Ice."

"I won't."

I gently place Seth on the grass and lie next to him.

Juan Carlos takes the pic. "Dude, I didn't know you were that strong."

Click.

I just stare at the sky, happy to have this moment again with my brother.

Juan Carlos walks toward the house. "I'm going to the bathroom."

"Seth's is the closest," I say.

I'm glad he's leaving us for a minute, because I haven't reached out to the wish granter in a while, and I need to talk to him. I take my brother's hand as we stare at the sky together. *Thanks for bringing Seth home. I'm sure you saw him lift his head at therapy, so thanks for that, too. Please help him do more. And help Dad keep his cool today.*

When Juan Carlos comes back, I get up. "We should take a picture of you in your Jeep."

I get my arms under Seth's head and legs, bend my knees, and lift him.

Juan Carlos snaps another picture. "It's got to be all that hay you're tossing around."

"He's really not that heavy," I say, strapping Seth back to his chair. "Ready? Okay, let me take one of you, and then one of you and Seth."

Click.

Then Juan Carlos kneels next to Seth's chair and poses. "Dominican Chocolate!"

Click.

The last pictures we take are of Seth petting Dolly and Buster with my help. And I roll his chair as close to the chicken coop as I can before snapping a pic.

"We should head back inside. He's had enough fun out here," I say.

Juan Carlos holds up my phone. "He needs a good picture of you. One with just your face, so he can stare at it. Where do you want to take it?"

I shrug. "I'll just stand here. It doesn't matter."

Click.

I can't wait to load the pictures into the talking board. I'm going to take a bunch more so I can switch them out as we wake up Seth's senses.

While Juan Carlos watches a movie with Seth, I upload

the pics. I also add some everyday things like *Hello*, *No*, *Yes*, and *Music*, and then say the name of each picture before I hit "Save."

Juan Carlos touches the pic I took of him and Seth, and my voice says *Juan Carlos and Seth*.

"What? That's dope!"

"I know!" I look around Seth's room. "We need something to set his voice board on that will fit over the arms of his wheelchair."

Juan Carlos nods. "I'll look outside."

"Okay."

I hold up the board so Seth can see it. "Let me show you how this works."

I press each picture twice so he can hear what it is. But then he squeezes his eyes closed so tightly that my stomach muscles tighten.

"Seth? Are you okay? What's wrong?"

His eyelids relax, and so does my stomach.

"Are you tired? Let's rest a minute."

I put my earbuds in but keep my eyes on Seth just to make sure he's okay. His eyes are still closed, so I don't want to bother him. Ten minutes later, Juan Carlos comes back with a board long enough to cover the arms of Seth's chair. "Will this work? I found it in the barn."

I nod, looking from the board to Seth's wheelchair. "I think it might be perfect."

Seth's eyes open, so I unstrap the belts from his head and arms and hold his head until it slowly droops. Juan

Carlos lays the homemade table over his chair, and I rest Seth's arms on it.

"I'm going to put your new voice board on the table so you can see it up close."

With Seth's head down, he's able to see the collage I made of family, friends, and our animals. I hold his pointer finger and press it to the picture of him and his best friend.

My voice says, *"Juan Carlos and Seth."*

Juan Carlos answers jokingly, "What do you want, Ice Pic?"

We do this twenty times before we stop. "That's enough for now. I'll do it again tonight with my picture."

Juan Carlos grins. "I'm feeling really good about this."

My elbow accidentally moves the voice board. "Whoops, my bad, Seth, I—"

Seth's eyes move to find the voice board. As I move the board back toward me, Seth's still tracking the pic of him and Juan Carlos.

"His eyes are moving!"

But when Juan Carlos looks up, it's not happening anymore. I try moving the board again, but Seth's eyes stay fixed, just like they've been for the past month. I must've imagined it.

CHAPTER FORTY

When Mom and Dad come in, Juan Carlos and I are excited to show them what we did, but the way Mom drops her purse on the cocktail table and Dad loosens his tie, it changes our happy vibe to red alert.

Mom forces a smile. "Juan Carlos, thanks for staying with Seth and Isaiah this morning. Our afternoon meetings were postponed, so we're home for the day."

Juan Carlos grabs his keys. "No worries, Momma Abernathy. I'll be around."

As soon as he leaves, Dad storms to his room and shuts the door. I'm heading that way, too, when Mom calls out to me and motions for me to sit with her on the sofa.

"Isaiah, today was a rough day. I can't handle many more like this one."

I sit on the sofa and give Mom all my attention. "You want to talk about it?"

"Yes, maybe that will help. We got to Trish's office a whole hour early because Hannah, Pastor, and his wife wanted to pray over us before the depositions."

I nod. "That was nice of them."

"Yes, it was. BMP had seven attorneys seated on one side of a long table in the conference room. On the other side was your father, me, and Trish. The BMP attorneys kept staring at us. I thought Ray was going to invite them outside, but he stayed calm."

"Good for Dad," I say, but my stomach's bubbling.

Mom keeps talking. "The first deposition was Johnny Earl's."

Snapsickles.

"When he first walked in, I didn't recognize him because he'd lost just as much weight as Seth has. His face was sunken in, and his eyes were bloodshot, like he hadn't slept in a long time. As soon as he saw your father, he burst into tears and couldn't stop. He just kept apologizing over and over and asking for forgiveness. It hurt me so bad, and when I looked over at Ray, there was an emotion in his face that I've never seen from him before."

No wonder they're home early. Johnny Earl must've caught a combo meal from Dad.

"He kept crying and begging Ray to forgive him. I took Ray's hand, but he pulled away from me, pushed back his chair, and got up."

My heart's in my back—at least that's what it feels like,

and I don't know what to do. "Mom, are you okay? You don't have to tell me the rest."

She wipes her eyes. "Yes, I do. Your dad walked over to Johnny Earl and wrapped his arms around him. They cried together, and everybody in the room needed a break before we even got started."

I'm stuck in stupid, trying to get my head around what Mom just said. How can Dad forgive Johnny Earl? How could he show him love like that?

Mom takes my hand. "I was so proud of your father. BMP thought he was going to get violent, but instead, your father offered forgiveness. After Johnny Earl's deposition, the next statements came from Mr. Douglas, your father's boss."

I roll my eyes. He's the jerk who acted all concerned when Dad went back to work and told him he could work part-time, then laid him off. "What did he say?"

Mom shakes her head. "Right after he got sworn in to tell the truth, Mr. Douglas pulled a paper from his jacket and said he wanted to read from it. The BMP attorneys looked confused, and so did Trish. Mr. Douglas read that he has known Ray for fifteen years and that Ray was a model employee. He then said that right after the accident, he was called by the corporate office to join a meeting where he was told to include Ray in a layoff because it would scare the other employees into staying quiet about their unwritten incentives. The BMP lawyers objected, even threatened to end the deposition, but Trish held her cool, and so did Mr. Douglas."

Mom goes on to tell me that Mr. Douglas admitted that "there and back in a dash makes more cash" was an "under the table" incentive they offered Johnny Earl and other drivers they knew needed extra money. After he said that, Mr. Douglas ended his deposition by reading his letter of resignation, right there on the record!

I'm getting hyped. "Dad must be lit, right? His boss finally told the truth."

Mom shakes her head. "BMP hurt him. He needs time to deal with that. Trish asked that we continue the rest of the depositions on another day. The BMP lawyers agreed, and so we came home early."

We sit quietly, letting everything sink in, then Mom gets up. "Did you and Juan Carlos change Seth's clothes while I was gone?"

"Five minutes before you came home. He's washed up and smells great."

"Good, I'm going to go take a nap, okay?"

"Sure, Mom. I'll hang out with Seth."

I shuffle into his room, and his eyes lock in on mine. I freeze.

"Seth?"

I move a little to the left. His eyes follow so I take his hand. "Squeeze twice for yes."

Nothing.

There's no doubt he's locked in on me, and there's no way I'm going to waste an opportunity to apologize.

"I want you to know that I'm sorry for hitting you last month."

I wait for a response, but eventually let go of his hand, sit in the recliner, and google more therapy ideas while trying to act casual. I want him to keep looking at me because I've waited a long minute for him to see me again.

After he falls asleep, I add *I'm sorry* and *I forgive you* to his voice board just so I don't miss an opportunity. Then I write up all my therapy notes and send them to Zurie.

Seth looked at me. Followed my moves. It's happening. He's changing.

She sends a quick response.

Crying. So happy.

I send a text to Juan Carlos telling him the same thing. His reply is quicker.

Seth's breaking through. Video everything for proof so we can wrap it like a gift and send it to those nonbelieving doctors for Christmas!

When Mom and Dad wake up, I take their pictures so I can load them into the voice board. I don't tell them about Seth looking at me because if I tell them and then he doesn't do it, they'll think I imagined it. Dad and Mom sit down together on the sofa but before they get comfortable, I take a stand for my brother.

"Seth needs to be in here with us, just like at dinner. He's changing, and we need to see those changes happen."

Dad pats my shoulder. "You're right, Dr. Abernathy. Nicole told us that same thing in her email yesterday about

Seth's therapy sessions. She also told us that you're doing a wonderful job. I'll go get Seth."

Yeah, this feels right, all of us sitting in the living room together. I'll have to ask Nicole and Trinh why the changes don't stay. But it's all good—I know if we just keep him involved in the mix, even if it's something small like sitting in the living room, he'll find his way back. One change at a time.

CHAPTER FORTY-ONE

Monday afternoon at therapy, Nicole smiles as I roll Seth past the reception desk and into the backroom. "How was your weekend?" she asks.

"Amazing!" I show her how I reprogrammed Seth's board with all the pictures we took, and how I worked with him on just a few exercises instead of all of them.

Nicole holds out her fist for a bump. "Nice job!"

"And check this out. I was doing my homework in Seth's room, and when I looked up, he was staring at me as if he'd said something and I didn't answer. I was too scared to move or else I would've filmed it for you. But he hasn't done it again since. Why not?"

"We call that a window. It's when something opens up in the brain, and then shuts down and doesn't happen again for a while. Thanks for telling me. Now that he's done it once, I'll watch for it to happen again."

Instead of moving him to a mat, Nicole keeps Seth in his wheelchair. "Today I'm going to give Seth a few simple commands, just to see where he is mentally."

She sits next to him, removes his straps, and puts a ball in front of his feet. I hit the record button on my phone.

Nicole kicks the ball to him. "Hi, Seth. Let's play. Can you kick the ball?"

Nothing.

Nicole keeps trying to get Seth to respond to the ball, but I notice his eyes are tightly closed again.

"Are you okay, Seth?" I ask, then turn to Nicole. "He did that on Saturday—closed his eyes so tight that it scared me. Why does he do that? What if he's hurting somewhere and we can't help him?"

"It could be a lot of things. It may be something internal—maybe he's feeling confused or frightened. Or maybe something is becoming clearer to him but it's hazy in his head right now. Unfortunately, it's impossible to know."

Nicole moves her chair closer to him and gently rubs his hand. "It's okay, Seth. You can't have a good day every day, and we understand. Keep up the great work."

I stop recording. "Thanks, Nicole."

Trinh strolls over and sits on the matted table. "Is Seth okay? Why is he making faces?"

I shrug. Trinh talks softly to him as she places a tray over his chair, then puts his hands on top of it. "Nicole and I talked about trying some one-step commands with Seth today."

"Yeah, he didn't do so good," I say. All the excitement I felt when I got here fades away. "I'm going to the restroom. I'll be back."

Inside the men's room I duck inside a stall. It's quiet in here, and if I could, I'd just cry it out. I can't believe Seth's not showing *any* changes today. And if he's in pain and can't tell us, that's even worse. Maybe he's done all the changing he can. Maybe I'm pushing him too hard.

I come out of the stall, splash cold water on my face and try not to look at my reflection in the mirror. I'm the worst brother on the planet. Maybe I'm the one who needs to change, not Seth. I've been making him do twice-a-day therapy sessions, watch videos, and listen to music, but never told him that if none of this worked, if he never got better, everything is still between brothers because I'll always love him, and I'll figure out ways for us to have fun together no matter what.

That will never change.

I go back to the therapy room, ready to drop this truth on my brother, but Trinh's just sitting there, holding Seth's hand. I try to stay upbeat but I'm too tired. "He's not responding to you either?"

Trinh pats the mat. "Come sit next to me."

She continues to hold Seth's hand in one of hers, then puts her other hand on my knee, and moves her face closer to mine.

"I just gave Seth a command, actually the same command twice. I don't want to get your hopes up, but both times he tried to do what I asked."

I'm not sure how to react. "Are you saying Seth's following instructions?"

"He's definitely trying. It makes me think his expressions aren't about pain, but more about something in his brain trying to rewire. I've asked Nicole to come back when she finishes with her other patient. I'm hoping we can try some things together."

My heart's pounding. "Did you say rewire? Like how a person can rewire a computer to use a keyboard instead of a mouse?"

Trinh smiles. "Exactly."

"Oh my gosh, can I quote you on that? For my science project?"

"You sure can, but I'm still bothered that he won't open his eyes."

The sun's glaring so hard through the window that I have to cover my eyes because . . . of course!

I rush to Seth's backpack and grab his sunglasses. While Trinh watches, I stretch the plastic arms over his ears and make sure they're sitting right on the bridge of his nose. "This should help."

A lady walks over. "Here I am, Trinh. Did you need something?"

"Oh, yes!" Trinh turns to me. "This is our speech therapist, Kris. She's also an expert with voice boards."

Kris smiles at me. "Hi. What's your name?"

I open my mouth to tell her, but before I can, someone else does it for me.

"Isaiah."

My head jerks around. Even though I can't see his eyes through the sunglasses, his head is raised, and I can feel him staring at me.

"Seth? Did you—"

His head slowly lowers again as his hand presses the same picture.

"Isaiah."

I grab my phone, shaking as I hit record, then rush to his side and drop to my knees. I stare at his face, doing my best to hold on and record what's happening. We're both trembling. I don't know if he's cold or afraid, so I wrap myself around him and try to take care of both at the same time. "I'm here. Don't be afraid." I turn the phone to face me without letting go of him. "Today is Monday, October eighteenth, and Seth just . . . he touched . . . never mind, I can't right now . . ."

I turn off my phone, drop it on the mat, and rest my head on my brother's shoulder as I free a heavy cry that's been sitting in my chest for over a month. "I've missed you so much. I love you, and I'm so sorry."

He touches my picture again. *"Isaiah."*

A hand pats my shoulder, but I brush it away. "Isaiah, it's me, Nicole. I saw what just happened and had to come over. Let Kris talk to Seth. It will only take a few minutes."

I let him go and back up to stand next to Nicole and Trinh. We all watch Kris as she sits in front of his wheelchair and talks to him.

"Hello, Seth. My name is Kris."

His hand flops over and touches a picture. *"Hello."*

I'm crying again, just knowing he understands.

Kris continues. "It's so nice to meet you. Have you seen Isaiah today?"

It takes him a moment, but soon he presses a picture. *"No."*

Kris stays calm. "Are you sure?"

He stares at his board and touches a picture. *"Dolly."*

"Seth, are you sure you didn't see Isaiah?"

"Buster."

I stop filming, feeling totally defeated that he forgot about me so fast. Trinh must see it in my face because she answers the questions I haven't yet asked.

"It's part of his brain injury. Sometimes a patient's memory short-circuits, and they can become confused, or completely forget what just happened, or even something that happened six months ago. But the brain is an amazing thing, and with good therapy and repetition, it can rewire."

I nod, knowing she's telling the truth. Seth just proved it.

Kris asks a few more questions, then she thanks Seth for talking to her and says goodbye. As she walks toward Nicole and Trinh, I go back to my brother and remind him that I'm still here. But I can hear the therapists whispering.

"I'm going to request more therapy days for Seth," says Nicole.

Kris agrees. "It's time to take his therapy up a notch."

I hug my brother and whisper. "It's okay. We all make mistakes. If you get lost again, just listen for me. I'll help you find your way."

CHAPTER FORTY-TWO

When Dad pulls up, I'm almost too excited to talk. Him and Mom are chatting about which documents they need to send Trish for the lawsuit. Once they finish, I chime in.

"I've got another video."

I'm still trying to keep my tears in check as my parents let their emotions out. When they see Seth looking at me, pushing the button on his voice board, they burst into tears. I lean forward and tell Seth. "They're not sad. Those are happy tears."

Dad reaches over his seat and pulls me closer to him. "I love you, Isaiah. Look what you helped your brother do, after the doctors said he never would."

"Thanks, Dad. Abernathys don't quit, right?"

"Right."

He and Mom watch the video twice more before we

head home. I talk the whole way—I wish I had put Seth's voice board in his lap because then maybe he could've said something, too. Instead of calling Zurie and Juan Carlos, I text them the video. I get five different happy emojis from Zurie. Juan Carlos's response is different.

My boy is back.

Me and Juan Carlos—we know *our* brother. All he needed was a chance.

On Tuesday morning, I give Mr. Williams an update on Seth.

"I can't wait to tell my wife." He grins. "Thanks for letting me know."

At school, I tell Mr. Whitaker, and my principal, Mr. Cochran. Shy Guy must've packed up and moved out because I'm a talking machine now, blabbing to everybody about my brother.

When Zurie shows up to have lunch with me, I tell her everything again as we eat our sandwiches and chips. She acts as if it's the first time she's heard it.

"It's like a fairy tale except you've got the pictures and video to prove it."

"Kind of like a yearbook," I say. "It's Seth's yearbook of his most important year."

"And it's everything we needed to complete our science project! Seth rewired, just like we hoped. Trinh said he did, and we've got the data and pictures to show our work. That was the last piece we needed. Seth deserves an A plus, too."

I nod. "Yeah, and it feels really good."

"This is going to make the dance even more fun! We'll have a reason to celebrate!"

"And I'm going to look so fly."

She rolls her eyes and laughs. "Whatever."

That afternoon, I'm strutting as I push Seth to therapy, wishing people would look at him now, chillin' in his shades, and the only strap he's wearing is his seatbelt. I changed his voice board to include pictures of cars, trucks, and stoplights, and when we spot one, I grab his finger and we press the picture together. Rhino waves from across the street, so we walk over to him and Uncle Jerry.

After we reintroduce ourselves to Uncle Jerry, he talks to Seth, while Rhino checks out Seth's wheelchair.

"Got those straps off," he says. "And he looks stronger! That's what's up! And that board talks, right?"

I nod. "Yeah, he's making progress. Uncle Jerry still in training?"

"We'll be training until the day before the race. He loves it, and I love running with him. Seriously, Abernathy, I bet if you asked Seth and he could answer, he'd tell you to sign him up. Anyway, see you inside."

Uncle Jerry waves bye to Seth before jogging with Rhino the rest of the way to the clinic. Seth and I continue our nice, easy stroll.

Nicole's waiting on us when we get there. "Hello, Isaiah. Hello, Seth," she says.

I stop the wheelchair, and Seth's hand moves across his board. *"Hello."*

She grins. "Very nice. We got approval for more therapy, so I emailed your parents and told them we're moving to a more aggressive program where the focus is on balance, posture, and standing. Follow me."

As we follow Nicole, I lean down and whisper, "Dude, you graduated to the next level!"

Nicole opens a door toward the back of the big therapy room, past the weights. I hadn't noticed that door before, especially since it's painted the same color as the walls.

"I want to begin this program with Seth using the standing frame because it has so many benefits. It will help strengthen his hips, legs, and posture, and even help his digestive system work better."

Whoever created this standing frame is a boss! It looks like a desk in the front and a wheelchair in the back, with a crank lever on it that—I don't know what it does, but I'm so excited for Seth!

Nicole explains everything as I help her transfer Seth from his wheelchair to the standing frame. I take his hand.

"I'm right here. We're trying something new today."

Nicole smiles and stands in front of us. "All right, Seth, now that you're seated, we're going to strap your chest to the back of the chair and secure your feet. These kneepad-looking things will protect your knees as we crank your seat from a sitting position to make you stand. We'll do this slowly so it doesn't affect your blood pressure." She checks the safety straps one last time. "Here we go."

Nicole slowly cranks a lever that looks like it should be attached to a water pump. I use the shutter speed on my phone to take fast pictures that show everything in freeze frames. As Nicole cranks, the chair of the standing frame straightens into a one-piece board and lifts Seth while keeping him straight and secure. My thoughts drift to that awful day when Dr. Parker dropped bad-news bombs on me about Seth. I was all in my feelings until Juan Carlos made me say Seth was coming back. Now, I'm crying happy tears because for the first time in over a month, Seth's standing next to me.

Nicole calls out. "Hand me his voice board. He can do activities while he stands. Eventually, Trinh will do the same thing, and so will Kris when he begins speech classes."

I'm snapping pictures, making videos, even ready to do a happy dance. "How can I get one of these standing frames for our house?"

"They're expensive. We don't even have one to loan."

"So how am I supposed to help him stand at home?"

"You can't without lots of help from some really strong people," she says.

It's not going to help him if he can't do this over and over like the other exercise. How is doing this once a day, and zilcho times on the weekends, going to help?

Nicole lets Seth stand for ten minutes while he and I play on his voice board. The loud honk of an eighteen-wheeler's horn startles me, and I glance out the window as the truck breezes by. When I turn back to Seth, his eyes are tight again.

"Hey, Nicole, something's going on with Seth."

She nods. "Maybe it's time for him to come down. He tolerated the standing frame really well. Next time we'll try for twenty minutes."

As Nicole cranks Seth back to a sitting position, I record it so I can show Mom and Dad the pics and the video.

Nicole unstraps the safety belts, and I help her put him back in his chair. "Great therapy today, Seth. Did you like it?"

He looks at his board, then presses "*stoplight.*"

"No, that's not the right answer," she says.

I look at my brother's face and hold up a hand to Nicole. "I don't think he's talking about therapy right now."

"Okay, sure," she says.

"*Stoplight.*"

Seth's made wrong choices on the board before, but he's consistently hitting this picture. I remember the horn we just heard. Oh no. Is he remembering the accident? I take a knee, like football players do, then put my arm around him as Nicole nods and leaves.

"It wasn't your fault. Johnny—somebody ran a stoplight. I'm so sorry for everything, Seth, and that includes hitting you."

We stay right there until Trinh comes for his next therapy session. When it's over, and we're heading home, I tell

Mom and Dad how he kept pressing the word *stoplight*.

"He may be having flashbacks to the accident. I better tell Trish," Dad says.

"And tonight after dinner, when we're watching television, I want Seth out of his wheelchair, sitting next to me on the sofa," says Mom.

I nod because I totally get what Mom's feeling. I don't know how to help Seth deal with that memory. I guess trying to bring back the old Seth brought everything, and there was no way to separate it.

CHAPTER FORTY-THREE

I'm glad it's Wednesday because tonight, Juan Carlos will be here to help me with Seth. I can't wait to tell him about the standing frame and everything that's happened in therapy.

Right after Mom and Dad leave for prayer service, I unload the awesome news on him. He starts pacing. "Okay. If they're going to take his therapy up a notch, then we need to do the same. It's time he sees a live race, smells the track, hears the crowd, know what I mean?"

"Yeah, I think you're onto something, but how are we going to do that? Just sitting in his wheelchair at a cross-country race could make him depressed instead of helping him get better."

Juan Carlos stops, shrugs, and nods. "Good point. Seth's never been one to just watch sports. When he spent the weekend with me last month, he tried to play baseball.

Even though he stunk at playing right field, he didn't care. He just wants to be in the game."

"But right now, watching a cross-country race live is the best he can do," I say.

Juan Carlos agrees. "Truth, but I think your point about him getting depressed is legit."

I take a seat. "I know."

I'm thinking so hard that my head hurts. I'm about to give up when Rhino and Uncle Jerry run through my mind—and I couldn't be happier to see them in there. "I've got an idea."

I don't know enough about Woodbridge's Thanksgiving Turkey Trot to tell Juan Carlos about it. And even after he's gone home, and I'm in bed, I'm still not convinced this is the right thing to do. But I'll know better tomorrow.

After school, I help Nicole with Seth's therapy by lifting one of his arms, moving it above his head, then back down again. "Hey, Nicole, what's up with that flyer about the Turkey Trot race I saw in the reception area?"

"It's fun! You and Seth should enter," she says.

"But Seth can't run yet. Heck, he can't even walk."

"The Turkey Trot is for *all* abilities. That means walking, running, in a wheelchair, amputees with prosthetics, on crutches, it doesn't matter. Everybody's welcome."

That's what *all abilities* means? Snapsickles! But I still need more answers.

"I can't picture myself bolting down a track, pushing

Seth in his wheelchair for three miles."

She laughs. "Seth would need a racing stroller. It's a smooth ride and an easy push! I can get you a permission slip."

"A permission slip? For what?"

"Your parents have to sign one for you and Seth to enter the race."

It took Dad two whole years to sign my yearbook permission slip. Seth doesn't have that kind of time. I need a plan to prove how important this is to help my brother be Seth-sational again.

"I'll get back with you on that," I say.

Mom and Dad loved going to Seth's cross-country races. It was a family thing. But with all this therapy, and working, and the lawsuit, they haven't seen much fun. Seth and I can bring family time back! That should make them sign in a hurry!

The ride home is a quiet one. I think we're all tired. But after dinner, I make sure Seth gets his therapy, and while I'm exercising his arms, I tell him what's on my mind.

"I'm going to a dance on Saturday. Do people really dance at those things? And I have to wear a suit. I wish you could give me some pointers on what to do."

After we're finished, I drag to the study and fall across my bed without taking off my clothes. What feels like two minutes later, my alarm goes off. I get up, clear the sleep from my eyes, and go feed the animals. I'm on autopilot now, doing everything the same way just to make it through the day.

When Friday evening comes, I'm so happy to park on the living room floor near Seth's wheelchair and relax. We're all watching *Law & Order* when I notice the two guy detectives are wearing suits. Snapsickles! I almost forgot!

"Dad, can I borrow a tie?"

"Sure, go in my closet and get one. Make sure it matches your suit."

"You'll tie it for me, right?"

Seth bangs my pic on his voice board. *"Isaiah." "Isaiah." "Isaiah."*

I touch his shoulder. "I told you I'm going to a dance tomorrow. I don't have a tie."

He keeps banging. *"Isaiah." "Isaiah." "Isaiah."*

"What? Why are you—"

At that very moment, it's clearer than ever that I need to do more than just hear my brother bang on his voice board. I need to listen to him. I sit on the edge of the sofa.

"Seth, may I borrow your clip-on?"

His hand gently presses one picture. The automated voice says, *"Yes."*

"Thanks," I say with a grin. He may not be talking the way I hoped, but at least we're understanding each other.

Dad chuckles. "Some things never change. Still looking out for his little brother."

We all still have each other's back, and we're getting

more comfortable taking care of Seth. Mom's sleeping in her own bed again, and it's been two weeks since I cried myself to sleep.

When Saturday morning blows in, I'm up, excited, and ready to move around! I even practice my dance moves as I feed the animals. Dad stops his truck at the pigpen, rolls down his window, and gives me ten bucks. "On my way to work. Have fun tonight. You deserve it."

"Thanks, Dad."

Juan Carlos is right on time, and the music pulsing from his speakers has me dancing in my seat. He pulls up to the gym and hands me another ten. "Text me when you're ready to go."

"Thanks, Juan Carlos."

I've got a money swag driving my strut as I step up to the gym doors, where there's a man collecting cash. Zurie's there, too, holding two cameras and wearing a beautiful blue dress.

She shows the man our badges. "Yearbook photographers."

He smiles. "Go on in. Have fun."

Inside, orange and black balloons dangle from the ceiling and refreshment table while Frankenstein's monster, Little Bo Peep, even Superman show off dance moves on the gym floor.

Zurie yells over the music. "You take the right side, and I'll take the left."

"Got it!"

I climb the bleachers to take panoramic pictures and a few close-ups.

"Abernathy!"

It's Rhino, dressed like Mario, and soon, we're both chuckling watching Luigi on the dance floor. "Mr. Cochran invites him every year."

I nod. "That's so cool. Hey, I'm thinking about getting Seth into that Turkey Trot race."

Rhino nods. "What's there to think about? Just do it."

We talk about the dance and how much I'm enjoying taking pictures.

"You're good at it, Abernathy, especially all those pics on Instagram." He looks around the dance floor. "Uh-oh. Need to check on Luigi. Later."

Rhino weaves through the crowd. Zurie signals me to come down the bleachers.

"It's time for a break. Are we going to dance or what? Come on!"

My heart pounds as Shy Guy returns and tries to convince me that I look absolutely ridiculous and that I need to sit down. But I ignore him and let go like I do when I'm dancing at home with Seth.

After two songs, Zurie and I get fruit punch, snap selfies, and watch everybody having a great time. Before we get back to work, I just have to ask her.

"Hey, I'm thinking about entering Seth in a race. I'd push him in a racing stroller, which sounds kind of cool.

Do you think it would be dumb to sign up?"

Her eyes widen. "No! It sounds fun! What can I do to help?"

"I don't know yet. I'm going to ask Juan Carlos to train me. I hope he says yes."

"Me, too. I'm sure he will." She looks around the floor. "We'd better get back to work."

I'm having a blast with the camera, capturing special moments for our yearbook. But when there's a "last dance" call, I find Zurie and we get back on the floor.

When the song ends, and the bright lights come on, everyone floods toward the doors. I walk Zurie outside, and she points across the street. "My ride's here, but before I go I want to know what you thought about the dance."

My insides squirm because I'm not sure this is the right thing to do—and I wish I had Seth to ask, but I don't, so I bend down and give her a hug.

"I loved it. I'm glad you were here with me. Thank you for being my best friend."

She grins. "You're my BFF, too. Look, I've gotta go. See you on Monday."

Once she's gone, I notice Mario and Luigi saying their goodbyes to the other students. Luigi's holding balloons from the dance. They can't be walking home, can they? It's too dark out. I text Juan Carlos and jog over to them. "Rhino, you guys need a ride?"

He takes a selfie of him and Uncle Jerry smiling. "Naw. Unc likes to walk."

"Dude, it's dark out here! You and Uncle Jerry could get hurt."

He chuckles and holds up his phone. "Watch this," he says, and posts the selfie on Instagram with a caption. **The dance is over. On our way home.** Suddenly, as far as I can see down the street, porch lights, yard lights, even living room lights come on and brighten the once dark streets around us. Rhino takes Uncle Jerry's hand and nods.

"Scarboro strong, baby," he says. "Everybody watches out for me and Unc. Day and night. They'll watch out for you and Seth, too, if you let 'em."

CHAPTER FORTY-FOUR

Moments later, Juan Carlos pulls up to the curb. "Looks like you had a good time."

"It was incredible!"

"Seth and I had fun, too. We did our thing," he says with a grin.

I let out a mind-made-up sigh. "I found Seth a race."

"Perfect! Which one are we taking him to watch?"

"He's not watching—he's going to be in it. I'll push him in a racing stroller."

Juan Carlos's eyes dart from me to the road. "What? Is that like a baby stroller?"

"I'm not really sure, I haven't seen one yet."

"Oh. How long is the race?"

"Three miles. Do you think I'll have to, like . . . train for that?"

He's quiet for a moment and then blasts me. "Do you

think running three miles is easy? It's not just physical. You'll have to use your mind to push your body—and Seth!"

I stare at the floorboards, knowing I just changed the vibe inside his Jeep. "My bad. I wasn't trying to hate on runners. Will you help me train?"

"How much time do we have?"

"It's a Turkey Trot on the morning of Thanksgiving."

"That's only four, maybe five weeks away! You can't train for anything in five weeks."

"Dude, I learned how to shoot free throws in two!"

He's quiet for a while, but then smiles. "And you crushed it. Okay, I'm in. Are you willing to do what I tell you?"

"Yep."

"Is Momma Abernathy cool with this?"

"She'll love it," I say.

"Okay, then I'll train you. I'm sure that's what Seth would want me to do. I may not understand a lot about therapy, but I've got a black belt in distance running. Look for my texts and be ready to start tomorrow, early."

"Okay, I will. Thanks again."

Mom and Dad are on the sofa watching the news when I walk in.

"How was the dance? Come tell me all about it," Mom says, patting the sofa pillow.

"It was legit, but I'm wiped. I'll tell you about it in the morning."

When I look in on Seth, he's asleep. Maybe this race will make him happy. I've got to make it happen for him.

My mind flashes back to what Rhino said. *They'll watch out for you and Seth, too, if you let 'em.*

I sit on the edge of my bed, hoping I'm not making the biggest mistake of my life. Dad warned me to stay out of conversations about Seth because of the lawsuit. But I think Rhino's right. Scarboro will support Seth, whether he's running cross-country or riding in his wheelchair.

I upload the video of Seth raising his head when I fell, to Instagram, along with pictures of him petting Dolly and Buster with me. I also include the reel of him pressing my picture on his voice board. It still gives me chills.

I run my hand down his clip-on tie, and then create another reel.

"Hi. This is Isaiah. I've uploaded pictures of Seth working hard in therapy. He's making progress. Thanks for your support. I'll keep you posted."

I create a hashtag #SupportforSeth, and tag as many followers as I can, especially @Scarborostrong since that's the one Rhino mentioned. Moments later:

Ping. Ping, ping.

I don't want to hear all that tonight, so I silence my phone. As I change out of my suit, I notice a text from Juan Carlos.

WEEK ONE: Sunday, Wednesday, Friday early mornings after feeding the animals: Load the

wheelbarrow with ONE bale of hay and push it while running to the mailbox. You have twenty-five minutes. Do it again in the evening when the sun goes down. You have thirty minutes. Record your time and text it to me. Don't lie. I'll know. Tuesday and Thursday: Light jog to the mailbox and back two times in the morning and evening. Thirty minutes max. Saturday and Monday: Rest. Stay hydrated. No sodas or sweet drinks. Water only.

What? A bale of hay is seventy pounds! I should've kept my mouth shut. I'm already dragging every day when I get home because I'm so tired. Now I've added a huge training camp to my days! What have I gotten myself into? Thank God tomorrow's Jesus Jail. I'll have longer to rest.

But at six a.m., my phone buzzes. It's another text from Juan Carlos.

Get up. It's not all about your physical body. Get your mind ready to run.

I'm not sure what that means, since my mind is always running, but I roll out of bed and feed the animals, then fill the wheelbarrow with a bale of hay. I tap my clock app to start the stopwatch, turn the phone's ringer back on, grab the handles of the wheelbarrow, and take off.

Pushing the wheelbarrow is much lighter than I thought it'd be. *Ping.* Twenty-five minutes to finish. No problem.

Ping, ping. I must be getting some Instagram followers from that post I made last night about Seth.

I head down the hill, get past the animals just fine, but when I turn onto the gravel, the rocks make the wheelbarrow harder to push, and it's messing with my rhythm. I hit a patch of gravel that throws my balance off, and now I'm struggling to stay on my feet. As I crash across the rocks, the wheelbarrow falls on its side, and my bale of hay rolls across the gravel like a tire. I check my arm for cuts and flick pieces of rock off me.

"Dang it!"

I scramble to put everything back in place. How much time have I lost? I run faster to make up for that stop, but halfway back, my thighs burn and the hay feels like bricks.

When I get to the end of the gravel road, our apple tree looks twenty miles away. I lean over and grab the bottoms of my shorts. Dolly and Buster are staring at me. Buster's standing on Dolly's left side like he always is.

Like he always is.

He never stops watching out for his mother, just like I'm never going to stop watching out for Seth. "Good boy, Buster!"

I grab the handlebars of that wheelbarrow, and as I make my way up the hill, Dolly and Buster trot with me. The pigs squeal as I jog by. I can hear my divas in the chicken coop. It's as if they're all cheering for me.

I pass the apple tree and keep going all the way to the barn before letting go of the handlebars, huffing so hard I can barely catch my breath. I stop the clock on my phone. Thirty-two minutes. Dang it. I send the time to Juan Carlos, and he texts me back.

Good job. Take it easy today. No workout tomorrow. See you Wednesday.

My legs tremble, threatening to give out, but I drag my worn-out body into the house. Mom's in her room, so this is a good time to let my brother know what's going on.

"I'm getting you back in the game. It's a cross-country race, and I'm going to run with you. Juan Carlos is training me, and—and he told me to get my mind ready to run. I think you need to get your mind ready, too, whatever that means."

CHAPTER FORTY-FIVE

Monday morning, when Mr. Williams opens the bus door, I raise my lunch to him. He raises his back, and so do the other riders. Seeing all the support for my family is a great start to my day. After advisory, I shuffle by Mr. Whitaker on my way to yearbook class.

"You did a fabulous job at the dance."

I'm trying not to grin, but I can't help it. "I had a blast. Can't wait to do it again."

"I checked out the pictures you and Zurie sent to me. You have a soft, caring touch behind the lens that makes you an excellent photographer."

"Thank you."

Seth said my soft is hard-core, so I walk like a boss into class.

Zurie's waiting for me, smiling like she's got a secret.

"Hey! Here's a draft of our science project. We crushed it! Check it out and let me know if I need to change anything."

The awesome photography and artwork Zurie added to the cover is worthy of an A+ all on its own. She even slayed the title! "Rewiring: The Astounding Similarity Between the Brain and Modern Technology." She also added my charts, notes, and quotes from Trinh and Nicole.

"This looks amazing!"

"You and Seth did all the hard stuff. I just organized it," she says.

I flop into my chair without taking off my backpack. I'm uncomfortable, but I'm too tired to care. Maybe sitting here a minute will help me recharge, but I'm already getting exhausted just thinking about my evening workout and all the other things I have to do before I can go to bed. It's as if I'm a robot, programmed to feed the animals, help get Seth ready to leave with Mom, get myself ready for school, and walk almost a mile to the bus stop. All that before the sun comes up.

But at least I know why I'm tired. The most important people and things in my life—my parents, my brother, and the animals—need me. And everybody rooting for Seth needs me, too. That's why I make a bigger effort to post on Instagram to let everyone know how Seth's doing. And just for laughs, I post a reel of my diva hens clucking to "The Chicken Dance."

When Wednesday rolls around, Juan Carlos and Seth come outside to watch me run while Mom and Dad go to Bible study.

When I finish, Juan Carlos says, "Good job, Ice Pic! Keep it up."

But he's wrong—I'm not doing a good job. He hasn't noticed that I haven't changed Seth's info sheets on the wall since Monday or that Seth's voice board is nowhere near him. And I'm too tired to even ask for help.

By Thursday, all my days are running together. But the biggest issue is that I'm down to four weeks before the race. As I run down the gravel road with the wheelbarrow, I wonder if I'm doing the right thing. Which is more important for Seth, evening therapy or training for the Turkey Trot? Therapy is super important, but a race might help Seth rewire enough to talk. I can't decide. Maybe I just need a break. So I send a text to Juan Carlos.

I'm wiped. I need a break. Tomorrow, I'm skipping my morning and evening run.

On Friday after therapy, I'm looking forward to a little vacation! After dinner, I sit down to relax and watch television with everyone. Except Dad doesn't turn on the television. Mom is sitting next to him, and I can tell something's up just by the look on their faces.

"Do you remember when your mother and I went to those depositions?"

"Yes, sir."

"The following week, the judge presiding over our case ordered us to attempt mediation. That's when the plaintiff and the defendant meet with a mediator—who kind of acts like a referee—and we try to settle the lawsuit. That meeting is happening tomorrow, and the BMP representatives and their attorneys want to see Seth. We're taking him with us."

I shouldn't have skipped my run. This news is heavier than two weeks of running combined. "Do I have to go?"

"No. You'll go to school, but we just wanted you to know. The meeting begins at eight in the morning, and we should be back in time for Seth's therapy."

I nod. "Okay."

Someone knocks.

"I'll get it," I say.

It's Juan Carlos. Awesome! Maybe he came to hang out with us. He strolls in, man-hugs me, and walks over to my parents. "Hello, Mr. Abernathy, Momma Abernathy. What's going on, Seth? It's late, but I just need to talk with Ice about his training real quick."

Mom and Dad look at each other. The quiet in the room bangs like cymbals, and I can feel the heat from Juan Carlos's eyes on the side of my face. My head spins as I scramble for a lie.

"Oh, uh, yeah, I meant to tell you that Juan Carlos is teaching me how to run to help with my stress, and you know, make me relax more."

Dad nods. "That's nice of you to look out for Ice like that."

Mom smiles. "Thank you, Juan Carlos."

Juan Carlos smiles, too. "You're welcome." But when he turns back to me, the smile's gone. He gives a hard nod toward the door. "Get your shoes on."

The bass in his voice lets me know he's not asking me, so I grab my shoes. I've already got a mindful of drama thanks to this mediation thing, so I hope Juan Carlos isn't going to add to it.

Mom waves. "You boys have a nice walk."

We barely get past the apple tree before he goes off. "So you're quitting?"

"I didn't say that! I just need a day off. I'm exhausted."

"I know how much you do around here, and I completely understand. I'd be exhausted, too. As your coach, your friend, and your brother, I want to do everything I can to help you."

I shrug. "I don't know what else you can do."

He stops and turns me by my shoulders. "I can't let you quit."

"What are you talking about? You know Abernathys don't quit!"

"That's what you say, but you've only been in training

for a week! You already get two days off! You're letting your body speak for you, but your mind needs to be the boss."

I shake my head. "I don't even know what that means."

"I'm going to teach you by example. You're sacrificing, and I need to do the same thing. We're in this together, Ice Pic. We only have four more weeks. Both of us need to stay mentally strong."

"But I don't know how," I say.

He puts his arm around my shoulders. "Here's what we're going to do. We're going to jog to the mailbox, then back to the house. We'll find a good pace, a good rhythm. I want you to focus on breathing in through your nose, out through your mouth."

I light up. "Oh! Smell the flowers and blow out the candles!"

He hesitates, but then chuckles. "Yeah, exactly. Let's go."

I really am exhausted, and it's dark out here, but after what Dad just told me, running may be just what I need. So we take off, and I get in rhythm with Juan Carlos until we sound like one pair of feet hitting the gravel. Dolly and Buster trot with us inside their pasture.

After we turn onto the gravel road, Juan Carlos asks, "So where are you going to get one of those racing strollers for Seth?"

Snapsickles!

"I'm, uh, working on that with his therapist," I say,

hoping it sounds truthful.

When we get to the mailbox, Juan Carlos points to his temple. "On the way back, let your mind control your running. Your body will lie, make you believe it can't go any farther. When that happens, remind yourself why you're doing this, and that you're strong. Your mind holds your truth, and a reserve tank of energy. That reserve tank is connected to what runners call 'the runner's high'—when you reach that level, you'll feel like nothing can stop you. Let's go."

I've been working so hard on helping Seth rewire his brain, and here I am, learning how to rewire mine too. We stop near Juan Carlos's Jeep and catch our breath.

"We all need a break sometimes. Life is about pacing, understand?"

"Yes. Pacing. Got it. Thanks, Juan Carlos. See you on Sunday."

"Oh, and one more thing. Do your parents know what we're *really* training for?"

If there was a lie detector on my forehead, the arrow would point to *Pants on Fire*, but I smile and hope he doesn't smell the smoke. "Sort of. I'll give them more info this weekend."

"You better, because Momma Abernathy looks like she can bring the funk and the noise, and I don't want any of that. You do what you need to do, or I will."

"Don't worry, I'll tell them. I've just been so busy that I

forgot, that's all. I'm sure my parents will be excited seeing Seth back on the track."

As I watch the lights on Juan Carlos's Jeep disappear into the night, the permission slip weighs heavy on my mind. Maybe Nicole can email one to me to print out. And when I give it to my parents, I'll make a big deal about how Seth's come so far. They're going to be super excited, like I am right now, knowing my brain is stronger than my body, and there's nothing that can stop me.

CHAPTER FORTY-SIX

Juan Carlos keeps his word about training with me. In just three weeks of his coaching, I feel stronger and more confident. But this permission slip drama is making me sweat more than my running because I can't find the right time to talk with my parents about it.

Mediation keeps getting cancelled, then rescheduled, just to get cancelled again. Mom's wearing down, complaining about everything, and Dad's yelling all the time for no reason. They snap at each other, then quickly apologize. It's so stressed in the house that Dad prays for patience and Mom asks God for guidance.

But today, the last Friday before Thanksgiving break, mediation is finally going to happen. I'm looking forward to an easy day at school. I need it, knowing Mom, Dad, and Seth will be in that mediation meeting, trying to settle the lawsuit. I wonder what Seth's thinking. I hope Mom's not crying and Dad has his emotions in check. With all that on my mind, I'm glad today will at least be a fun day at school.

In second period, Zurie, Rhino, and I team up and crush everybody in a game of trivia. In fifth-period science, Zurie makes a big deal out of turning in our report. She places it on our teacher's desk and gives me a hard high five before sitting next to me.

When school's out, I jog the path I usually walk to Center Street Church. Even though I'm tired, I need to know what happened in that meeting. I have to make sure Seth's okay and check on Mom. They're waiting for me inside the church.

"How'd it go? Is the lawsuit over?"

Mom shrugs. "There was a whole lot of arguing, and we must've taken five breaks just so the lawyers could cool down. But Trish held her own. When we left, they were still there. I made your dad bring us here because I didn't want Seth hearing it all. Are you okay?"

I try not to show my disappointment. "I'm sorry the lawsuit didn't settle, Mom. I better get Seth to therapy. See you later."

I jog a little as I wheel Seth down the street, hoping it clears my mind. Halfway there, a woman runs past, pushing a baby in a stroller. It reminds me to handle my business. So when Nicole puts Seth in the standing frame, I start firing questions at her. "Hey, is it too late to get a permission slip for the Turkey Trot?"

She smiles. "Nope. Stay here with Seth, and I'll get you one. But you have to get it back to me before next Tuesday so I can add you to the list of participants. Can you do that?"

"Of course!"

While Nicole's gone, I upload a new picture to Seth's voice board. It's him, running in a cross-country race. I add my voice to it and then warn him. "Not a word to Mom or Dad, okay?"

He pushes it immediately. *"Run."*

"I know! I'm trying to make that happen for you. Let me handle it!"

Nicole hands me a permission slip, and I stuff it in my pocket. "Oh, and where can I rent one of those racing strollers? How much do they cost?"

"We've got three in our supply room. You can borrow one. When do you want it?"

I perk up immediately. "For real? How about after therapy on Monday or Tuesday?"

"That'll be fine, but make sure you get that permission slip signed first."

"I'll get it back to you before Tuesday, I promise."

I'm trying to think what else I need to do to make this race work for Seth. What else will he need?

While Seth and I wait on Mom and Dad, I tap my Instagram app and make another reel.

"Hey, it's Ice Pic. Seth and I are training for the Woodbridge Turkey Trot! Seth's been working hard to get back in the game, and he's got everything to make that happen! Well, everything except his fans. He really needs you, so please come support him on Thanksgiving morning at the Woodbridge Community Center! I've posted the flyer on my page. Thank you, and I'll see you there."

I upload my reel just as Mom and Dad pull up. Thank goodness they're clueless about social media. I'm not worried about them finding this post, but I am sweating about the permission slip.

Later that evening, when Mom calls Dad and me to eat, I roll Seth to the table and take a seat. After Mom feeds him, and we all finish eating, I rub my stomach.

"Mom, those pork chops were so good!"

"Thank you. Oh, and speaking of good food, we're going to the special Thanksgiving service and candlelight dinner at church on Thursday. I volunteered to make green bean casserole. Hannah's making the yams. It's going to be beautiful. Do you realize this will be the first time we've been in church together as a family since the accident?"

Dad winks. "Trish is joining us for lunch on Thanksgiving before the service, so tidy up the study, okay?"

I take a deep breath. "Sure. You know, Seth's making huge progress. He's raising his head, moving his arms and hands, and that voice board . . . he's really figured out how to use it."

Mom giggles. "He sure has."

"You and Juan Carlos have done a wonderful job," Dad says with a smile.

I smile back. "Thanks. But I think he's ready to do more. I've got a surprise!"

I put the permission slip on the table. "After talking with Nicole, we think Seth would really enjoy being in the Turkey Trot race on Thanksgiving morning! I just need you to sign the permission slip, please."

I put my hand on my brother's arm. "You ready to do this?"

He searches his board and then presses a picture. *"Run."*

I grin. "I know, right?"

Mom hands the slip back to me. "I don't think that's a good idea. He could tip over."

A knot forms in my stomach. "He'll be in a special racing stroller, with seat belts. I won't let him crash. I promise. You used to love going to his meets! The race will give us a chance to do something fun again as a family."

"It still sounds dangerous. I can't allow anyone to hurt him again," she says.

"Mom, please—"

She gives me a stern look. "The answer is no."

The room is quiet. This can't be happening.

"But, Mom—"

Dad's voice makes me jump. "Isaiah, you heard your mother."

I'm out of options. "May we be excused from the table?"

Dad leans back in his chair. "Yes."

I roll Seth back to his room as he keeps banging the board, *"Run!" "Run!" "Run!"* I close the door and pace, rubbing the top of my head, trying to figure out how to get around this, but Seth keeps pressing that same picture, distracting me. I touch his hand, and he stops. Before I speak, I make sure I'm calm, but I tell him the truth. "I'm salty, too. Let me think, okay?"

"Dolly."

Great. He's so mad he checked out on me. I don't blame him. He wants this, and so do I.

That evening, Juan Carlos reminds me to find my rhythm and use my mind, but it's hard because I've got to break this bad news to him. When we're finished, he reaches inside his Jeep and tosses me a Scarboro High cross-country jersey. I can't tell him. I just can't.

"I got this from Coach. You can wear it in the race when Seth wears his, right?"

That's Juan Carlos's way of making sure I let Seth represent the team.

I fake a smile. "Of course."

"You had a good workout today, Ice. I'll see you on Sunday."

Two months ago, Juan Carlos was just Seth's cool and funny best friend. Now, I don't know what I'd do without him, and I feel horrible not telling him what Mom said.

But what Mom, Dad, even Juan Carlos don't know is that I already made up my mind to run with or without their permission. Before the accident, Seth made all the decisions about what we did as brothers. He was the oldest. He was in charge.

I grab the pen on Dad's desk and use it to forge his name on the permission slip.

I'm the big brother now. I'm making the decisions. And we're entering that race.

CHAPTER FORTY-SEVEN

Sunday night is my last run with Juan Carlos before the race. Instead of one bale of hay, I toss two into the wheelbarrow. "This feels closer to what Seth weighs," I say.

I mentally see myself pushing Seth in a racing stroller. That's all the visual I need to pace with my mind, not my body, and when we finish, Juan Carlos bumps my fist.

"You're ready. No doubt. Rest tomorrow, and on Tuesday and Wednesday, just do a light jog. I can't be here with you because I have to help my dad get the house ready for Thanksgiving. But there's no way I'm missing that race. See you there."

"Wait!" My shoulders drop, and I come clean. "Will you pick us up on Thursday morning? Seth and I need a ride. We have to be there by seven."

His face is full of disappointment. "You parents said no, didn't they?"

This time, my expression can't cover up the truth, and his can't hide the disappointment.

"Dude, I can't go against your parents' wishes! You worked so hard. I'm sorry."

As he drives away, so do my chances of getting Seth back in the game. How will I find a ride, and also hide Seth's racing stroller so Mom and Dad don't see it?

I send an emergency text to Zurie.

Hi. I need a huge favor.

After telling Zurie my plan, she sends a text back.

It's risky, but I'll be there.

That night, I lie in my bed wondering if this is what stepping up looks like. If I get caught, it's probably going to be a punishment-for-life kind of thing. Maybe this is how all great people feel the night before doing something important.

I get out of bed, open the window, and stare into the night. Our front porch light brightens everything all the way down to Mom's apple tree. I've had so many good times under that tree with Seth. I'll never forget crying my guts out to Zurie there, too. She listened to things I'd never told anyone. As I stare into the darkness, I can remember the moment she made me feel better.

Everybody makes mistakes. Always leave space for grace. Mom told me that.

Getting Seth into that race could be my space for grace, my chance to forgive myself. This one good thing could cancel that one bad thing I did to him and make things right "between brothers" again. I close the window and go back to bed.

Early Monday morning I feed the animals. Then, since school's out, I get in Dad's truck so he can drop Mom, Seth, and me off at the church. Seth and I get stuck in one of the offices, and after only ten minutes, I'm ready to go. I can't believe he has to sit here all day, every day, doing absolutely nothing. We watch movies and music videos on my phone until I can't take it anymore. When Mom finally lets us leave early, it's as if me and my brother just busted out of Jesus Jail.

As I roll Seth to therapy, I feel like the scheme I'm masterminding is scrolling across my forehead. We get to therapy just moments before Zurie.

"Hey, thanks for coming," I say.

She looks around and whispers, "I'm worried the plan isn't going to work. My cousin said she'd be back to pick me up in twenty minutes because she has things to do."

My knee jumps. "So we'll have to talk fast."

The therapy room door opens, and Nicole smiles at us. "You ready? Hi, Zurie!"

So far, so good. As I roll Seth back he bangs on his voice board and hits a picture I forgot to remove.

"I like big butts."

Zurie side-eyes me. So does Nicole. Two men in the reception area chuckle.

"See, we were at church—" That sounds even worse. "I'll take that one off."

Nicole grins. "Good idea."

Once she gets Seth in the standing frame, I hand her the permission slip. "Here you go. All signed and ready. Can I get the stroller today?"

She looks over the permission slip, and I freeze. Does my cursive look adult enough to her? If Nicole calls me out, I'll squeal like a pig.

"I haven't sanitized it," she says, still checking the permission slip.

I'm ready to oink. "We can handle that," I say.

She smiles. "Perfect. I'll be right back."

Soon she returns, rolling a bright red-and-black stroller with two monster tires in the back, and one smaller tire in the front. If I could spray-paint racing stripes down the sides, I could turn this thing into the baddest three-wheel drag racing stroller on the planet.

"He's going to love riding in that," I say.

Zurie slowly walks around it, looking at everything. "Does it fold?"

Nicole nods. "The tires pop off, then you can fold the frame. Here, I'll show you."

She demonstrates, and it's so easy that Zurie and I fist-bump, but then her phone buzzes. She checks it and then turns to Nicole. "I can sanitize the stroller. It's my way of being a part of the Turkey Trot team."

Nicole's head tilts as she smiles. "That's so sweet. Just be super careful with it."

"I promise! My ride's here. I'll get it cleaned up and bring it to the race."

She pulled it off! Now I've only got one transportation issue left, but it's huge.

After dinner, I go straight to my room because I can't risk being around anyone tonight, as I firm up my plans. All the work Seth's done, and all the work I've done, can't be for nothing. I tap a pen on Dad's desk, trying to think of someone—anyone—who would step up and help us because we can't do it on our own.

Suddenly, I drop the pen. My thoughts are sketchy at first, but the clearer they come in, the more excited I get. I listen for Mom and Dad to leave Seth's room. Once they're gone, I step inside his room, close the door, and use the remote to raise the head of his bed so he's sitting up., I'm losing the rhythm in my breathing because the more I think about it, the angrier I get. We wouldn't be in this predicament if my parents would've just given me and Seth a ride. It's a race, not a smash-'em-up monster truck demolition derby. Juan Carlos chumped out on us, too, but he did get one thing right. I worked hard. So did Seth. We deserve this race.

I don't know if Seth's looking at me or not, but I lay it all out there for him. "I got good news and bad news. The good news is, we're running in a race on Thanksgiving morning. The bad news is, we'll need to borrow Dad's truck to get there."

CHAPTER FORTY-EIGHT

I've never planned anything this outrageous, but I don't think there's ever been a time in my life when I needed to. I've been sneaking the stuff we need out of Seth's room—one thing at a time—to put in the bag I'll take with us to the race. Milk, feeding tubes, wipes, blankets, extra clothes, a hat, even a diaper. Every evening I've made it a point to jog, then watch television with the family and talk at dinner so they won't get suspicious.

Late Wednesday night, I wait for Mom and Dad to go to bed, then I creep into Seth's room to get him out of his pajamas and into his cross-country shirt. I won't put his pants on until the morning, just in case he needs a diaper change. I check off everything on my list of things he'll need, so I lean down and tell my brother what he needs to hear before I go to bed.

"You've got a cross-country meet in the morning. We've

got to leave early. Be ready."

In the study, I put on the clothes I'm wearing tomorrow, then get into bed and close my eyes. But they just flip right back open. I lie awake, going over the plan again, including everything Seth and Juan Carlos showed me about driving. We're leaving so early in the morning that most people will still be asleep. The streets should be empty.

It'll be just like driving to the mailbox.

Thirty minutes before my alarm vibrates, I cut it off and ease outside to get Dad's truck ready because once I get Seth we'll have to move fast. Back in the house, I tiptoe into Seth's room, turn on the small lamp, grab a diaper, and pray for nothing in the one he's got on now. It's dry, but I put another one over the dry one to avoid a pit stop during the race.

"Dude, wake up. It's time to run, and I need you to help any way you can."

I slip on the rest of his clothes, then transfer him to his wheelchair the way Nicole showed me. I've got to hurry because Mom will be up soon. I roll Seth to the living room and check for noise. Mom and Dad's door is still closed, so I grab the keys, turn the chair around backward, and carefully bring Seth down the ramp.

Once I open the truck door, I slide one arm under the back of Seth's knees, and the other across both shoulder blades. "Ready? On three. One, two . . ."

I lift him into the passenger seat of the truck. After I

click his seat belt, I angle his legs to the center of the floor-board so that I won't accidentally close them in the door. I drop his bag filled with everything I need to take care of him between our seats. Before closing his door, I lean in and whisper, "You good?"

His right hand slides to a picture on the board and then taps it. *"I'm good."*

Just as I'm about to close the door, the automated voice speaks again.

"I like big butts."

Dang it! I forgot to switch that picture out. I put my hand on his shoulder. "That was hilarious when we were watching videos, but don't press that one today, okay?"

He doesn't respond, and I'm not sure he understands why this isn't the time for jokes. I slowly shut his door, and then bump it with my hip. From the passenger window, I look at my brother wearing sunglasses in the dark. His body stays exactly where I put it.

I collapse his chair and lift it to slide into the back seat, but accidentally clang it against the door and freeze. If Dad wakes up and sees me stealing his truck, things could get ugly fast. I rush around to open the driver's side door and stand just inside it.

Closing my eyes, for the tenth time, I go over everything Seth and Juan Carlos taught me about driving, mentally check off the things I packed in his bag, and remind myself why I'm doing this. I really wish my brother could talk to me. I turn toward him, the only light we have comes from the moon, and I speak my heart.

"Once we roll down this dirt road, there's no turning back. You understand that, right?"

Silence.

I must've overloaded his brain with too many things at once. But his hand flops hard onto the voice board. It slides across the pictures that I can barely see, but Seth seems to know exactly what he's looking for and presses it.

"I forgive you."

That one cry—the one I've been holding for seventy-seven days—gushes out of me. "Thank you, Seth. I'm so sorry."

"Between brothers."

I sniffle. "Let's get gone."

I put the truck in neutral and hop in when it starts to roll. As soon as we get to the bottom of the hill, I switch to park, start the ignition, and take off down the gravel road. When I get to the street, there's a car coming, and the driver flashes bright lights at me. Oh no, I forgot to turn my headlights on—no wonder it's so dark! A turn of a knob lights up the darkness, making the street so much easier to see. "I'm nervous, that's all. But I'm going super slow and doing everything you taught me."

The voice of the GPS lady calms me. She doesn't wait until the last minute to tell me to turn or keep straight. We're on Main when she says, *In a half mile, turn right onto Center Street.*

My breath catches. There's got to be another way to get

where we're going. I take turns looking at the road and then at my GPS map. There's no other route. The sun rises at the absolute worst time, showing me everything I don't want to see as my curiosity makes me look. I don't think Seth's been at this intersection since the accident. He's sitting as still as he was when we left the house. I can see through his sunglasses that his eyes are open.

I pull over and cut the ignition. The memory of that day comes back as I try to explain everything to him.

"It happened right here. You were in an accident, but it wasn't your fault."

I sit for a moment and let that wrap around my head again for the thousandth time.

"Isaiah."

I try not to tear up, but it's important for him to know. "You're different in some ways than you used to be, but I love the Seth you are now just as much, maybe even more."

I start the ignition, turn my blinker on, and merge back onto the road. The GPS sends me toward Interstate 45 South, but there's no way I'm getting on that. I've been in the car with Dad when cars sped by doing ninety, weaving in and out of traffic. He always says, "On the freeway, drivers act like using blinkers are a sign of weakness."

The fastest I've ever driven is twenty-five miles an hour. There's no way I'm cranking up to fifty-five. I try taking side streets, but the GPS lady keeps rerouting me, and I hit the steering wheel in anger.

"We can't get around it. I've got to take the freeway. Hold on!"

I take quick looks in all my mirrors, but cars that weren't there a second ago honk as they zoom by. I turn on my left blinker, and the arrow blinks on and off inside the car. It looks like Mom's face, and I grip the wheel so tight it hurts.

Come on, exit. Where are you?

Now there's a car riding my bumper. I wish it would just go around me. What if it's a cop? Can I get a ticket for driving too slow? If that *is* a cop behind me, I'll soon find out because twenty-five miles an hour is where I'll live until the GPS lady tells me to exit.

In a half mile, take exit twenty-seven.

"That's what I'm talking about!" I turn on my right blinker, take the exit, but that same car is still behind me. I look closer and realize it's a van, not a car. I don't think police officers drive vans.

At the light, make a right turn.

I slow down to ten miles an hour before making that turn.

In two miles, your destination is on the left.

There it is. The Woodbridge Community. Their huge parking lot is packed with all sorts of vans—minivans, custom-made vans, huge vans with high roofs that looks like a canoe sitting on top of it, or with wheelchair lifts connected to the back. This place is amazing. The grass is dark green, with trees and flowers everywhere. There are at least twenty handicapped parking spots. I find the closest one and pull in.

I'm so hyped about my driving skills! I open the door and step out, feeling proud and successfully sneaky. As I'm on my way to get Seth's wheelchair, I look up—and all the blood in my body rushes to my feet.

Dad is standing at the back of the truck.

CHAPTER FORTY-NINE

I think I need one of Seth's diapers. "Dad, what are you doing here?"

His face is full of mad. "That's a question I should be asking you, don't you think?"

"Yes, sir. See—"

"You've been lying to your mother and me. I knew you were up to something with Juan Carlos, running with all that hay in the wheelbarrow. And when Nicole emailed saying she was looking forward to seeing us at the race this morning, I knew you forged my name after we told you no."

"Dad—"

"I'm not finished! Do you realize you could have killed both yourself and your brother?"

"I know how to drive! Seth and Juan Carlos taught me, and they let me drive to the mailbox all the time."

Dad rubs his forehead. "The freeway is nothing like our gravel road. Seth was an excellent driver, but a stupid mistake by someone else almost cost him his life. I can't go through that again."

I can't, either, and now I realize the bonehead mistake I made. "I'm sorry, Dad."

A voice blares through the sound system. "Ladies and gentlemen, welcome to Woodbridge Community's 5K Thanksgiving Turkey Trot, a three-mile race for people of all ages and abilities! All competitors, please check in at the registration booth."

"Dad, I wish you understood how important this is to us."

He nods. "I do understand. And that's why I didn't stop you. I was okay until you took the ramp onto the freeway."

My eyes widen. "You saw that?"

"I was behind you the whole time. I cried when you pulled over on Center Street."

I break down again. "I told Seth what happened to him. Even if he doesn't remember, I'm never going to forget. But I really think this race will help him get better. That's the only reason we're doing it. We've worked so hard, Dad. I can't let him down."

Now he's crying, too. "Isaiah, I've watched you leave the house to feed the animals before the sun comes up, go to school, and then take your brother to therapy. You got your training in with Juan Carlos, and you did your homework, helped your mother—the list goes on and on. And you never complained. Watching you take on so much helped *me* keep going."

He reaches in his pocket and pulls out a medal. "I picked this up from the Worthing Rec the day I got laid off from my job. I was planning to bring it home to you after work, but I got so depressed when BMP let me go. I needed something to motivate me, and all I had was this medal. You worked hard to get it, and that reminded me to work harder, so I did. I'm sorry for not giving it to you sooner."

"No, it's okay."

Seth bangs his voice board. *"Run." "Run."*

Dad puts one hand on me, and one on Seth. "I'm proud of the love between you boys, but, Isaiah, even though you made it here safely, I'm still going to punish you for taking my truck. You could have hurt yourself, or Seth, or someone else. Your mother's furious. She's getting dressed right now. I'm going to go get her. We'll be back in time to see the race."

I grab Seth's bag from between the seats and hand Dad the keys. "Yes, sir."

He backs the truck out and leaves the parking lot.

"Ice!"

Zurie comes toward me with Seth's stroller. It looks brand-new with a shine on it as strong as the sun.

"Special delivery," she says.

I give her a long hug. "You're an amazing friend."

"So are you! I brought my camera and zoom lens, and I'll record you on my phone, too."

I look around, and my shoulders droop. "I thought there'd be a lot more people here rooting for Seth after I posted that reel on Instagram."

"It's Thanksgiving morning. Give 'em time. People might still show up."

Seth won't stop hitting the picture on his voice board. *"Run." "Run."*

I transfer Seth from his wheelchair into the stroller. "Will you keep his wheelchair until my parents come back?"

She nods. "See you at the finish line! Go get 'em, Seth!"

At the registration booth, a lady pins papers with the number forty-six on my back and on Seth's racing stroller. The lady next to me has one real leg and a prosthetic one.

She looks our way. "This is always so much fun, isn't it?"

I shrug. "It's our first time."

Before she can say another word, a familiar voice startles me.

"Hi! What's your name? I'm Uncle Jerry! Do you want to run in the race with me?"

"Run."

I hold my fist out for Uncle Jerry to bump. It's the slowest bump in the history of fist bumps, but I don't care.

Rhino man-hugs me. "Glad you made it."

A woman in a racing stroller like Seth's pulls up, but her wheels are close enough to her that she can push on her own. "I look forward to this race more than I do eating turkey! This is my eighth time! Each lap is a mile, so it goes pretty fast."

I nod like I understand, because I do. A short thin guy walks over to us, his grin as big as his face. I'm ready to say hello when I realize he's not paying attention to me at all. He taps Seth's voice board, and it responds.

"Hello."

He lets out a big laugh. "I love it! I'm Henry. What's your name?"

"Seth."

Henry pats Seth on the shoulder. "Nice to meet you, Seth. Good luck in the race."

"I like big butts."

Henry's eyes widen, and Uncle Jerry squeals with laughter as Henry covers his mouth to hide his giggle and hurries back to the starting line. I lean over Seth.

"Cut it out. We're already in enough trouble."

The announcer speaks again as an ASL interpreter signs next to him. "Runners, the race is about to begin. Please take your place near the starting line."

I close my eyes and try to think of what I should say to my brother to rev his engine. And then it comes to me. I lean down and let him know.

"It's time to release the fire-breathing dragon and that club-carrying cyclops!"

"Run." "Run."

"Runners on your mark, get set, go!"

CHAPTER FIFTY

Instead of taking off like a herd of buffalo, everyone patiently waits for the runners in front of them to start. It feels like fun from the beginning, and I like it. But not long after the race starts, dark clouds take the sky hostage, and soon it looks like evening outside instead of morning. Nine minutes into the race, Seth and I come around to finish our first lap, and the crowd has gotten larger. People wave, and I wave back. We spot Mom and Dad near the first aid tent. Dad waves and whistles.

I lean down to check on Seth. "You good?"

His hand slaps a picture. *"Run." "Run."*

It starts to sprinkle, but I've got Seth's bag hooked to the handles of the racing stroller, so I just grab his hat and cover his head. We make our second lap a little faster than the first one, but the rain makes me cautious. Just to be safe, I slow my pace since we only have one more lap to go.

But the stroller doesn't slow down as quickly as I thought it would. I lean down to check the back wheels, and as I do, the front wheel leaves the path, making the stroller tilt and ride the edge of the asphalt. I try to keep Seth from falling, but it doesn't work.

"No!"

I slip and skid my knee as I tumble. Seth's stroller ends up on top of me. I'm face-to-face with him as he shakes uncontrollably. "Seth! I'm sorry! I'll fix it. We're okay."

Since he's still strapped in, I push the stroller off me, grab his voice board from the grass, and get back onto the path. Runners stop and offer to help, but I tell them we're fine. My knee stings enough to add a limp to my jog. I feel around my pockets for my phone to turn on the flashlight. Double dang it! I left it in Dad's truck.

"Let's just try to finish, okay?"

"Run." "Run."

I haven't even jogged fifty feet when one of the back wheels begins to wobble. Seth's so excited about being in the game again, it can't end like this.

"Abernathy?"

Uncle Jerry runs to me. "What's your name?"

The pain has me talking with my eyes closed. "Isaiah."

Rhino puts his phone light on my leg. Blood's racing down my left knee, and Uncle Jerry gets upset. "Isaiah, you need a Band-Aid. I'll get you a Band-Aid. Come on, Rhino! We have to get Isaiah a Band-Aid!"

Rhino checks me out. "What happened?"

"We tried to go off-road, find a quicker route."

Rhino laughs. "Right. It's the last lap, so the quickest route is this one! Let me keep going with Unc, get him out of the rain. I'll send someone to help."

We're out here, on the opposite side of the finish line. It's two-in-the-morning-dark out here, and I'm sure the clouds are going to open soon and drench us. Two more runners pass, holding their phones up for light. I wave and smile, hoping to convince them we're fine. I take slower steps, but the wheel continues to wobble. I don't know what to do, but then—

"Ice Pic!"

Juan Carlos rushes over and checks my knee. "Uncle Jerry said you need a Band-Aid."

"Don't worry about me. Something's wrong with the back wheel on the right. Watch what happens when I roll it."

I push Seth forward so Juan Carlos can see the wobbly wheel. He shakes his head.

"It's going to come off. Where's your phone? We need the flashlight."

"I left it in Dad's truck. Where's yours?"

"The battery's dead, but don't panic. Wait here. I'll get Seth's wheelchair."

The pain and the disappointment both hit me at once. "No! We're not quitting!"

Seth's banging on his voice board, but not any specific word. *"Run." "Hello." "Thank you."*

Juan Carlos blasts me.

"That stroller's busted, Seth's drenched, and so are you! It's over!"

We stare at each other in silence. The rain makes us blink more than normal, but there's no way I'm losing this battle. I limp to my brother's side. Juan Carlos paces in front of me.

"What are you doing now?"

"We're finishing what we started! Go tell the officials not to end the race."

I face Seth, bend down, unbuckle his seat belt, and talk to him the same way I did when I put him in the truck. "On three . . ."

Juan Carlos gets in front of us. "I can't let you do that. It's too dark out here and—"

"One."

"Seth's clothes are soaked! Are you listening to me? That's too much extra weight."

"Two . . ."

Juan Carlos burns off toward the finish line. "You'd better not drop him!"

"Three! Aaaaahhh!" I power-yell strength into my legs, and raise my brother to my chest, hold him close, wrapped in his wet blankets.

"Here we go, Seth. You and me. Run, run."

Before Seth's accident, I thought I was a good brother, but I've only just begun learning about doing my best and caring about someone. Me and my brother, we've been through so much, together and apart. He's carried me my whole life.

Now I'll carry him.

Juan Carlos comes back, pushing the wobbly stroller with the voice board in the seat. "Okay, if this is what you want to do, then I'll help you! Your legs are strong. Your arms are solid. Get moving!"

I fight back tears from the pain. "Okay."

Suddenly, Seth's leg straightens and shakes in a bad spasm. I hold him closer and keep jogging. "My leg hurts, too, but don't give up on us, Seth. Between . . . between . . . ."

It's raspy, and if I hadn't already been staring at his face, I would have missed him saying . . ."

"Brothers."

I stop running. "Seth?"

Please don't let me be imagining this. I say it again. "Between . . ."

His voice is still raspy, but louder. "Brothers."

"Juan Carlos!"

He rushes back, pushing the busted stroller. "It's okay, I'm here! What? You need help?"

I'm trying to talk through a cry. "I know why he's making those faces. Watch him."

When Juan Carlos looks, I say it again.

"Between."

"Brothers."

Juan Carlos lets go of the stroller, and it rolls into the

grass, but it's time I let him know.

"Between brothers. That includes you, too."

We stand there, in the pouring rain, listening to a voice I was told I'd never hear again.

Juan Carlos tries. "Between."

"Brothers."

Juan Carlos and I cry together, his arms underneath mine as we hold our brother, knowing we just won whether we reach the finish line or not. As we stand there, a light shines on the side of my face, and Juan Carlos moves in front of me and Seth as if guarding us, then holds up his hand. "They're fine, and they're going to finish. They just need more time," he says.

Someone's walking toward us. My vision is blurry because of the rain, but Juan Carlos moves to let him by, and I finally see who it is. For a moment I'm unable to speak, and I'm not sure if it's because of the pain in my knee or the fact that I'm face-to-face with the same man who suspended me from school. He's soaked, wiping rain from his face with the bottom of shirt.

"No doubt you're going to finish," he says. "We're just here to help."

Principal Cochran turns on his phone light, and I can see a crowd of people, hundreds of them, some with umbrellas, some without. He points to the edges of the track. "Okay people, I need lines on both sides of this path, and then use whatever you have to light their way to the finish line!"

Adults and children move to stand shoulder to shoulder like a human fence. My heart's banging in my chest, and I'm not sure of what's happening, but I hold on to Seth and trust Juan Carlos to protect us. Suddenly, one by one, flashlights and phone lights illuminate the route, just like the lights that helped Rhino and Uncle Jerry the night of our school dance.

Bruce, who rides my bus, waves and yells out, "You can do it, Ice!"

A lady I don't know gives us a thumbs-up. "You're going to make it!"

Rhino was right. We're Scarboro strong, and right now, my community is proving it.

Juan Carlos turns to me. "It's time. You ready?"

I try to move through the pain, but my legs won't budge. Seth feels extra heavy, and I fight the need to cry as Juan Carlos tries to keep me going.

"You're doing great. Now run with your mind, just like we practiced."

I take a step, then another, but the pain is too much. I look into the eyes of people I know, and some I don't know, lighting our path to help us finish something I'm not sure I can. And then I spot Dad, wiping rain from his eyes and keeping his phone light steady on our path. His voice separates from the others.

"I know it's hard, but you can do it, son. Just—don't give up."

I think about all the times Dad could've given up, but he

didn't. He kept walking, and so will I. I grip Seth tighter, switch mental gears, and force my feet to jog. Juan Carlos runs next to me, no longer talking calm but yelling at the side of my face like a drill sergeant.

"Keep moving! No more stopping! Don't listen to your body! Make your body listen to your mind! Why are you doing this, Ice Pic?"

I look down at Seth. He's my reason, and I won't quit on him. "Let's goooooo!"

Seth's body wiggles, and his left hand tries to bang his voice board, but Juan Carlos has it. We must be close to the end because with or without a brain injury, Seth knows the sound and smell of a finish line.

And as phones light up the darkness brighter than a lightning bug reunion, the three of us cross the finish line together. The crowd celebrates, and Juan Carlos slaps high fives with his cross-country teammates before coming back over to me.

"That's what I'm talking about! We did it!"

CHAPTER FIFTY-ONE

I limp through the crowd as people pat my shoulder, clapping and whistling for us. Dad brings over Seth's wheelchair, my phone, and an umbrella. I gently place my brother in his wheelchair.

"I'm so proud of my sons."

I'm still catching my breath. "Thanks, Dad."

I put Seth's voice board in front of him. He bangs it over and over, hitting different pictures without looking. It's his way of celebrating, and I'm happy to see him happy.

Just like that, the rain stops and the sun appears again—but here comes Mom, and she's got a tropical storm brewing on her face.

"Well, I hope you enjoyed yourself, Isaiah, because it's going to be a while before you have an opportunity like this again."

"Yes, ma'am. But you should know that this was

between . . ." I look at Seth.

Seth's voice is getting stronger. "Brothers."

The tropical storm downgrades to a gentle breeze as she covers her mouth and lets out a joyful cry. "Ray, our baby's talking."

Dad hugs her. "Yes, he is, thank God. But we need to thank Isaiah, too. Even though he was wrong for disobeying us, he was right about his brother. For that, we need to celebrate."

That's what I'm talking about. Dad gets it. He understands.

Nicole, Trinh, and Dr. Ramirez stroll over. Seth's therapists hug him and me.

"That was absolutely amazing," says Nicole.

"I loved it," says Trinh.

I wink at Seth. "If you thought the race was amazing, watch this. Hey, Seth, between . . ."

"Brothers."

Dr. Ramirez blinks several times before grinning. "You know, sometimes it feels wonderful to be wrong. Seth has an appointment with me soon. See you then."

He shakes Mom's and Dad's hands and then mine. "Happy Thanksgiving."

As he walks away, Nicole leans down and speaks to Seth. "You know what this means, don't you? I'm requesting another block of therapy time! I'm so happy for you, Seth."

"Me, too," says Trinh. "See you two next week. Happy Thanksgiving."

The announcer turns on his microphone. "All participants please come to the stage area."

Nicole and Trinh wave goodbye and move closer to the
stage while I go get Seth's ribbon. People clap as the names
of the first-place winners are announced. Zurie finds us,
and I spot Rhino and Uncle Jerry not far away and call
them over.

"Rhino, Zurie, check this out. Between . . ."

Seth answers. "Brothers."

Uncle Jerry claps. "He's talking to me! Look, Rhino!"

Zurie covers her mouth. "Oh my God!"

Rhino slaps me a hard high five. "Look what happened
when you got your boy back in the game. Trust me, bruh.
He's not tired yet."

"I believe that, too," I say. I hold up my phone. "Let's
take a selfie!"

Rhino, Uncle Jerry, Zurie and I, crowd around Seth's
wheelchair and smile.

Click.

Uncle Jerry takes Rhino's hand. "I'm hungry. Let's go
eat."

Rhino rolls his eyes as Uncle Jerry tugs at him. "Happy
Thanksgiving, y'all."

Uncle Jerry pulls at Zurie, too. "Come eat! You can eat
with me."

She nods. "Okay, I'll be right there, Uncle Jerry."

Zurie kisses Seth on the forehead. "Congratulations on
getting back in the race."

She looks up at me. "Bend down so I can kiss your forehead, too."

I do, and she pecks my lips instead and giggles. "See you in class."

I'm grinning so hard that I can't talk. I puff my chest, enjoying my instant swag upgrade, and even take a few steps forward to test whether a new walk came with that until Dad makes me blush.

"Ah sookie, sookie!"

Seth bangs on his voice board again. I reach over and bang on it, too, and we all laugh.

"We have to get home. Trish is waiting on us for lunch," says Mom.

On our way to the truck, Juan Carlos stands with the entire cross-country team, fists over their hearts as Seth passes by. I put my fist over my heart for my brother, too, and nod at Juan Carlos. "See you Sunday."

"I'll be there," he says.

When we pull up in front of the house, Trish waves from her car. "How was the race? Sorry I missed it!"

"We didn't win, but we finished," I say with a grin.

"Finishing what you start is important," she says.

She doesn't know how true her words are for me and my brother.

Inside at the dining room table, Mom unzips a bag and takes out everything she needs to feed Seth and freshen him up. One of the last things she pulls out is a can of chocolate milk.

My eyes widen. "Is that for Seth?"

"Yep! Found it online."

When she finishes, we all go in the living room, where Trish has opened her laptop. She looks at both my parents, and they nod. What's going on? Aren't we eating lunch?

"Isaiah, I need your undivided attention for the next thirty minutes or so."

I've already given all I have today, and I may have even dipped into what I have for tomorrow. Mom puts her hand on my shoulder, but that doesn't help. I just can't.

"Trish, I'm so tired that I might have to skip lunch, and I don't usually miss a meal."

She smiles. "Unfortunately, my plans have changed. I'm not here for lunch. Your parents asked me to summarize the mediation meeting for you."

The last time I heard the words *summarize a meeting*, it was from Dr. Parker, who dropped bomb after bomb on me. I can't take another summary like that, and I'm already feeling a certain way about my parents for thinking I'll be okay with it—especially on Thanksgiving. But I don't have any choice.

CHAPTER FIFTY-TWO

Trish shows me a bunch of charts and graphs and a timeline she created. "After the accident, BMP got bombarded with protestors, boycotts—even their own employees lashed out, especially after your dad's boss resigned during his deposition."

I glance at Dad, but he seems fine as Trish keeps talking. "The judge presiding over this lawsuit ordered us to attempt mediation. After several reschedules, we finally had that mediation last Friday. Even though your parents and Seth had to leave, the negotiations continued throughout the evening and even into the weekend. We were close to settling the lawsuit, but BMP wanted something specific before they would agree."

I check out Mom's and Dad's faces to make sure the happiness from earlier isn't about to disappear.

I can't tell, so I ask. "What did they want?"

"Proof, through original pictures and video, of how much the accident changed Seth's life," she says. "All your parents had were school pictures. The BMP attorneys said that wasn't enough. Then your father showed me Seth's voice board, and a family file called 'Countdown to College.' From those videos and pictures, this is what I gave them."

Trish presses the remote. Music plays as the words *Meet Seth Abernathy* appear on the screen followed by pictures of my birthday breakfast a few months ago. I remember the timer going off before I was ready, and we all laugh at the expressions on our faces.

"I love that picture," says Trish.

I grin at the pics from Redd's Barbershop of Juan Carlos, Seth, and me.

Next is a video of Seth taking first place in his cross-country meet as Mom claps. I look over at my parents. Their eyes stay glued to the screen as they hold hands.

But the last one makes me lose it. Seth's got a good beat going, Dad's bobbing his head, and I'm rapping about Mom's spaghetti and meatballs followed by Dad dancing with Mom around the table while Seth and I watch. There was so much love in the room that day.

Trish turns off the television. "Isaiah, those pictures and videos sealed the deal. I have the settlement papers right here. I'll leave them for your parents to look over and sign."

"The lawsuit is over?"

"It's over," she says with a smile.

"BMP has to pay for all Seth's medical bills, right?"

"Yep. And he'll even have money left over for anything he might need in the future."

I start rattling off everything I can think of. "He needs a standing frame right away. And what about school? I'm sure he lost his scholarship for cross-country. What's he going to do all day? He can't just sit in his chair at the church. And he needs lots of chocolate milk."

Mom joins in. "Trish contacted the Woodbridge Community Center weeks ago, and we met with them about Seth. His application was accepted!"

I can't stop grinning. "Will he have classes? Like at a college?"

Trish grins with me. "He will, at his own pace. Seth will also continue therapy at Woodbridge, make new friends, learn a skill, even attend parties!"

I lean over his wheelchair and hug him. "You did it! You're still going to college!"

Trish looks my way. "A Woodbridge Community shuttle will pick him up in the mornings and bring him home in the afternoons. And we didn't forget about you, Isaiah."

I'm crying. Seth's new normal could be as amazing for him as his old one.

"A portion of the lawsuit money will be placed in a trust fund until you graduate from high school. Once you do, those funds will be released for you to attend the college of your choice. Seth once told me you want to be a veterinarian. Is that true?"

"Yes, ma'am," I say.

"I've got a feeling you're going to be a good one," she says.

Mom and Dad nod, and I turn to Seth. "Between?"

"*Brothers.*"

Trish gasps. "He's talking? When did that happen?"

"Today, during the race. When he said it, I almost dropped him! That's all he says right now."

"But that's okay! More words will come. It's a miracle," she says.

"Yes, thank God," says Mom.

"Actually, I thank the wish granter," I say.

Dad laughs. "The wish granter? I haven't heard that in ages! The wish granter was my father's special name for God."

A wave of chill bumps cover my body, and my mind rewinds to all the times I lifted my head to the clouds and poured out my heart, asking for help. He answered my parents' prayers, and he answered mine, too, even after I doubted that he was real.

I look at Seth's old boss. "Thank you, Trish."

"Thank you, Isaiah, for showing us that even when circumstances change, love doesn't." Her phone buzzes and she takes a look. "Gotta get to my parents' house. They're waiting on me. But I'll be back next week."

I reach out and hug her. "Happy Thanksgiving."

She hugs me back. "Happy Thanksgiving to you, too, Isaiah."

Dad and I take her equipment back to her car and wave as she drives off before joining Mom and Seth in the living room.

Dad sighs as if he's been holding it for months. "Glad that chapter is closed."

Mom sniffles. "Me, too. So much to be thankful for today. I need to work on that huge green bean casserole for the church dinner, but I kept lunch warm in the oven."

I wipe my face. "What are we having?"

"Spaghetti and meatballs," she says with a grin.

Dad looks my way. "Your punishment for taking my truck is—no second helpings."

Mom's spaghetti and meatballs go hard, and this punishment is too much. "Can't you just ground me for life? Don't take away my second helpings! That's abuse!"

Dad grins. "I know, right?"

I side-eye him, grab the handlebars of Seth's wheelchair, and roll him toward the table. "I got my mind on it," I say with a grin.

"Me, too. Break me off a beat," Dad says, putting his arm around Mom.

Seth bangs on his voice board, hitting all kinds of words. I find his rhythm and add some of my own as we rock the house like old times with the Abernathy anthem for pasta.

I got my mind on spaghetti, got spaghetti on
    my mind.

AUTHOR'S NOTE

Many of you know me as an author who writes humorous stories. I love making people laugh! Laughter is medicinal, and it's free. But that doesn't mean it comes without a price.

Some time ago, I read a passage from a novelist named Émile Zola, and his words really resonated with me. He wrote:

"We are like books. Most people only see our cover. The minority read only the introduction. Many people believe the critics. Few will know our content."

Even though I have published five novels, *Between Two Brothers* feels like my debut because with this one, you will know my content.

It took eight years to finish this story, and ironically my youngest son was eight years old when a catastrophic incident changed the dynamics of our family forever. The mental and physical changes on my son were apparent, but the effect on the rest of my family was not so obvious.

We all needed freeing, or at the very least, distractions.

For my oldest son, his diversion was sports. For my husband, work. Writing humor allowed me to mask my pain. It all seemed to work until I tried to write something more heartfelt, and I knew the only story I could genuinely tell was the one I was living. For years I had tried to write it without help, but couldn't.

Now, though, I'd have support. I knew my agent and editor would help me find my words, give me time to write them, and encourage me to tell my story. I just needed to figure out a way to get through the difficult memories.

So, in an effort to protect myself and my family from reliving those horrific events, I chose to make the plot, characters, dialogue, and most of the names in the story fictitious. (In a few instances, I have named fictitious characters after the real-life heroes who inspired them.) However, the heartaches, the anger, the hopes, and triumphs experienced by the characters are real, and that is the content I've chosen to share with you.

This story is about a lot of things, like making mistakes and owning them, dealing with failure, and rejoicing at even the smallest of victories. Most of all, it's a story about accepting but not settling, and the power of a family's unconditional love.

In the midst of our ashes, my family found beauty. From our brokenness, we mended each other, grew stronger individually and together. And through it all, we learned to love life again, understanding that every day is a gift and a blessing.

I hope you enjoyed reading *Between Two Brothers*. Thank you for taking this journey with us.

Much love,
Crystal

ACKNOWLEDGMENTS

I'd like to thank my Lord and Savior, Jesus Christ, for everything and everybody in my life, especially my husband, Reggie, for giving me the time I needed to write. Thank you, Joshua and Phillip, my precious sons, for just being you. I love you so much.

Thank you, Kristin Rens, for your patience, your understanding, and your willingness to help me pen this important story, not just for me—but for others to be encouraged and know anything is possible.

Jen Rofé—thank you for being beside me for every step of this journey. I couldn't have done it without you, not just because you're my kick-butt agent, but even more because you're my forever friend.

No one writes a book alone. I'd like to thank and acknowledge the following people for their time, expertise, and love during this journey:

Nicole Miranda, PT, DPT

Trinh Phan, OTR

Kris Conley, CCC-SLP

Patricia Haylon

Christine Taylor-Butler

Kenneth Taylor-Butler, MD

Chris Tebbetts

Lynne Kelly

Dara Sharif

Eileen Robinson

Ann Broyles

Kari Anne Holt

Sharon Draper

Kristen D. Brown

Joy Preble

Neal Shusterman

Donna Gephardt

Tameka Fryer-Brown

Laura Ruthven

Michele Bacon

Varsha Bajaj

Dixie Keyes

Luke Bedwell

And if I accidentally forgot someone, I acknowledge you right here. Thank you.

ALSO AVAILABLE BY CRYSTAL ALLEN

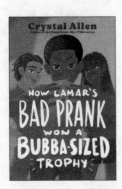